KGB

... KILLING GEORGE BUSH

by Mike Palecek

Published by:
CWG Press
1204 NE 11th Ave
Fort Lauderdale, FL 33304
www.cwgpress.com

978-0-9801354-6-6
Originally published in 2001 by Publish America

Reprinted by Permission of the Author
 by CWG Press and Seventh Street Press

Newest edition: January 2019

To the children of El Salvador, Panama, Iraq

"There can be no reward for aggression. Nor will there be any negotiation. Principle cannot be compromised."
— George H.W. Bush

"Bad boys, bad boys. Watcha gonna do, watcha gonna do, when they come for you? Bad boys."
— "COPS" theme song

Just saying:
John Hinkley Jr., the attempted assassin of Ronald Reagan, while George Bush Sr. was vice-president ... well, his family is big friends with the Bush family. The family of Osama bin Laden is big friends with the Bush family, and business partners as well.

[FOREWORD]

I LIKE KGB BECAUSE IT TELLS the forgotten story of prisoners and conspiracy theorists and people slaughtered by Bush Sr. in Panama and women and children in jail visiting rooms and other stuff.

I would like to say something about KGB.

I would like to ask why there is such a stink about even talking about the killing of a rich "leader" in a fictional story — and yet, the real-life slaughter of thousands, millions, of poor people goes by without a whisper, a passing breeze in the trees that is gone and forgotten by the time the hot dogs on the grill are ready.

I am not for the killing of George Bush Sr. or George Bush Jr. or George H.W. Bush or George W. Bush or George X.Y.Z. Bush.

I am not for killing. Period.

But I do think it is within the parameters of fiction and good taste and morality to allow the characters in a novel to discuss what they might do if they ever discovered how they came to such a desolate place in life.

In KGB we hear from his victims in El Salvador, Panama, prison, jail visiting rooms.

In KGB we have a pronounced preference for the poor, as it should be.

I am not for killing.

I only wish the same were true for George H.W. Bush.

— MIKE PALECEK

[PROLOGUE]

THE MEN IN THE WOODBURY COUNTY JAIL sat below grade.
They inhabited the middle earth between hell and heaven.
They smoked, crossed their legs, and stared through the
bars into the hallway.

Above them the television blared.
The commercial boomed. The noise and the soap and
the lovely women had nothing to do with the men. They
watched the set as they would the stars in their backyard,
because it was there.
"Turn that damn thing off!" hollered the young blond guy,
barely a man, with the tattoos up and down his arms. He
held his cards over the metal table, his limbs and the yellow
circle the same scarred motif.

He stroked his mustache from the middle of his nose to his
chin, fanning his thumb and first finger.
Another guy reached up to switch the station.

An older man, at least forty to his cellmates' teens and
twenties, dealing with his back to the set, twisted, crunched
his homemade cigarette in his teeth, squinting his eyes
against the smoke.

The "old" man said nothing and the guy pulled back his
hand from the set. He stepped away and leaned into the
bars, skinny enough to get half his body in.

The men in D-Block watched the replay of the black con-
vertible moving slowly through the packed crowds in
Dallas, then watched Walter Cronkite describe the scene,
succumbing to tears. They watched the announcement
of the President's death by a man in a black suit standing
outside the hospital.

The old man of the block turned back and scooped his cards.
The others followed suit as the guard wheeled the lunch cart down the cement hallway.

"Let's play cards," said the blond young man with the tattoos and the bushy mustache.
The old man looked over his hand into the younger man's eyes, not blinking.

He pushed a paperback book across the table, keeping his eyes keen. The younger man seized the book and flung it into his cell without looking. The book plopped on the taut grey blanket and stood on end.

The younger man, hearing the meal cart squeaking behind him, slammed his cards on the table and hurried to be first in line.
Twenty-three years later, a tall man with a receding yellow hairline dealt spades with his back to the dayroom cell door and the television above it.

He sang. "Goodbye to my Juan, goodbye Rosalita, adios mis amigos … hmm, hmm, hmm, hmm, hmm-hmm."
He bit a cigarette in his front teeth as he counted the cards out the sides of his mouth. The men around the grey table watched and counted to themselves. A young man picked at the table, revealing yellow underneath.

In the mid-morning hours the trusties mopped the hallway. The guard complained about walking through water en route to C-Block.

"You got any more tattoos?" A young man asked the dealer, touching the smiling catfish riding atop an eagle on the man's right shoulder.

The blond dealer crushed his eyebrows, sending deep rivulets flowing from his eyes. His worn hands fidgeted independently. His feet got themselves ready to move. His stomach tightened and his heart revved. The ears knew to listen down the hall and around past the kitchen.
Keys jingled.
"No," he said.

A black special report graphic replaced "The Price Is Right" ribbons and bows.
The dealer saw the men's eyes connect with the screen.

"Geezuz fuck," said the young man.
"Whoa. Boom, boom, boom," the black man punched the air and weaved.

The dealer looked over his shoulder and caught the replay of the space shuttle popping like a dud firework, then falling away from a tail of smoke.

As the men venerated the television, the brown man in the hall rested his mop in the bucket, against the wall and retied his stone-black ponytail. A friend from Minneapolis handed a tailor-made through the bars. They whispered in the corner, laughing behind enemy lines.

On his way back, the chunky guard pushed his cheeks into the dayroom and wheezed, catching his breath. His face pressed into the bars in folds, like warm bread dough dropped on a sewer grate.
"Oh, shit. Shit," he said. "Oh, man. Can you believe it?"

He scooted away, dabbing his forehead with a damp white handkerchief, his hips swooshing back and forth to the rhythm of his new brown pants wearing sores between his legs.

"My God. Shit. What next?" he muttered his way down the hall.

The screen returned to Bob Barker and the blond man spun around.

"All right. Bid, my man. Bid 'em like you got 'em."

ONE

"You don't know how lucky you are, boys."
— Beatles, "Back In The U.S.S.R."

Twelve years followed because they had no choice.
Day after day.
The blond man, now halfway through his forty-fourth year, his arms covered in orange, sat at the orange D-Block dayroom table.

A California surfer-type who had never seen an ocean, he dealt solitaire facing the twelve-inch color television above the cell door.

He counted three cards and turned the last one up.

He held it between middle finger and thumb, passing the card like a wand over the layout, then pressing the card into the slush pile.

In front of him two black men ranted.

He decided not to hear.

A Mexican-type sat at the table with the blond man, his elbows on the tabletop and his legs stretched ahead.

Another young guy paced up and down, his greasy hair stuck to his forehead, drumming with two pencils on each cell he passed, then tapping the air in between.

He hummed and sang, "Na na na na, na na na na, hey, hey, hey, my, my."

The card player listened to the young man's routine through "The Price Is Right" and "Love Boat."

"It's goodbye," he said without looking up.

The young man skidded to a stop.

He wore blue boat shoes without socks. His orange jumpsuit came to the tops of his ankles. He wore his collar turned up like Elvis Presley. His sleeves were rolled tight over his thin biceps.

"Say what, dude?" he said.

He leered down at the older man, beard coming through in white nubs.

"Am I bothering you, man?" the young man said.

He put his foot on the bench seat and leaned a forearm on his thigh. He led his invisible band, tapping his pencils on the table to a magnified beat.

"No, the song. It's hey, hey, hey, goodbye," the older man said, still studying his cards.

"Who asked you?"

The young man's face flickered, then flamed. Red spots appeared on his neck.

He leaned to glare into the heart of the older man.

The older man looked away from his cards and into the soft eyes and the dried snot in the nostrils, the redness around the nose.

The older man's various parts became ready, like a submarine crew called to general quarters late in an eleventh month at sea.

All the younger man noticed was a slight tightening of the other man's jaw, like tendrils in the shoulders of a lion.

The eyes of the blond man mesmerized the young fellow, the older one as impassive as a house cat observing a black bird out the window.

There was no hatred or affectation in the older man's face. Like the cat he would rip apart his prey without emotion.

The young man did not see the left fist that hit his right temple and crashed his head against the cell bars.

He saw only a flash of the blue shoe that sent blood gushing from his nose.

Then the shoe thudded against the clenched stomach and the other shoe landed in the groin.

The older man returned to his table.

He drew a homemade cigarette from a Marlboro pack.

One of the black men offered a match.

Bobby Ford, who had been standing nearby watching the TV, grabbed the young man lying on his side with his arms locked between his legs.

Ford hugged him from behind and dragged him into his cell.

Ford gritted his teeth and fell with his load onto the bottom bunk, then grabbed the legs and flipped them onto the bed. He hurried out of the cell as the guard's hard shoes clicked down the shiny hall floor.

The Mexican-type shot up and faced the guard through the bars.

"Hey, man," he said. "I got court today-man?"

The short, stocky guard leaned to see around the prisoner.

He examined left then right, leaning, leaning.

He paced back and forth, looking in each cell, squinting to see the ten feet into the dark rooms, homes.

"What's wrong with him?"

He stopped and pointed a size 20EEE walkie-talkie at the man on the bunk with his back to the door. He shined his flashlight.

"Sleepin," said Stephen Baltimore, one of the black men.

The other black, Martin Mumford, walked over to the cell door and hollered.

"Hey, dude, wake up. Wake up. The man here wants to talk to you."

No. No, s'okay," the guard said. "Musta been C-Block. A-gain. Sonofabitch."

"Ah heard that, Burt," said Stephan. "They make a racket."

Ford walked over and reached to turn the television down.

The blond man passed another card over his game and laid it on the ten of hearts, trying to sneak up on his breath.

Don Burton waddled away and turned the corner. He stopped and listened.

The men in D-block waited until they heard the keys again.

The salesman Bobby Ford turned up the sound.

He stood directly under the TV with his arms folded, trying to see under the dresses of the women on the screen. The changing scenes on the set reflected off the spot in the middle of his head.

Stephan called Bobby "ER" because the bald spot resembled an alien landing zone where the cows are found surgically mutilated.

Bobby wiped the palm of his right hand across the spot, leaving his left arm across his chest. He got a rash whenever he came to jail. He returned the right arm to the waiting left one and moved in closer, tilting his chin toward the ceiling.

"He's got hairs growing out his nose," Bobby looked back to Mark Pontiac at his card game.

"Uh, huh," said the blond Pontiac without looking up. He ran off three torn cards. "Who?"

The television news showed the Sioux City courthouse.

Each head in the block shot up.

Martin and Stephan pointed at the set.

Bill Mourning Dove appeared in his cell door drying his hair with a thin white towel.

"That guy."

"That's the courthouse," said Mourning Dove.

"No shit, chief," said Mumford.

"Turn that up," said Baltimore.

Ford didn't move.

"Fucking freak," Mumford stepped in and turned up the sound.

Two young policemen in dark blue pants and light blue shirts, followed by a phalanx of stern men in suits and sunglasses, pulled a medium height, middle-aged white man with a large nose and coal black hair down the court steps. The police officers aimed for the car while the man watched the crowd.

The scene switched to Dan Rather in Washington.

"Michael Zags has been charged with threatening the life of President George Bush."

Rather read from the paper on his desk. He wore a pin-striped shirt with red suspenders. Though only morning, his red tie was loosened. Behind him two spring Columbia graduates holding blank pieces of paper hurried every which way, grinning at each other.

"Sources say federal authorities are preparing charges of conspiracy against Zags. President Bush is schedule to visit Sioux City in the coming months. Bush, a former World War II pilot, will fly a Stealth B-2 bomber from Washington, D.C. to the Sioux City National Guard wing. The 185th Air Guard will become the first unit in the country to employ a Stealth."

The screen showed a batwing B-2 taking off from Fort Bragg.

"Authorities say Zags, a laborer for a Sioux City construction firm, made comments to fellow workers which were threatening to the president. He was arrested at the job site, the Sioux City Irving Elementary school's new gym."

The scene turned to footage of the job foreman talking to a police officer.

"Zags is being held at the Sioux City jail. We'll have more on our evening report. Now we return you to your local programming."

Bobby Ford twirled on his left heel. His arms remained folded at his chest. He squeezed himself tighter and shuffled to the card table.

"He's comin' here," Ford leaned over.

Mark Pontiac asked Ford who he was.

"The guy on TV. He'll be comin' in here. They got to put him in the felony tank. Said he was bein' held in the city jail and he ain't here yet, so he'll be comin.' I ain't takin' no roommate. I like it like it is. It's already crowded," he whispered.

When Pontiac didn't respond, Ford dropped his hands and asked Mourning Dove for a light. The rounding Indian disappeared into the shadows of his cell. His mid-section jiggled with his steps. He returned with a new pack of matches and flipped it to Ford.

"Keep it," he said.

Ford picked a butt from his jumpsuit pocket and lit it with a barely shaking hand.

"Catfish really fucked up that fuckin' Al," said Ford.

The Indian stood in his underwear, holes surrounding the elastic like melting ice.

A homemade India-ink-and-needle-thread tattoo of a lance and eagle feather covered his chest from his collarbone to his left nipple. His tar-black hair, now glistening wet, hung to the middle of his back.

Mourning Dove stared at the back of Pontiac's head, curled over the table, passing a lone card over his game.

Mourning Dove flipped his head back and let out a high-pitched pow-wow chant.

"Hi … yi-yi! Hi yaaa, yaaa. Hi yiyiyi … Hiiiiii!

Ford fell backward, caught himself and shuffled the few feet to the bars, next to the hall.

Mourning Dove watched the man dealing cards to himself.

"Catfish" Pontiac laid out three more cards and flew the fourth in a low run over the stacks.

The black men watched the Indian.

Miguel Mendez lay on his back and set a neatly rolled towel across his eyes.

Not betraying facial expression, Mourning Dove thought

of Pontiac once saying he was part Indian, and that he wanted to "get into" Native spirituality.

Pontiac looked back and Mourning Dove stared until Mark turned away.

Mourning Dove smiled to himself, pirouetted slowly, showing off his aquiline profile, and melted into the darkness. The light in each cell was supposed to burn night and day, dimming at 10 p.m. and brightening at six. Mourning Dove's cell was on the far end. The guards hadn't noticed the light out. He hadn't mentioned it.

The turnover was low in the felony tank. People got to know each other. Sometimes getting to trial or transferred to a federal facility would take over a year. By now the D-block prisoners knew more about each other than they cared.

In cell five lived Bobby Ford, the car salesman going to jury trial for raping the 15-year-old daughter of the Sammy Sindelar Ford dealership owner.

In cell four was Mendez, from Del Rio, Texas, waiting for the INS to return him to El Salvador.

In cell three lay Al Arthur, the great-great grandson of the first mayor of Sioux City. Al's grandfather owned seventy-five percent of the railroad line in the region.

Al managed a countywide methamphetamine ring, once the largest in the state.

Cell two housed Mark Pontiac.

Stephan Baltimore and Martin Mumford bunked in the first cell, right across the lone door to the block.

Baltimore was a student at Morningside College. He was charged with burglarizing apartments in the married student housing complex.

Mumford had been living in the Jesus Saves shelter when he was dragged out of his cot one night just before supper.

The prosecuting attorney said Martin was seen with a man whose body later bumped into a tour pontoon on the

Missouri River full of kindergartners from Saint Agnes Elementary. Martin's case would be going to jury selection very soon, his lawyer said.

Voir dire, said Martin over supper last night, loud enough for the others to hear.

Mark Pontiac's first mother named her boys after the four gospels.

She hoped it would keep them safe or perhaps give them pause.

Then she died.

She also said they could claim some Indian blood, way back.

Their dad said the name came from the Lakota god of compression.

When Mark's father married Martha, his AA sponsor, the old man wondered is she was too young for him.

Martha had plunged into the opportunity to raise boys headfirst, like skinny-dipping on Corn Creek.

Pontiac was now the oldest in D-Block.

"Catfish" had come to jail for drunken disorderly for the past thirty-some years, at least once a year. His record was six.

D-Block was once the misdemeanor tank. Pontiac got used to cell two, and even when it became the felony block he demanded to have his old house back.

They let him stay as long as he signed a sheet saying the city was not liable if he sustained any injuries while incarcerated.

Each time he arrived, Betty or Jennie would tear a fresh page from the pad of forms printed just for him, and then add it to the mess of papers in the manila envelope in the wire basket below the front desk, marked in white tape and black marker: Pontiac, M.

The jail squatted beneath the Woodbury County courthouse, invisible as a good boy to those walking outside, known only for the white vans disappearing into the yawning jaws of the off-white overhead door to the enclosed parking lot.

Each weekday morning the door would groan and open, just enough for the van to reappear to take inmates up the street to the federal courthouse.

Those prisoners needing to appear in county court would walk. They would crowd handcuffed and shackled into the elevator in the jail front lobby with two guards for the ride up two floors.

The door would open into the world of color, people in a hurry, people whose days "flew by." People with smiles on their faces, people with faces serious about nothing.

The door would open and reveal the load of orange men with scraggly, matted hair, men with no reason to shave, who had just walked into a department store holding the hand of a little girl and the girl asked the sleeping man what she could have and he said, nothing, and he woke up in jail with real tears coming down his cheeks.

The door split in two and revealed to the hurried people a crowded little room of orange men who were the reason for the huge building of marble and concrete and stone and hardwood and the salad bar in the lounge.

These almost-men with their bowed heads and tangled hands propped in front of their waists like they were hiding a wet spot shuffled crossway over the lanes of traffic with difficulty, like passing through a cornfield against the rows.

Two brown men stood on the sides of the orange men, keeping them from the hurried people who carried papers concerning the lives and children of the orange men.

In three seconds, four, the orange and brown men slipped inside the lonesome door that led to the damp holding tank outside the rear courtroom door.

Above the stomach-clenching courthouse, after the orange men had been locked in yet another small room, an eagle played on the waves of heat rising from the small city.

She dipped and lowered her wings and never worried about being spotted. The focus of the ground creatures was down.

The eagle admired the town square pattern around the courthouse, the row of barbershops and salons: Sam's Shop, Wave This, the corner grocery store, bookstore, city offices, Wilbur Aalfs Library, and five banks.

The eagle let the heat from the downtown mid-day traffic take her up another whoosh! She saw the schools, public on the east side and Catholic downtown. The eagle loved to admire her black and white feathers in the sun and her face reflecting in the wing mirror, so far above the ground.

The ground.

The eagle imagined Sioux City as a place for bovine types, carpenters, salesmen and ministers who held only shared thoughts, when they told each other what they thought, they always already knew.

These people.

Just lucky to be able to be able to soar above all that.

The smell from the wiener factory, sweet like burnt molasses over manure pancakes, kept the eagle from the south edge of town. She climbed a winding staircase. The motion below slowed and slowed until it stopped.

Mark Pontiac fondled a single card.

The keys rattled in the hall, Stephan and Martin sat on the floor in front of their cell, their arms splayed over their knees.

Miguel Mendez perched on the steel toilet in his cell, his jumpsuit around his ankles, reading a Sports Illustrated laid flat on the shiny smooth green cement floor.

To a new person the block smelled of years of cigarettes and shit and piss.

But it did not bother the men. The long-time prisoners smelled with their memories rather than their noses.

Bill Mourning Dove crouched on the floor of his cell with his feet under his bed using a flattened Marlboro carton on top of the mattress for a writing table. He sat on the limit of three New Testaments.

At the table, Bobby Ford sat across from Pontiac with his back to the cards, facing the television. He jumped up and grabbed the bars when he saw Burton leading a prisoner.

"We get store today?" asked Ford.

"S'posed to," answered the guard.

He spoke into his walkie-talkie and the outer sally port door opened with the sound of a pyramid vault. The prisoner walked in and the outer door closed . The inner door opened.

The prisoner walked in carrying a grey blanket, pale green sheets, toothpaste, toothbrush and black comb, like a dead child in his arms.

Each man studied the new man's arms and determined if he was weak or strong, a potential friend or enemy, whether he had cigarettes.

The man sported thick, black eyebrows and a mischievous half grin like Abbie Hoffman walking into a courtroom.

He didn't appear to care about the stares.

No one spoke to him and he didn't attempt any pleasantries.

He walked into the cell with the knocked-out Al on the lower bunk.

He shinnied up and knelt on the thin mattress of the top berth, like a sailor joining the ship two stops down the line. He began to make his home, kneeling in the middle of the mattress, folding it back, tying the two ends of the sheet in a knot, then repeating at the bottom.

The new guy fitted another sheet and pillow case and smoothed out the scratchy blanket on top.

He stretched out with his hands behind his head, his legs crossed at the ankles.

The toothpaste, toothbrush, and comb fit nicely on the side between the mattress and the steal frame.

Stephan and Martin walked past, staring in.

The dark-haired man's orange suit was crisp, clean, new. He wore black socks inside his slip-on blue tennis shoes.

Pontiac continued dealing.

Mourning Dove wrote.

Bobby Ford walked up to the new man's cell door. Careful not to put a foot inside, Ford leaned on the bar.

"We saw you on TV, man."

The man gazed at Bobby in silence.

"The feds bunking you here, then?"

"Yeah."

"What's your name?" asked Ford.

"Zags, Michael."

"Zags Michael?" Ford said.

"Michael, Zags," said the man. "Same either way."

"Acey-doocey!" shouted Mumford.

"Oh, yeah, like Boy George," smiled Ford.

The man sat up on the edge of his bed. He pulled an unopened pack of Marlboros from his jumpsuit pocket. He wore a white T-shirt underneath.

"Palandrone," said Pontiac, barely audible.

"Need a match?" said Bobby. He reached up and handed Michael a pack with one match left.

"Get one a those?" said Ford. "We're supposed to get store today." He looked into the hall.

The two black men walked past slowly, staring up at the man on the top bunk. Michael folded his pants leg up and flicked the ash in the cuff.

"How long you been here?" he asked Ford.

"Nine months. I'm about due, huh? Going to trial pretty soon. I'll be getting' outa here."

"Mmm, mmm," hummed the new guy. He nodded his head.

"You been charged yet?" said Bobby.

"No. I don't think so. The marshals said they'd be back," said Zags.

"Your cellie had kind of a rough morning," Bobby nodded at Al, now beginning to rally.

Al sat to the edge, his head bowed to fit under the top bunk. He rubbed his eye with the heel of an open hand, then noticed the feet dangling in front of his face.

He jumped up and confronted Michael Zags.

"What? Oh, ma-an!" he said. "What you doin' here? Shit."

He unbuttoned his fly and with eyes closed took a leak in the stainless steel toilet with no lid. He leaned over, pushed the knob above the stainless steel sink, and leaned over to suck a drink from the faucet. He stood and wiped his mouth, looking up at Zags.

"When you get here?"

"Just now," said Bobby Ford, stepping inside the cell.

"Am I talking to you?" said Al. "The man can talk, can't he?"

"Just now," said Michael.

He puffed the cigarette in his left hand and ashed in the cuff.

Keys jingled.

Burton appeared in the hallway, head down, arms pumping, walkie-talkie in his right hand, clipboard in the other.

He stopped at the cell door.

"Chow time!"

He hollered then spoke into the machine.

The men lined up at the door.

"Chow time! Chief! You coming?"

Mourning Dove stood in his door and combed his hair. He slowly buttoned his jumpsuit and flipped the comb back on the bed.

The first door opened. The men crowded inside the sally port.

Mourning Dove moseyed down, then inside with the rest.

Burton spoke into his walkie-talkie and the door closed as if he were speaking to the iron bars.

KGB

The outer door opened and the men elbowed their way into the hallway to begin fast-walking, followed by a panting Burton, speaking into his walkie-talkie, telling the front desk he was taking D-block to the cafeteria.

TWO

"THE WAY THINGS ARE GOING, THEY'RE
GONNA CRUCIFY ME."
— JOHN LENNON

Paul Novotny sat in traffic counting the steps on the water tower.

The noonday glare pissed him off.

He clenched his teeth and slammed down the visor.

It's the sensitive types who climb the water tower with high-powered rifles, Paul resumed his reverie. They drive us to it. The bastards.

Hiking his sweat pants into the fold between his ribs and chest, Paul raised his chin to view himself in the rearview and see if he was gay.

Paul strained to tune the radio.

In his peripheral vision he saw the light switching to yellow. He sensed the cars around him sliding away, leaving him.

The white Camry with gold piping behind him shouted its horn.

Paul held up a finger to the rear window and continued to search the dial with his left hand.

"Paul Harvey … good day. Sghtietbt. You look wonderful to-night. Wwwierbnvvv. Sirhan-Sirhan. With atrazine. Ggggll. I'm Bob Edwards."

"And you're not," whispered Paul.

The Camry edged up, nudging Paul's tan Escort.

Paul decided to dis' the out of state plates.

He leaned into the brake pedal, motioned the Camry around and walked the radio arrow right.

The right lane cleared, but the Camry driver beeeeeped his horn, rolled down his window and shouted at Paul to get the fuck outa the way!

She had to be there.

The light clicked to red.

The lanes filled in around Paul. The Camry inched back. A black and white Sioux City police cruiser slid up next to Paul. Paul dragged the shifter into first and stared straight. Paul turreted his head right. The black officer glared until Paul looked away.

He watched the light while moving the knob with his right hand.

The light clicked to green.

Paul moved away within the flow.

What if I could go-gay right now? Shee-it.

He spread his thighs and picked his balls free. He signaled and moved to the right lane. He put his left hand to the window and gave the Camry a no-look finger as it moved past.

Paul turned right, down Nebraska Street. Looking up the hill he saw the walkway between Norwest and Penney's, the sidewalks littered with walkers, lingering fog, orange and yellow blinkers.

Paul steered with his knees while he lit an Old Gold. He rolled down his window.

The KZOO morning show, Mike & Ike, went to commercial.

Paul eased in behind a purple mini-van and tried again. He heard crackling. His arms ached.

He noticed a familiar tone. He backtracked and fine-tuned.

"Good day, my friend," the deep female voice brought the day's first smile.

Paul cranked the wheel and on the green cut off a Yellow cab to park on the curb.

He put the car in gear, stopped the engine, then turned the key and sighed in relief at the return of the voice.

"This is Radio Free Siouxland, broadcasting the underground seeds of the revolution with legs astride the weather ball in downtown, on top of the Terre Center, Sioux City, Iowa. America.

Paul pulled the lever to recline his seat.

"You can get no further into the heart of America, the beast. This is it, the stomach, the belly, the soul, the lungs, the gut.

"Here in the slaughterhouse, and all parts of the animal are put to use, for no good whatsoever."

Paul tugged the emergency brake and pushed the button locking all doors. He pried each heel from his tennis shoes and watched the road and foot traffic from below the low bill of his cap with steely, narrowed eyes.

He strained to see the weather ball on top of that one building next to the cop shop.

"When the weather ball be red, we all be dead. The weather ball be green, Wall Street obscene. Weather ball is blue, they come lookin' for you. Weather ball be white, no brothers in sight.

"Yes, the weather ball is black, bad times ahead. But you know that rain is good for the crops, don't they say?

"But today we play! We're going to send out some Jackson Browne, Lou Reed and Mr. John Prine for you this morning.

"This is Elana, at KFU."

Pretending to sleep, Paul watched a mail carrier in shorts and knee socks coming down the sidewalk with an antenna sticking out of his bag.

"Remember, all next week, I'll be on a live clandestine remote from the Southern Hills Mall. Bring your Walkman and we be jammin'!"

The mailman passed without incident.

Paul swiveled his head slowly and saw two brown men on the corner, a line of sweat down both of their white T-shirts.

Ahaa! thought Paul. Wetbacks.

He turned up his radio as a sheriff's car sped by.

Paul scrunched farther down.

"You know, as I sit in my window and watch you all hurrying to work I wonder if we've used up all our tokens, you know?

"If we're coming to the end of the line.

"You been hearing about the Truth Commission in South Africa?

"Why don't we have a truth commission in the United States?

"Who killed Bobby Kennedy?"

Paul shot up and worked the knob as she drowned in static.

"You killed Martin King? Why? Excuse me, Mr. Haig, Ms. Kirkpatrick, Mr. Abrams, just how many people did we kill in El Salvador? And did we care that they had their heads cut off, their organs stuff into their mouths as they died? Not-a-problem? Hmm."

Paul stuck his right hand into his front pocket. He dug way down, fishing for a cigarette. He pulled up what looked like a watermelon Lifesaver. He picked off what lint he could and stuck the candy into his mouth.

"Yes, Mr. Clinton. How you doing? Why can't Leonard Peltier get a fair trial? Paul curled his toes as his lady of the radio went on and on.

"What is the FBI really up to around here? Let's organize a Cub Scouts tour of the Hoover Building and that CIA compound and that National Security Agency thing.

"What's this all about? May we help you, citizen?

"Well, yes. I'd like to read that file that I paid for, and that one over there, too.

"And I'll take two of those chartreuse folders with the burgundy clips.

"Ye-ees, honey, Mr. Director, come sit on my lap and you tell me what you've been up to today, now, chil'. Such a big boy."

Paul felt motion. He felt as if he were slipping off the planet, like Apollo in free-fall.

Boom!

His rear bumper hit the front bumper of the Yellow Taxi behind him. Paul jerked around and saw the car was empty. He started his car and pulled up a few feet.

"… you know what I'm saying?" she said.

"Poverty is not the problem. It's the solution.

"We need to look for the lie, friends, look for the lie, in the eyes, on the tongue.

"Listen, y'all, I got to be gone.

"I hear the pitter-patter of little jackboots. Lou and John will have to stay the night with me. Seems that we're out of time. No more tokens to play today. Here's that Jack Browne I've been promising.

"Lives in the balance. I've been waiting for something to happen.

"Y'all be good.

"Until tomorrow … stop obeying."

As the music played, Elana Usak swiveled the chair to look out her window. She tried to guess the vehicles with her show tuned in. Maybe that pickup, that garbage truck, the El Dorado in front of the bakery with its motor revving.

The station went to static before the song finished.

Paul opened his eyes and moved his seat up.

He flipped the visors and turned off the radio.

He released the park brake and started the car. He looked in the mirror and turned into traffic, causing a Budweiser truck to slam on its brakes.

Paul checked his side mirror and moved to the middle lane.

KGB

He moved up the hill in jerks, stopping at each light, keeping his right foot on the brake and half on the gas.

When he reached the top, the sun chimed nine o'clock, the sidewalk people sat down at computer terminals and the beer truck lurched into a grocery parking lot.

Paul chugged over the crest, past the Catholic high school, and disappeared down, into a maw of white houses.

THREE

"We are not deceived by their pretenses to piety. We
have seen their kind before. They are the heirs of all the
murderous ideologies of the 20th century. By sacrificing
human life to serve their radical visions, by abandoning
every value except the will to power, they follow in the path
of fascism and Nazism and totalitarianism. And they will
follow that path all the way, to where it ends, in history's
unmarked grave of discarded lies."

— GEORGE W. BUSH, SEPT. 20, 2001,
SPEECH TO CONGRESS, DECLARING WAR ON TERROR

E lana saw Paul Novotny pull in front of the beer
truck. She saw the Woodbury County Sheriff,
Jeremiah Williger, driving slowly past.
From her second floor perch Elana noticed the navy blue
Ford and the two insurance men who could have been
Federal Communications Commission agents in another
life. The springtime morning air chilled the sweat on her
forehead.

She closed her eyes, sucked down the pancake aroma
from The Nebraksa Café below her and considered her
good fortune. The wind today floated past from the north,
keeping the hog slaughtering smell of South Sioux City
across the river. She twirled back, shut down her equipment and walked into the kitchen for more coffee. Her

living room was full of plants and radio machinery, second hand stuff, microphone, mixing board, transmitter, cart machine, CD players she had picked up at a ham operators swap meet during the Sturgis Rally summers ago, all on a bare, shining hardwood floor.

The antenna ran up the inside wall to the roof and connected to the line running up the side of the First Security Tower, giving her use of the largest building in the city.

They were getting close.

She felt it.

She thought about staying off the air for a while.

Returning to the office living room, Elana shook her head to get the sticky hair out of her eyes. Holding her cup with both hands in front of her face she stepped close to the poster of a bridge in Prague hoping to see her father. The laminated newspaper columns and her diploma from the "U" attempted to fill the south wall and cover the pockmarks in the legal pad yellow texture.

She moved in swaying elephant steps to the bookshelf, uneven strips of boards from the alley Dumpster supported by chipped bricks and concrete blocks. She had lifted them from the Firststar Bank site on Western Avenue and hauled them up the two flights in her backpack on successive August solo Hamm's Lite party nights.

She scanned the titles for something new: Journalism texts, Radio For Dummies, The Complete Manual of Pirate Radio, Radio Free Berkeley Yearbook, Basic Electronics, FCC Rulebook, Czech Book of Verbs.

A year's worth of the Sioux City Journal, Des Moines Register, Sioux Falls Argus Leader and New York Times was stacked neatly in piles next to the bookstand.

Elana returned to the window, the sidewalks and streets now empty. She shook her head and snorted softly. She was probably the only person, in history, ever to move to Sioux City to get away from the Twin Cities.

She put the cup under her nose and breathed deep,

expanding her economical chest. She squatted and set the smoking cup on the window ledge, and resting her chin on her arms welcomed the chill of the spring morning.

Why did that angry little man park at the curb each morning? Was the beer man single or did he have three kids and a house with no trees up on a hill east of the mall. What would it be like to be the older man there in the suit, walking with a briefcase from the '50s from his brick home and grandkids in Morningside.

Maybe she could become a teaching Franciscan at Briar Cliff, eat with a group and play cards or walk giggling to a movie in the evening. They'd excuse one lil ol' abortion, forgiveness is their cash crop, for Jesus-mageezuz. Ride in a station wagon to the dog races in Omaha on the Fourth of July. Drink keg beer from flowered cups on a fairy tale June evening sitting on donated lawn chairs in one humongous wooded backyard.

Elana sipped her coffee and spilled on her top. She patted her breast and saw that the square Ford sat empty.

She leaned her forehead into the screen and saw the heel of a black shoe going into the building. She sprinted into the dining room, flopped onto her stomach and pressed her ear to the floor. She heard a flurry of scuffled thuds hurrying up the stairs.

Shh. Shh. Boomboomboomboom.

Elana sprang. She grabbed her jacket from the wall, scooped tapes into her backpack, unhooked the screen, lifted it and brought it inside, setting it against the wall.

Two alternating hammers beat the door.

"FCC! Open the door!"

A plastic photo ID slid under the door along the wood floor.

She got on all fours to read it.

Damn. Why were good looking guys always mad at her?

Elana stepped through the open window, grabbed the ledge and eased herself down to hang.

A retired farm couple from east of Sergeant Bluff, seated in one of the front booths, was startled when the toes of Elana's white Reeboks popped down to slam the middle of the front café window.

Elana heard her door crashed down and let go.

She hit the sidewalk and flexed her knees.

She hurried into the café, stumbling, catching herself on the building.

She sat down at the counter and ordered coffee with pancakes. She reached into her jacket pocket for paper and pen.

In an exaggerated right-hand scrawl she began to take down the details of the scene around her.

The diners heard above them the banging and slamming of furniture.

A flurry of squad cars skidded to the curb and officers rushed in, pounding up the stairs opposite the south wall of the café. Puffs of plaster poofed down from the textured ceiling like fairy dust.

Elana continued to jot notes in her white rectangular pad tucked under her saucer.

Elana's transmitter exploded on the sidewalk.

The café owner wiped red hands down the back of her pants and stood by her front window talking to the couple in the booth.

Elana slurped her coffee and watched her pancakes steam in the serving kitchen window. The remainder of the dozen customers stood by the front and south windows kibitzing the law.

A Channel 4 television van jumped the curb to park on the sidewalk. The Channel 9 crew squealed and stopped crossways in the street.

Boom! Boom!

Elana's CD players landed in the street. Shrapnel tinked against the café window. Down came her speakers and microphone. Out flew her books and shelves, diplomas and family photos. The old couple jumped and raised their hands to their heads. The crowd at the windows ducked as if a plane were buzzing them.

Yellow plastic ribbons connected the café to the parking meters and the rose bush in the Egyptian pot outside Bobby's Barber Shop.

The café owner herded her customers back to their food. She found Elana's pancakes and set them down.

Elana asked for more coffee.

The owner met a line of customers at the cash register.

The old couple looked through the "C" and "A" at the pile of life on the walk.

There was a stack of pink and blue underwear carried out by fingertips by a female U.S. Marshal and dropped on the stack. A Hispanic FBI agent from South Omaha had two halves of Elana's Prague poster in his hands as he came down the enclosed steps, turning sideways to allow a TV cameraman past.

A circle of uniformed officers kept news crews away from an interior circle. Woodbury County Sheriff Jeremiah Williger conferred with Special agents Don Hargrove and Jeffrey Fry of the FCC. The cameramen filmed from beyond the outside circle and the reporters shouted questions.

The auto da fe complete, the pastel FBI units one-by-one pushed away and disappeared.

"She's not far," said Williger. "Shit, we had 'er right in 'er winda."

Hargrove held an open can of Skoal. He put a three-finger pinch in his lower lip, closed the can and returned it to his shirt pocket. He searched the skinny sheriff's balding head for dandruff.

The sheriff carried his round hat with its plastic rain cover.

Hargrove shook his head at the sharp-toed cowboy boots.

"All right. You want some lunch?" Hargrove looked at his gold watch.

"This stuff OK here?" Williger waved his hat over the debris on the sidewalk.

Hargrove looked up and down the streets.

"Yeah."

Hargrove, Williger and Fry moved through the milling herd of stout black and white city police. They stopped in front of a bright camera light.

"This was an illegal radio operation," Hargrove answered a question.

"We call these tiny stations pirates. They reach barely a few blocks, but they jam the radio frequencies for the authentic operators and offer a threat to the public safety."

Hargrove let a stream of spit splat on the cement.

"They are a public nuisance. They serve no public good, often act as a focal point for drug dealers to sell their products."

"But can you stop them? asked a reporter.

"This one won't be up and running anytime soon. She walked the plank. The sharks'll get her," Hargrove chuckled.

Hargrove held the screen door for Williger and Fry.

The owner poured coffee for Elana. The older couple stared at the large men in the brown and blue windbreakers. The men moved to the booth in the corner, behind the couple, able to look below the "E" into the street.

The owner forced a smile, scooped her pencil from the counter and took the men's order.

The old man in the booth motioned to his wife. He nodded toward the men behind her. She twisted her napkin. Elana's heart beat a rap song she didn't know she knew. The deep bass with the car widow down on a summer night stamped its rhythm in her chest.

The owner stopped in front of Elana on her way to the kitchen.

"The guy in the corner," she said nodding.

Elana began to slide from her stool.

"He says give you a refill on him. Such a sweetheart."

Elana looked over at Fry, who saluted her. Elana looked away. She breathed, closed her eyes: thousand one, thousand two, let it out.

With gritted teeth the old man pushed up from the table. With great effort he straightened his back, then went crooked as soon as he began to shuffle the few feet to the law officers. He continued to stare at his wife, who smiled at Elana when he looked away to concentrate on the next step.

The man grabbed the plastic chair behind Hargrove's shoulder. The lawmen stopped talking. The old man positioned himself between them, leaned in to the table, steadied himself with his right hand and pointed with his left back at the counter where the owner was collecting her tip and wiping up Elana's spill.

Elana Usak tore out of the café to the corner, took a left, sprinted and hung another louie, then crossed the street dodging traffic.

She jogged into the front door of the City Hall, feeling the breath of the hounds on her neck, tap-tapping across the interminable marble hallway. She exited on the next block, crossed the street and entered the library, where she hurried to the women's restroom.

She sat in an empty stall with her pants around her ankles waiting for her heart to stop.

The door opened.

It took all day long in closing.

Elana grabbed her pants with both hands.

Slow steps, hard-healed-sole steps, clicked across the tile.

Something heavy hit the door.

The water began to run.

"Mommy-I-go-potty-now," a little voice announced.

Elana flushed, zipped, buttoned, and unlocked the stall.

She nodded to a white woman washing her son's hands, and opened the door a slit.

Elana walked with her chin to her chest to the pay phone.

She huddled up to the booth, curling her shoulder, tucking her hand into her scant cleavage. She dug for change and called Martha Pontiac at work.

The phone rang across town in the sociology department of Morningside College.

Elana sat on the high stool, watching her tennis shoes without seeing, fingering the pattern on the front of her Timberwolves T-shirt and cried when she heard the voice.

She squeaked the chair around and burrowed into the scarred booth.

"Martha. I need to talk," she said, wiping her nose with the back of her hand.

Elana huddled in a corner of the entrance until the Yellow Cab pulled up.

She pursed her lips and hurled herself out the door like a celebrity seeking sanctuary.

The black driver said, "Elana?" and opened the back door for her as if they had rehearsed.

She flopped inside and lay on the seat.

"You goin' to the college?" he said. "They said don't worry about paying. You a student?"

"No," she said.

From her back she watched the buildings pass. She saw the black electrical tape on her former antenna.

They turned left and she slid her head to the door, a right sent her toward her feet. They sat in traffic and she tried to be invisible by closing her eyes. They roller-coastered over the viaduct, where Elana caught a glimpse of a billboard for the Channel 9 personalities.

She saw overhead wires and cloud wisps that turned to trees, and they entered the Morningside neighborhood, the middle class working folks east-edge backbone of Sioux City.

The driver tuned to KZ98.

"Officials say they broke up a major methamphetamine ring this morning in the downtown. FBI, FCC and Woodbury County officials joined with Sioux City police to raid the second floor apartment of Elana Usak, 211 Nebraska Avenue, during the mid-morning drivetime.

"Usak is being sought. Anyone with information that leads to her apprehension will be eligible for a CrimeStoppers CrimeDog Award, which includes a box of steaks from Vision World and three orange Jell-O salads from the Hy-Vee Deli."

With narrow eyes Elana watched the top edge of the front seat.

She closed her eyes. She recalled her last day on her previous job.

Every time this happens I can't believe where I've just been.

She had backed her peach Ford Explorer out of the drive.

She and Mitch lived on Minnetonka Boulevard in Minneapolis, the perfect, tall-tree-taller-houses avenue that evokes thoughts of Disney movie sets, perfect Christmas eves and summer walks serenaded by the applause of water sprinklers on night cycle, with the inferred deep sighs of blue jays.

Beyond Minnetonka was Lake Street, which Elana took to work each morning to get the feel, she said.

Mitch grabbed the freeway.

Elana drove past all the colors and conditions of the world moving up Lake, past the stares of the early bird drug dealers and the groups of kids heading to school, then crossed the Mississippi into Saint Paul.

She then turned right, past the College of St. Thomas onto Summit Avenue because she liked the feel of that, too.

She curved around the Basilica down into the city past the Science Museum, the Fitzgerald Theatre and over to the parking ramp and The Pioneer Press.

She and Mitch were columnists for the paper.

Mitch covered the Twins.

Elana wrote about whatever she liked.

Her column ran top to bottom on the first column of page one every day of the week. Her photo was the first thing readers saw every damn day of their lives.

Elana liked it that way.

She liked being known without having to know people; being able to talk to people without having to sit down and listen to them.

She didn't mind the one-on-one interviews, but put her on a long table over drinks at a staff Christmas party or trapped with a group of people walking the same way down the street and she was soon looking for the first mother-fucker to Kung Fu in the Adam's Apple to get herself the-fuck-free.

On her last day she had been called into her editor's glass office.

While looking out the forty-yard-dash-length window overlooking the Mississippi, the editor began to cry. She said that Elana's series of columns "Among the Hmong," that they had thought was going to win awards, was now the reason she would have to fire Elana.

The editor had received calls, and as it turned out, one of the sources for the last in the series of fourteen columns was not a commentator for Minnesota Public Radio, but a barmaid in the Orion Room on the top floor of the IDS tower in Minneapolis with a taste for powerful men, if you understand what I'm saying, the editor said. Elana should have checked it out more carefully. The editor was sorry, she said.

Elana and Mitch had not wed. They wanted to live the good life before they settled down, they agreed.

Elana moved out, lived in an apartment above a Laotian grocery store on the corner of Lake and West Humphrey.

For weeks she sat in her room and watched people out her window, clutching her tea cup to her chest.

At night she would walk all over town, down Hennepin Avenue, out to Lake Minnetonka, down Nicollette Avenue.

Once she looked both ways, strode to the middle of the street, and tossed her clothing rack stocking cap in the air. The wind caught it and she never saw that fucking orange thing ever again.

Once atop the world, astride the Twin Cities, she was now humiliated.

Talk radio shows, Star-Tribune and Pioneer Press reporters, and gossip columnists made "Elana U-suck" jokes for weeks, grateful for the opportunity to chop her down to size.

After three months in the apartment, three months of staring out the window and three months of walking all night, she came to feel blessed by her humiliation. She had not deserved fame. This was who she really was, no better than anyone else. No one to be driving past in the shiny, waxed automobile taking notes through locked doors and windows.

She thought she had begun to understand.

She did not deserve the Twin Cities. She deserved to start again, this time at the beginning, the bottom dollar. Alaska? No, cliché.

She began to wonder why nobody ever talked about Sioux City, Iowa.

And that made her want to go there. She needed to be punished.

The car turned and curved, then stopped.

"Here ya go-ooo," the driver sang a dropping-off-ditty.

Elana sat up and let herself out. She thanked him and looked around at students strolling in one's and two's with arms stuffed with books and basketballs.

In one of the windows she saw Martha waving with both hands and smiling.

She motioned for Elana to come inside and pointed stabbing daggers toward the door.

Martha whisked around the desk and opened her arms for Elana to enter.

They hugged as a crowd of students surged out of the building, straining toward the bright spring light at the end of the hall, weaving around a wave of incoming headed to their next class.

Elana felt warm inside Martha's thick, loose sweater.

Martha kicked the door closed and asked Elana to sit in the deep chair amid the plants.

Elana brushed aside a leaf and plopped.

She looked around at the posters, plaques, stacks of loose papers, padded walking shoes. Two walls were filled with leaning stacks of paperbacks, textbooks, novels.

"I heard about you, girl," said Martha.

"You've had yourself a busy morning."

"You did?"

Elana slid down in the chair.

She shook her head and stuffed each hand into the sleeve of the other.

"What the hell-happened!" said Martha.

She got up to close the blind.

"The sun's right in your face. I can't see you, but everyone else can."

Most people looked like someone else, Martha had decided long ago.

Elana resembled that perky woman who fakes the orgasm in the movie in the restaurant.

And she thought she herself looked a lot like Susan Sarandon with long graying hair. Her husband had wanted her to cut it. Made her look like a hippie, he said, which she was not.

But she was, Martha understood.

And it was funny how some things took on importance once you were on The Big Slide, that ethereal Wal-Mart dressing room in which people change their shapes, their sizes, maybe their souls, and come out not recognizable to someone who sat next to them at The Big Game.

Martha's hair had become her thing. She'd hated it as a

kid, cut it short as a boy's just to be rid of it, out of the way. Now she bathed it, combed it, read to it, wore it up, down, all around.

She had noticed that her male students, the young boys with an eye for such things, took an interest in how Martha wore her hair. On Fridays she had taken to leaving an extra button undone on a sweater, with no shirt underneath and letting one side of her hair flow into that mysterious crevice. She could see the young boys dying in their seats to find out where that hair had gone. Those dirty young boys and she such on old hippie woman. And she liked that.

"They came."

Elana began to tear up again.

Her lower lip quivered.

"You would not believe it," she said.

"I took notes."

She reached into her pocket and touched her notebook.

"What will you do?" asked Martha. "Is there anyone in the group you could talk to?"

Elana closed her eyes, tilted her head toward the floor, and put up a hand like an aggravated traffic cop.

"No. Don't go there. Those people are nuts."

"Perhaps they could help. Have you considered coming back?"

Elana shot up.

She leaned on Martha's desk with both hands.

"You think I'm crazy. Don't you? You're just like them.

"Well, I'm not. They really did come for me."

She stood and put both hands on her hips, inverted, the way some people can do.

"They put my underwear … on … the … street!

"Lucky I just washed last night."

She sat in the big chair, crossed her legs and looked away at nothing.

"Just because you're paranoid, doesn't mean," her voice dropped into the planter.

Martha walked to the door and turned the latch, then tried it.

She returned to her desk and crossed her hands on the desk.

"Agoraphobiacs some times …," she began.

Elana reached for the stack of "The Progressive" magazines on the floor to her right and fired three at Martha. They flew around Martha's head like a dysfunctional teal family attempting to take off in a sleet storm.

"Sometimes experience events from … an …," Martha plowed on, ducking more magazines.

"From an … disparate point of view."

Elana pounded both feet onto the floor at once and squeezed the chair arms.

"Which means?" Elana said.

Martha breathed deep.

"Which means, that whatever happened may not have happened to quite the degree you are experiencing it," she said.

"Have you got a car?" Elana said.

"The Chevy," said Martha.

The doors squeaked and the tires were dusty and bald, but Martha was afraid to get a new one. She didn't want to find out if the kids loved her for her car or vice versa. They stuck bumper stickers on the front and back. They wrote messages in the film covering the olive green body — love letters to each other and day-to-day stuff: "I thought you were going to call." "I left a note on Martha's car. I had practice."

The back fins took another half parking space both ways. Martha's abnormal psyche class decorated it each fall for the homecoming parade. She drove, students filled the inside and three could fit on each fin. They tossed those spin wheels with the never-ending circles to the little kids.

"Let's go," said Elana.

Elana got in the passenger side while Martha squeaked her door open and threw her dress and hair inside and followed.

"Go to my place," Elana said.

"I thought," said Martha.

"I know what you think, just drive."

Elana gently place her hand on Martha's thigh.

"Please. Drive."

Martha slowed at the café.

Elana ducked.

The crime scene yellow ribbon still flapped in the breeze, and Elana's under clothes were scattered along the curb and gutter. Her equipment pile filled the walk under the window. The café owner swept pieces from her property.

Martha leaned low and saw people in the window upstairs.

Two empty police cars hugged the curb tight.

Martha gained speed. Elana pushed up.

Elana put her arm in her window and let the wind play with her hand. She stuck her head out and shook her hair. She watched herself in the side mirror.

"You'll stay with me," said Martha while watching the road.

She signaled a right turn with her arm, then used both hands to crank the wheel.

Elana smiled and let her hair blow as Martha went fast.

FOUR

<u>DALLAS. OGLALA. WACO. MEMPHIS. RUBY RIDGE.
LOS ANGELES. NEW YORK CITY.</u>

D-Block filed inside the block after lunch. Don Burton sang high to himself, "In the garden of Eden, baybay."

After the cell door banged and the walls shuddered, Burton walked away with Bobby Ford following him from inside the day room like a tiger cub in a zoo.

"I get any money on my books yet?"

Burton said he didn't know. Ford asked if he would check for him. Burton said he would when he got time.

"I 'preciate that," said Ford.

"Fat fag," said Ford when Burton was gone.

Michael Zags sat down across from Mark Pontiac.

Stephen Baltimore and Martin Mumford stood on opposite ends of the table. Miguel Mendez lay on the floor he had mopped that morning, his hands folded on his stomach.

Bill Mourning Dove, the last inside the block, began chanting a pow-wow song.

"Corn dogs ... hi! hi! ... with white bread ... and white boys ... the other white meat."

"Shuddup," came a voice from down the hall.

"Doing the lunch thang with you just makes me want to sing, Burt," Bill shouted, pitching his chin into the hall.

44

"M.D., Doctor Eagle Feather," said Baltimore. "Come over here. We got ourselves a political prisoner in our mother-fucking midst."

Bill stood behind Mumford, peering around his shoulder at Zags lighting a cigarette. Mourning Dove walked away and chanted.

The high-pitch sent a chill down Zags' back.

Alford Arthur walked past the group and plopped into his bunk with his face to the cement wall. He plucked the pencil stub from the side of his mattress and crossed off another day on the calendar on his wall.

He lay with his left cheek against his pillow, a washcloth covering his eyes and the grey blanket pulled over his shoulders. He scrunched his knees to his chest and folded his hands under the blanket, saying Hail Mary's until he fell asleep.

Zags offered cigarettes to Pontiac, Mumford and Baltimore. Pontiac wagged his head no and kept dealing.

"What you say, you jus' told some guys you fel' like offin' the pres'dent and they put yo' fuck-nass in jail?" Mumford snarled.

Zags nodded and half-smiled.

He lit his cigarette.

"Ohh, they don't like nobody messing around with the president coming to town," said Baltimore. "Shit. A po-li-ti-cal. Like Ghandi. Mohandas K in orange jammies. Shiit." He waved both hands at Zags. Pontiac looked up at Michael Zags.

Pontiac saw the lines in the new man's face running from his eyes, away from his mouth, enveloping his nose.

He saw the long hairs stringing from the long nostrils. Zags took the strong fingernails of his creased right hand and pinched a group of nose hairs. With a dental yank he plucked them and examined them, white and brown, in his fingertips.

"Geezuz!" cried Pontiac.

"Ain't no thang," smiled Baltimore. "Ha! You see that?" he looked at Mumford.

The two black men each took a step back, turned their backs, then pivoted and marched back to the table, resting their third knuckles on the chipped paint.

"Who are you?" said Pontiac, looking at Zags.

"Nobody," said Zags.

"He's a muthafuckin' Cool Hand Luke," laughed Baltimore.

"Failure to communicate, that's what we got. Ha! He's just been out there ripping heads off parking meters, like it ain't no thang. Shiiit."

Pontiac almost smiled and pulled a perfect rolled cigarette from the Marlboro pack in his pocket. The tobacco Tampax was uniform in circumference from tip to tip with the seams in line.

Pontiac produced a match pack from below the table and lit his rollie.

He inhaled with eyes closed and held the cigarette in front of his face, pinched between the tips of the yellowed middle finger and thumb of his right hand.

"They said you work construction," he said.

"Hmm, mmm," said Zags.

"My dad laid brick and block, poured driveways," said Pontiac.

"I tended six bricklayers myself, includes mixing mud, raising scaffold. I kept them contented as babies in a crib. Not a peep."

"Commendable," said Zags.

Pontiac admired the cuts on Zags' hands, the lime stains, and the fresh Portland cement in his eyebrows. Pontiac noticed that the eyes were red. The lids bobbed like rowboats.

"You been drinkin', right?" said Pontiac.

Zags looked up.

"Just tired. We were out late. The Legion. I could use a nap."

"Why are you here?" said Pontiac. "Why would they bring in some square joe? What they tell you to find out in here? What do you get?"

The men stood at the sides of the table, fuses lit, like two Black Cobras ready to explode.

Zags looked into Pontiac's eyes.

Zags' eyes were no longer tired and droopy.

"I don't get nothin," said Zags.

He stuffed his cigarette out in the gum wrapper foil ashtray, rose and walked into his cell.

In one motion, like a cougar climbing to an afternoon sunspot, he reached his lair. He lay on his back with an arm over his face.

Within a minute his snores forced Pontiac to motion to Bobby Ford to turn up the damn sound on the damn television.

Like cake frosting melting in November the day somehow ended.

And without mercy another followed.

"You get three," the prisoner running the book cart told Pontiac.

Pontiac reached through the bars to touch old-friend paperbacks on metal shelves.

The trusty leaned against the bars, kicking the stuck wheel, watching the books as if they were his dead mother's personal collection.

Pontiac pulled out a Louis L'Amour without a front cover, "Walden," "One Flew Over The Cuckoo's Nest," and a New Testament.

"That's four," said the inmate librarian. "You get three."

Pontiac cupped the books in his right arms and walked to his cell. He exited with the New Testament, which he took to Mourning Dove's door and tossed it on his bed.

The trusty pushed the squeaky wheel down the damn hall.

Michael Zags and Al Arthur sat at the table playing rummy. Bobby Ford stared up at the TV. Stephan and Martin lounged in front of their cell, arms on their legs, catching a few rays from the hall light. Bill Mourning Dove leaned with his hands on the frame of Miguel Mendez' cell.

"Somebody oughta take him out," said Mourning Dove.

"Talk to protester. He's a hit man. He can do the job, man." Mourning Dove talked with his back to Zags and Arthur.

Mendez didn't answer.

He pushed off and walked through Mourning Dove to stand at the table, hovering over the card players.

"You kill people for money," stated Mendez.

"No," said Zags.

"But if you've got cash or a money order I'll talk to my old friend Mr. Alford Arthur and he can get back to you when it's convenient for both of you."

Zags picked the butt of a handmade cigarette with his middle finger and thumb out of the tinfoil ashtray. He put the stub to his mouth, sucked and squinted.

Mendez turned to Mourning Dove.

"He ain't about nothing," Mendez reported.

Zags heard "fucking punk."

"How much you got?" Zags said over his shoulder toward Mourning Dove's cell.

Mendez walked back and sat next to Zags.

"I want you to blow somebody away," he whispered.

"Unless somebody is in this block, I won't be able to help you, pardner," said Zags. "I'm not going anywhere."

"Why don' you jus' blow yerself?" said Arthur, glaring briefly at Mendez. He scooped up a pyramid of cigarettes he had rolled and stalked toward his cell.

Mendez grabbed Arthur's spot across from Zags. He leaned hard on his forearms resting on the table top.

"I don't like my wife's boss, man. I want you to shoot him, then stab him. I want you to cut off his dick and stuff it in his mouth. I will pay you a hundred dollars when I get out. I want you to put his balls in his hands and make him crush them."

Zags sighed. "Troubles. Troubles everywhere.

"You think it over, make sure what it is you want, and I'll double-check with our scheduling department. I thought you were being deported."

"My brother will send you the money. Will you do it?"

"Sorry, no," said Zags. "Darn tempting, though, hard to pass up. I didn't know you had a brother."

Pontiac sat down next to Mendez. Pontiac put his book on the table and read to himself. Mendez walked past Zags staring down at him.

"It's in the Indian's voice," said Zags. "Isn't it? I thought that was different."

Ford cast a glimpse at Zags.

Pontiac looked over the top of the book.

"They were just like us," he said. "In the book."

He held it up.

"Just by being in there, or here, they were saying no to the whole shooting match.

"Natan Sharansky. He said that by saying 'no' to the KGB he was fulfilling all requirements to God and life. He said that's a very rare feeling. He said you can't feel that in normal life."

"Oh?" said Zags.

"That's why we're here. You believe that, protester?" Pontiac continued.

"You know, for the cost of Star Wars, $91 billion, you could pay for Head Start for twenty-six years?" Mark said.

"How do you know that?" said Zags, immediately wishing he had not.

"You ain't the first motherfucker ever considered this stuff, Malcolm," Pontiac snapped.

"You believe we're just as good as you?" he continued.

"We are here because we said no. We refused to live within the compromises others tried to put on us."

He faked a punch at Zags.

He rose and stalked him up and down the run, making damn sure nobody took his eyes off him, he counted coup with direct eye contact.

"I come to D-Block every year," Pontiac stopped at the table.

"You ever been to D-Block before?" This is a big move for you, right? And you're a hero. Right? S'pose there was TV cameras and reporters when you went to court? We go to court and our wives and kids don't even show. No gas money."

"My grandmother used to come 'til she died," Mourning Dove stood behind Zags.

"Nofuckingbody knows we're in here," Stephan Baltimore hollered out from his cell. Martin Mumford stood up and walked to the table.

Zags smiled.

"You think that's funny?" Pontiac yanked a match out of a pack on the table and marked his place. He set the book on the table and looked hard at Zags.

"No." He paused. "I just had a hunch," said Zags. "I used to have this idea that I might find someone like myself in jail. Now I got all these good friends around me."

Pontiac made a move toward Zags.

Burton walked past and Mourning Dove let out a piercing war whoop.

He danced down the row of cells, kicking a leg up, sliding the other leg behind, his head bowed, open hand over his mouth, his face serious.

"I get any mail?" he asked Burton when they met at the block front door.

"I'll check," said Burton.

"You said yesterday you'd check," said Mourning Dove.

"And I'm saying it today," the jailer looked him in the eye.

"Or, you can wait till supper."

Burton smiled at the men gathered around the table.

"What's up?" he said.

"Catfish talking shit," said Mourning Dove. "Same tired bitch every time."

"Hey!" shouted Burton.

"Hey. You ever do it in the backseat of a Pontiac? Huh, Michael? Hey! Protester."

"What's that?" said Zags.

"You ever done it, you know, in the backseat of a Pontiac. Ha! Get it? Shit."

He walked around the corner and stood to the count of one-thousand-five. When his keys began to jingle Mourning Dove strode back to the table. He put his foot on the bench and leaned in between Mendez and Pontiac.

He showed Michael Zags the meaning of evil eye.

"You serious, or just playin'?" Mourning Dove said.

"About what?" said Zags.

"About killing George Bush. Would you do it?"

"I don't know. I was just talking."

"You was just talking," said Mourning Dove, keeping his left foot planted on the bench, straightening his back, looking down his eagle beak at Michael.

"Oglala, South Dakota. FBI's all around. I come from my grandmother's place, her trailer up by the tribal school. We was in a red pickup, pulled off the highway, past the Jumping Bull place.

"The FBI's followed us. We killed them. They were shooting at us. We were shooting at them. Joe Stuntz died too.

"But you never heard about that."

"You're too young," said Zags. "That was 1975. You would have been about five years old. You were there?"

Mourning Dove yanked his leg from the table and stood on both legs evenly.

"It wasn't about, would we kill them, would they kill us. We didn't have time to sit around and think it all over. They were killing us. My father, my sister, my grandfather.

"You kill or get killed. What would you do? Would you kill George Bush?"

"You're asking if George Bush is shooting at me," said Michael Zags.

Mourning Dove stared silently.

"I guess not," said Zags. "Nobody is shooting at me."

"Then why bother," said Mourning Dove.

He walked into his cell and plopped down.

"You're not one of the boys," said Pontiac. "You don't know what it's like not to fit in."

Martin Mumford came around to the hall side of the table.

He crossed his arms across his chest and stared at Michael Zags.

"You don't know shit, punk," said Mumford.

Zags' heart began a 440-yard sprint while he sat.

He tried to move slowly, taking a cigarette from his pocket, putting it in his mouth, sliding his hand along the table for the match pack, tearing off the match, rubbing it, lighting the cigarette.

He tried to make that act last a long time.

He could do this. He feared he had gone way too fast.

"Talking about killing people is serious business," said Pontiac.

He reached for the match pack in front of Michael Zags.

"People in the world might be afraid of you if you say that. We figured you was talkin' shit," said Pontiac.

Pontiac picked the deck of cards from the ledge on the bars.

"I sat in this cell and watched John Kennedy get killed. I sat here when they blew up that space shuttle. And I sat here when your picture came on our TV. Pretty boy news man and you.

"Everybody talkin' shit."

Zags crossed his right leg over his left.

He gripped his tennis shoe with his right hand. He smoked with his left.

Pontiac leaned in.

He loved Zags for the chance to talk like this in D-Block and grinned like Jack Nicholson with a hatchet.

"There are people who will kill for power," said Pontiac.

"And there are people who will kill for an idea.

"And … there's folks who kill just for practice. That's your George Bush."

He made a move to rise, then sat.

"RICO. Racketeer and Corrupt Organizations Act. Lots of people doing lots of time for that. But not George Bush. He was the head of a corrupt organization, making lots of money, killing when he had to, to stay in power," Pontiac said.

"The only real opposition in this country comes from abortion bombers and right wing survivalists. The only ones willing to put up a fight."

Pontiac began to get up. "We just wondered if you was one." Pontiac placed the cards back on the bars, gathered his smoking materials and returned to his cell.

The others also slowly scattered, like the witnesses to a car crash.

Michael Zags lit another cigarette and watched Bobby Ford turn the channels on the television.

"Somebody who would fight," Zags thought he heard Pontiac say.

FIVE

"Boring damned people. All over the earth. Propagating more boring damned people. What a horror show. The earth swarmed with them."
— CHARLES BUKOWSKI

On a warm Wednesday night in December 1989, Lt. Col. Ryan Mahoney sat on the bench in the officers gym at Fort Bragg, North Carolina. His team was ahead by ten in the middle of the last quarter. He leaned back on the bench with a towel over his head, recalling the shot from the left corner.

Both gym doors were propped open with cement blocks to let the night air blow through.

Mahoney put the towel up over his head, off his face, so he could suck in the male smell of the gym. He farted and inhaled. He looked at the south door and saw a few Salvadoran soldiers hanging around, staring in.

"Too dark for handball," Mahoney nodded toward the door.

"I thought the new bug zappers were supposed to keep the beaners entertained.

"Hey, Jonesy! That's a good foul!"

"They just want to kick the ball around," said the other officer. "Don't know how to use their hands."

Mahoney made a jerking-off motion with his right hand above his crotch. As time ran out on the game, the men began to move toward the locker, taking random long-range shots.

Errrr — errrr! Over the speakers around the base came a fog horn sound, short, insistent, like a fire truck demanding to get through city traffic.

The men sprinted to the locker room, leaving basketballs scattered around the gym floor.

The Salvadorans moved slowly into the gym, laughing softly.

"They left the lights on," one said in spanish.

They began to spread out and pass the basketballs back and forth with their feet.

As the alarm sounded at Fort Bragg and the bombers scattered at Fort Stewart in Savannah, Georgia, and the helicopter pilots aboard the carrier, parked in the Gulf of Mexico, hurried to the briefing room with hands full of Snicker bars, barbecued Fritos, and Coke cans, a young woman in Panama City scolded her children with a smile.

"Get in the house, now, mis hijos, andenle."

She looked in the sky to see the flashes and beams of light. She clutched her chest and jerked around at the crack as her youngest son kicked a flat soccer ball perfectly into a garbage can on his way into the house.

Paulo turned to her with his hands forming goal posts in the air and beamed.

She rubbed his raven head and held the door open.

She turned to watch a military jeep screaming down the littered dirty street.

General Noriega had made yet another speech that day, but they had no radio.

Her husband had been told to report for duty that afternoon, on his day off.

Inside the trailer the five children ran down the narrow hall to their bedroom, stripped off T-shirts and jeans and raced to the bathroom.

Maria Cordova scolded them to be careful with the hot water.

"Don't burn yourselves! Don't splash. Hey! Hey! You can't all fit in there!"

She brought cherry Kool-aid and PopTarts into the bathroom for the three as they sat naked on the backless bench waiting their turn. Their tangled feet played with each other like monkey tails.

She knelt by the side, washing the back of three-year-old Juanita.

She sang to her, "Des colores," as she heard the helicopters wap-wap-wapping over the trailer park. "Des colores se visten los campos en la prima vera …"

The little one stopped her struggling and looked up at her mother, noticing the face for the first time in her life. Juanita saw the smiling brown eyes and the swaying cascade of black hair around the pretty, perfect face. Her mother's teeth were white as milk flakes and her lips full and generous, red as ripe coffee berries.

Maria scooped up her 'Nita and swaddled her in a thin, pink towel. Pushing her off down the hall, Maria turned to walk into the kitchen. She stopped by the small hall window. She pushed back the yellow flower curtain with a red fingernail and bent down to see into the street.

Men in uniform stood in the back of a military jeep, clinging to the roll bar, searching the night sky. One shot his automatic weapon into the air and Maria saw the flash of the gun. Then the camouflaged Ford roared off down the street, disappearing in the blackness.

In Washington, George Bush sat behind his mahogany desk in the Oval Office. He spoke on the phone to General Colin Powell, who stalked the war room on Sherman Hall in a north wing of the Pentagon. Bush wore a grey cardigan sweater over a white polo shirt. He listened intently and pulled on his right ear. When he spoke his lips came to a dull point.

"Yes. Yes."

With Powell was National Security Advisor Brent Scowcroft, scrunched in a high-backed deep-cushioned chair and appeared sound asleep.

Powell stood and studied a detailed street map of Panama City. He and Bush had long ago decided to attack Panama in order to capture General Manuel Noriega.

Powell told Bush that the CIA knew of half a dozen locations where Noriega might be found, including the Fantigo trailer park on west Calle de Santiago, where Noriega was said to keep a shack house for personal concubines.

"You do what you need to do," said Bush.

"The American people are behind you. We salute you. We support the troops. I'm behind you. Barbara is behind you. We prayed for you and your men this evening. Vaya con Dios, may God go with you."

"Thank you, Mr. President."

The general hung up the special mauve phone and strode from the room in battle fatigues, toothpick in his mouth. Scowcroft remained hunched in his chair, leaning on his arm.

Lt. Col. Ryan Mahoney stood with his hand on the balance beam, night paint covering his face, his helmet tightened under his chin.

The fire in his eyes meant life, something happening.

He saw the two rows of seated paratroopers silently anticipating the jump into downtown Panama City. They seemed frozen, as if their arms and legs would never move again, gone dead.

But Mahoney had never felt so alive, so useful. Each brain cell and nerve in his body was on full alert, living in the moment, enjoying the day, centered, thriving on the Zen energy generated by the tingle of the hum of the engine through the skin of the airplane.

Mahoney again mentally checked his M-16, three grenades, knife, and city map in the metal tube on his side. His unit would set down on the edge of the downtown area and come in from behind the trailer park where Noriega might be, blocking any bashful departure by him or his troops upon the arrival of the unexpected company.

Noriega had known for hours the Americans were coming.

By monitoring the communications of the United States military compartments, and no word the past three days from the White House or his CIA contacts, he had known and had gone into hiding, leaving his undermanned troops to scan the skies with weak flashlights to highlight the bombs as they descended.

In Lincoln, Nebraska, in the Havelock neighborhood, a retired gentleman sat on his couch.

His wife was just returning with the popcorn as the news came on: Special Report.

She turned out the lamp to make it cozy, as her husband liked it.

She sat down and he got up and returned with two red and white Budweiser cans. He popped both and gave one to her as he got comfortable.

The screen was filled with the face of Dan Rather saying that a United States invasion of Panama was in progress.

Rather told about planes taking off from Fort Bragg and Fort Stewart, and that a fleet of destroyers and an aircraft carrier were in position for the assault of Panama City.

"The 82nd Airborne Division is, right this moment, dropping into the city," Rather said.

The man reached for his popcorn, keeping his eyes glued to Rather's.

The woman sipped her beer. She noticed a car door slam outside. She wanted to peek out the blind, but he liked her to stay put once they cozied in for the news, not bouncing up and down like some g.d. jack-in-the-box.

Maria Cordova went to the door to answer the banging. Her sister, who lived in a trailer down the lane, was excited and crying. She said the Americans were coming. She said she and her husband were heading to the community hall.

She said they were coming to kill Panamanians.

Maria comforted her sister. She told her to go to the hall if she wanted, but reminded her with a smile that it was a fair distance from here and dark.

Maria said she would be getting her children ready for bed. She would listen even though the military base was on the far side of the city and General Noriega had men out patrolling. She had seen them, just a while ago, Maria said.

"It has nothing to do with us," she said.

Maria's sister left. Maria watched her hurry in bare feet and disappear in the night.

Maria went back into the trailer and could not find her children.

"Come out, come out, wherever you are," she sang out.

She stood quiet in the hall, her hands on her hips.

She knew the little one would give the others away.

Soon Maria heard faint giggling.

She tip-toed to follow the noise, then bent over and crept into her own bedroom where she found five sets of eyes, like a row of raccoons, under her bed.

She did not laugh or scold them.

She got onto her stomach, stretched out her arms and pulled them close to her.

"Mis hijos," she said.

"Do not be afraid."

And then she led them in a rapid Hail Mary, Our Father, and Glory Be.

She said the Blessed Virgin would watch over them and reminded them that their father was out with the army making sure nothing bad happens in the night.

"You will wake up tomorrow and whatever is bad out there will be gone. We will play soccer and have a tortilla y quesadilla picnic.

"That is what Conchita was saying, that we should have a picnic tomorrow."

"No, mama," said Paulo.

"She said the Americans are coming with guns to hurt us. We need to hide. You get under here, there is room."

He tried to make his little voice deep.

Maria brushed the black hair from his brow and pinched her lips together.

"Stay here," she commanded the raccoons under the bed.

She hurried down the hall, peaking quickly out the window, then moving to the door.

She unhooked the latch and pushed it open a crack.

She looked into the sky and saw it ablaze with exploding fireworks and arcing lights, like a farmer with a flashlight trying to find his glasses in the dark. The military jeep was back in the street with men in the back firing their weapons into the sky.

Maria looked up and in the patched light she saw that the sky was filled with bits of dry dandelion, blown by the breath of God, floating ponderously toward the guns.

The men in the rear of the jeep cursed the driver.

The driver shoved the vehicle into reverse, rammed into a tree, pulled ahead and careened on two wheels down the street.

The dandelion bits meandered down, down as Maria gasped to see the black whale swimming above in the inky ocean with fireflies blinking around its wings and tail.

As the white parachutes floated down around her, Maria flinched at the sounds of their weapons tinging the sides of the trailer houses.

She ducked back inside, slammed the door, rushed down the hall, then turned back to close the door again.

When she reached the bedroom the back wall was in flames, Maria flung herself to the floor, reached under the bed and began pulling out hands and arms.

"Stay together! Hold on to each other!" Is this happening

to me? she thought. Am I a grown woman, under the attack of men dropping from the sky, trying to save my children by myself?

I can't do this. I am too small.

She told herself to move more slowly, to maker her motions controlled when she saw the terror in each of the faccs as she hauled them from under the bed.

One more set of raccoon eyes underneath, and the smoke in the room told her to send the children into the kitchen.

"I'm staying," said Paulo. "You go ahead. I'll be all right. Papa is out there. I am in here. You are covered. Take care of the children."

"You are child, too!" she cried.

"Come! You help me with the others."

Paulo accepted her hand, and they ran together down the hall that had pushed as narrow as an enclosed slippery slide.

Maria went to one knee in the kitchen and gathered the children in her arms as her bedroom became engulfed in the firestorm.

"We are going outside," she said.

"The bad men are out there!" one said.

"The fire is in here." She crouched and looked them each in the eye, her back growing warm from the blaze. They coughed. They dug at their eyes with toy doll fists. Juanita unlocked the door and opened it a crack to let their cat outside.

"Your father is out there, too," assured Maria. "And I will be with you. We will keep you safe."

She stood in front of them, one arm behind her encir-cling them all and one hand on the doorknob.

Something popped, then exploded in the hallway. She hopped out, to the metal porch and reached in and helped each of them over the gap between the first step and the trailer door. She heard the cries of her neighbors and the shouts of the men from the air.

Flame-throwers were burning the trailer homes as the white parachutes continued to fall like large snowflakes.

The green jeeps in the street were now filled with Americans.

Music by "Guns n' Roses" blared in the background.

Lt. Col. Ryan Mahoney had not landed in the downtown area, but directly over the Fantigo trailer park. Surrounding the trailers, the neighborhood was street after street of junky, dangerous barrio.

As he was landing, with his weapons spraying the ground below him, he was checking his map. When he hit the dirt street in front of Maria Cordova's home he had already decided that the whole area must be secured.

He ordered his men to fan out, close the perimeter and consider anything that moved to be hostile.

As Maria Cordova, crouched with her arms around five small children, came moving toward Mahoney in the alternating darkness, she appeared to him like a pair of soldiers advancing.

Maria shuttled her kids this way, then the other, like a mother goose looking for a way out of the lights of a car.

Mahoney snapped his M-16 to his shoulder and fired in one expert motion.

His bullet, made by a single mother temp worker for Alliant Systems in Hopkins, Minnesota, smashed Maria in the forehead.

The force of the little missile knocked her off her feet.

She floated for a long while, feet outstretched, arms swimming. She saw the stars winking and she beamed. Nothing more to do. Everything done. Chores and duties completed. She rested, at last.

She landed on her back, arms stretched outward in a cross, her legs curled in a figure four.

The children, covered by spots of their mother's blood, scurried and fell around her. Juanita cried. Paulo picked up his little sister and sang to her, "Des Colores."

While the men with blackened faces ran all around them, the children of Maria Cordova held her dead hands and recited a frightened Hail Mary, while Paulo continued to sing.

"Y por eso los grandes amores de muchos colores me gustan a mi."

Paulo cried while he sang harmony to the prayer. He licked the salt tears and tried to wipe the blood from Juanita's forehead, only smearing it.

Mahoney ran forward a few steps then leaned into the scene to make out the children.

He put his hand into the air to stop the firing.

But the action was on automatic.

His men could not see him, only the fire of fear, fed by a wild rage to live.

Mahoney crept ahead, slowly, in a crouch, his weapon on his hip as tracer bullets from both sides slammed into the Cordova children huddled over their mother.

A single bullet from a South Dakota teenager efficiently pierced the skulls of Paulo and Juanita.

The soldier turned to his friend, his mouth open, an excited, surprised smile covering his face, as if he had just killed his first pheasant.

The largest chunk of Paulo's forehead landed on his mother's chest, while a spray from two boys from the same high school in Kasson, Minnesota, keeping together for safety, splayed the other three children onto their front yard of weeds and broken glass.

The Minnesotans ran to their kill, pointed their weapons into the air and shot out the stars, whooping, counting coup.

The retired couple in Lincoln, Nebraska now had the popcorn bowl situated between them. They brushed hands while reaching at the same time, turned to each other and almost smiled. When the Mozart NBC invasion theme music played they tried to muffle their chewing.

KGB

The title "JUST CAUSE" filled the screen, while a United States Navy helicopter flew over the downtown of Panama City as Dan Rather told viewers that rebel Panamanian general Antonio Noriega was on the helicopter, headed for the United States federal prison in Miami.

"Likely, sources say," said Rather, "to be tried for drug trafficking."

In the morning the couple from Lincoln rose early to drive downtown for breakfast. They held hands across the seat.

The man stopped at the Lincoln-Star Journal box outside the restaurant and fed it quarters.

As he sipped coffee he read about the invasion.

His wife read the joke of the day and birthday announcements on the morning news sheet from the radio station.

General Colin Powell walked down Maria Cordova's street and from a distance saw persnickety crows picking at the bodies of Maria and her five children.

Lt. Col. Ryan Mahoney walked with him, still in battle dress, without helmet.

Neither had slept.

Mahoney accepted a black cigar from Powell.

The weapon he carried loosely was empty, his face smeared and sweaty.

His undershirt was cold from perspiration that had dried and now chilled him. He and Powell stopped their tour in front of the Cordova trailer, the metal porch now a rusted diving board into a smoldering pile.

The trailer park was gone, as was the neighborhood around it up to a ten-square-block area, said Mahoney.

"We secured this area in a matter of about an hour and a half," he reported. The two puffed together.

Powell and Mahoney scanned in unison to the left and to the right. As military vehicles hurried back and forth behind them, they continued their walk.

SIX

"People ruthless, people cruel.
See the damage that some people do
Full of hatred, full of pride
It's enough to make you lose your mind."
— NATALIE MERCHANT, "BREAK YOUR HEART"

Z ags!
"Michael. Zags."
The sound penetrated only to the one targeted.
Michael Zags laid the glove on the chair in his room after his last high school game and opened his eyes.

"Court!" thundered Burton.

"Zags, up. You got court. Marshals are coming. Let's go! Move it!"

Zags threw back his sheet and blanket and stepped down, using the sink and toilet as ladder. He pulled his jump-suit from between the bars and put his legs inside, then pulled it over each shoulder before buttoning the front. He reached back with both hands and folded his collar down.

Burton spoke into his walkie-talkie and Zags' cell door opened. Zags stepped out. The door clanged behind him. He walked to the first door of the sally port and stood.

A squawk escaped from inside Burton's handpiece and he turned red.

"Damn!

"Arthur! Alf! Court!"

He walked down the hall to stand even with Arthur's cell.

"Shut the fuck-up!" hollered Martin.

"Lay down, Burt!" yelled Mourning Dove.

"Arthur! Ar-thur!!" Burt yelled. He stuck his face into the bars.

"Yeah, yeah," came a tired kid's voice from one of the caves.

He stood in his worn, white underwear, looked like a high school boy getting ready for school, his eyes thin, his hair messed up.

The narrow, young man rose, turned to pee, then stood in his cell door, waiting for his mother to tell him once more, and then he would get a move on.

"Let's go!" said Burton.

Al tugged his orange suit over his shoulders. His hair stood on end, his eyes puffed. He staggered to stand by Zags.

He responded to a whispered request from Martin by placing a cigarette on Martin's cell door.

The sally port opened. They shuffled inside. The rear door closed and the front door squeaked open.

They moved into the hall, already feeling an inch more free than the others.

Al leaned his head against the wall with his hands behind his back. Zags began to move down the hall. Burton barked into his walkie-talkie and their cell door slapped shut — boom!

He hustled down the hall with his head down and arms now pistons firing.

Al Arthur wandered slowly down the hall, not trying to keep up, letting his finger follow a bed joint in the block wall.

Al lay on a bench in the holding tank, one arm over his chest, the other dangling to the floor. His snore resembled stadium crowd noise. Michael Zags paced back and forth, listening to the aggressive camaraderie shared by the guard and prisoners, the crackling of the radio, the changing of shifts, the electronic releasing of doors and slamming of doors, then the prescient jingle of keys — the king sound of the jungle.

A pile of chains dropped outside the door like The Ghost of Christmas Past on break. Zags turned to shake his cellie and bumped into Al staring at the thick steel door sure to open.

The door clicked and skreeked outward. In the hall awaited two men in suits. The young one now held the well-used chains in his hands. The older one blocked the hall, routing Zags and Arthur to his partner. The prisoners measured three feet from the wall and put their arms into the air, belly flopping toward the wall.

While leaning they spread their feet wide for the marshals to frisk them, running their hands up their legs, into their crotch, across their chest, under their arms. The prisoners let their hands slide down the wall to push back to stand.

The marshals scowled, shook their heads, cracked jokes and put handcuffs around the prisoners' ankles. They wrapped chains around their waists and connected the rings to handcuffs on the wrists, like dressing horses in bridles, bits and saddles.

The marshals nodded and smiled to the jail staff stuffing jail rolls into their mouths and followed the shuffling prisoners to the outer door and garage. The prisoners rode in the back seat of a green Ford the few blocks to the federal courthouse.

"Well, so you're the one don't like President Bush," said the young marshal as they walked from the curb to the side door. He held the door as Zags, then Arthur inch-wormed inside. The older man locked the car and finished a cigarette before coming along.

Zags did not answer.

"What's you got today, Alvin?" the young marshal asked. He exchanged greetings with a black man guiding a buffer. The young marshal swaggered, tapping on the desk of an oriental woman who looked like Babe Ruth, frowning into a phone receiver. He stood at the elevator and punched a number.

He whistled as Zags and Alford caught up. Zags looked back and smacked into the chest of the older marshal. The door opened. The young marshal boarded with the prisoners. The older man followed.

"You got sentencing today, Al?" he repeated.

"No. Don't think so."

"They're just bringing you over here to holler at you. Ain't that right, Alvin?" said the older man, who faced the others.

On the sixth floor the door split. The older marshal led the group down the hall to the marshal's office, past a voluptuous white-haired receptionist. Emmylou Harris, thought Michael. He looked away.

The older man unlocked a barred door and motioned inside. They entered a chilly block of three empty, shiny cells. The marshal unlocked the first cell. Al and Michael choo-chooed in . Michael sat on the bench as the door chimed shut and Al shuffled over to urinate.

They sat in silence for half an hour. The young marshal, modeling a wide gold ring, black tie and crisp white shirt, unlocked the outer door, then inner cell. He asked for Alvin.

"Al-ford," Arthur corrected. "Al."

Michael Zags lay back on the bench. He tried to fold his hands on his chest, but the wall was too close for his left arm. He put one arm over his eyes and let the other fall to the floor. A torn filmstrip of Christmas morning and playing baseball on asphalt showed on his eyelids.

He thought of how effortlessly some bricklayers put down a row, set their line for the next course, holler for mud and move on, joking, smoking, laughing all day long. What a life. Then beers afterward. Always laughing, smiling. Good times.

He jumped up when he heard keys. Al joked loud with the younger marshal. The door swung outward. Al walked in.

"Next contestant," he said. "Can I get a light?" he pivoted around. "After I take care of him," said the marshal.

The older marshal met them in the office. Michael walked between the law enforcement professionals through the office area, past marshal desks with scattered papers and family photos and secretaries who did not make eye contact with prisoners and a lunch room with an open box of Hostess Ho Ho's on the counter to a door marked in bold Helvetica letters: COURTROOM.

The front marshal opened the door.

Michael followed down a tube that turned from white tile and grey desks to crushed maroon carpet and walnut paneling. After ten yards the hallway, like the players entrance to a stadium, opening into a spelunker's paradise of sudden light.

A handful of people shuffled papers for something to do, and Michael, like a giddy racehorse, became frightened by the bright TV lights.

The marshal stopped by an aqua chair at a ten-yard desk as flashes winked and doors banged open and slowly closed.

Michael sat in the chair pulled back by the older man. He tried to sit in the chair, which kept slipping backward.

He sat with his buttocks halfway off the edge and gaped up at the front porch rising above him. The chameleon marshals now stood still as henchmen in back of Michael, their hands folded over nascent tummies.

The vacuum seal broke as a door somewhere swung open. The silver-service-coiffed judge ascended the steps to this chair, his robes flowing, his hair freshly blow-dried.

The white cuffs of his shirt showed just enough.

When he sat the room sat with him, the sound of an elevator stopping.

The judge, a "Big Chill," wannabe, chewed gum with a purpose. He checked things with a gold pen from an invisible sheet on the porch ledge. He arranged papers and combed back through his hair with the fingers of his left hand, showing a diamond and just how thick that hair was.

Judge O'Rourke picked gold wire-rimmed glasses from the hidden desktop and positioned them low on his Roman nose. He spied over the top of the frames at Michael trying to square his ass on the chair that kept scooting back.

The judge asked Michael Zags if he had a lawyer or would he request the state to appoint a lawyer for him.

Michael said, "the second one," while looking at the wheels on his chair to see how he could stop them from rolling.

The judge returned the glasses to the desk, asked the court clerk to have indigence papers prepared, checked a mark on his paper, pivoted his chair toward the exit, and rose, flowing down the steps like runny Jell-O and floating out through his office door as a poltergeist.

The door closed on its own.

Michael lifted his butt and leaped backward, reaching the backrest. His feet dangled a quarter inch from the floor. He smiled, took a breath, looked around the room at the reporters and prosecutors gathering up papers.

The older marshal gripped Michael by the left underarm. Michael's feet tingled when they hit the floor together. Michael followed the younger marshal out the back door while the older marshal trailed.

Inside the tank, Al got a light. He shook out the cigarette from a pack of Marlboros and offered it to Michael.

They sat in silence on the bench, straining to hear the talk in the marshal's office, then not wanting to hear.

"I'm not getting nothing," said Al, his elbows on his

thighs, his folded hands between his knees.

He looked over at Michael.

"They're cutting me off. My family. They're bringing papers for me too, to make sure I'm poor enough to get one of their kiddy lawyers."

"Sorry to hear that," said Michael. "I am."

"You're a protester, right?" Al said. "You should protest this. How can a family just forget you? I'll sue. I will."

They turned their heads to the door at the Pavlovian tune.

On the ride back to the jail both prisoners watched silently out their windows.

Al looked at a young girl waiting in the crosswalk. Michael at a guy watching his right foot move down the sidewalk with a blue glob of gum stuck to his shoe. The blinker pointed right and the car followed, around the corner, down the street, past the library, toward the jail.

Jeremiah Williger touched each of the dozen papers on his desk with his right index finger. The papers were laid in front of him in two rows of six. Above the rows, in the middle of the rows, sat his phone and intercom system.

His room, perhaps three times the size of Martha Pontiac's office at the college, told his story better than he could, he told elementary school tour groups.

The walls were filled with neat rows of diplomas from law enforcement seminars completed: small arms training, crowd control, noxious weed control, drug identification.

He wore a tailored grey suit in the office. In the closet hung four crisp sets of brown uniforms for the field. A glass globe paperweight anchored the top left corner of the large oak desk. Over his left shoulder two autopsy photos of John Dillinger were enclosed in a glass gun case, gifts of the Midwest FBI director sent by UPS after Williger attended a ten-day workshop at the FBI regional headquarters in Minneapolis.

A bookshelf within arm's reach to his left held color photos of his wife and three children. On the wall above the photos were a twenty-year plaque from the Sertoma Club and a twenty-five year certificate from the American Reformed Church of Iowa.

Behind the sheriff a screen saver American flag bristled in a cyber wind.

Jeremiah had been Jerry at Sioux City West High School. As a senior he quit his job helping his father clean the school in the evenings and joined the county payroll as a jailer. He became a patrol officer, then ran for sheriff when Susan Ferris quit to become a UCC minister.

When Ms. Ferris announced her intentions, Jeremiah had his own seminary application form addressed to Beyersville, Kentucky in his hand. He didn't want to appear a copycat. He tossed it away. Instead, he took the three-year deacon program at his church. Now he saved the county thousands of dollars by serving as jail minister in addition to his sheriff duties.

The top row of six papers had "Elections" stamped in red in each upper right hand corner. One was a letter to the editor of the Sioux City Journal announcing his candidacy in the upcoming Republican primary as a pro-life, pro-law enforcement candidate for sheriff.

The bottom row of papers were miscellaneous vouchers, vacation leaves, speaking engagements, supervisors meeting agenda.

Williger pushed his chair away, leaned back in his chair, placed his boot on the edge of the trash can, and stared at the letter in his hand from FCC special agent Hargrove. The letters on the page went out of focus and Williger wondered if the prisoners would like their clam chowder at noon. He blinked and began to read.

Hargrove asked that Williger consider the capture of Elana Usak as a prime concern. "A-Priority" the later stated in bold letters.

Williger reached for his gold pen, a gift from his secretary on the occasion of his 30th anniversary in law enforcement, and scratched a note at the top of the yellow legal pad in the flush right corner of the desk.

He would talk to each shift of officers about Elana Usak.

SEVEN

"In a couple of days they come to take me away, but the
press let the story leak; when the radical priest comes to
give me release, we is all on the cover-a Newsweek."
— PAUL SIMON, "ME & JULIO"

Michael Zags and Mark Pontiac shuffled back to the block after a breakfast of scrambled eggs and coffee.

Pontiac asked Zags if he was staying up.

"Yeah. For a while," said Zags. "Think I'll have a smoke."

Pontiac said he thought he might, too.

They sat across from each other, both thinking jail wouldn't be so bad if you could be in by yourself. In the quiet, with a cigarette in the morning, with time to think. Sure wouldn't miss going to work.

"So," whispered Zags, looking into Ford's cell. "What's up with him?"

Pontiac stuck out his jaw. He'd heard each of these guys' stories twenty times.

He rolled another smoke to begin.

Bobby Ford was a parvenu car salesman.

He drew the line. He was not an order-taker.

He sold cars.

He did not walk around behind sweaty couples up and down the rows scribbling down the names of their children.

74

He told them what they wanted.

Bobby knew what people wanted.

They had no fucking idea. He had no time for such people.

Growing up on a Mennonite hog farm in South Dakota, Bobby had always known what he wanted. Bobby Hofer left the compound during lunch one day and hitchhiked to Sioux Falls.

There he bought new clothes at the mall and caught a bus to Fort Collins, where he took the name of the Poudre Ford dealership across from the depot.

He got a job washing the new cars, starting over each morning on the same Ranchero he started on the morning before. Every morning a girl in a short dress wearing a Spice Girls backpack walked past and smiled at Bobby.

After a few weeks she stopped.

The next week he asked her if she wanted to see the inside of a new Mustang. He raped the eighth grader in the back seat and was caught by the sales manager climbing into the car to let a CSU industrial technologies professor and his wife test drive.

Ford went to federal prison because the state penitentiary was full.

Before the U.S. marshals picked him up Ford spent one year on the Poudre County Jail. Each night he heard the blacks in the mod swearing at him and he dreamed he was singing.

"We be jammin." And he would jump into the air ten-feet high in super slow motion and he would Kung-Fu kick on the way down, and he would be saving people in his dreams.

Singing and jumping and kicking.

He woke up singing, "We be jammin," and he threw back the one sheet and rushed to the vertical slit window of his cell. He pushed his nose into the glass until it should have stayed flattened.

He tried to hear if the blacks were laughing at him through their cell doors and under their cell doors. He heard them still talking, still whispering. Didn't the black devils ever sleep?

Bobby went to Terre Haute Federal Penitentiary, where he dreamed he was a snitch and all the Mexicans and Cubans and Salvadorans and Colombians in the world were housed in the same basement in-transit unit.

They would catch him masturbating in his cell and they would reach out their hands to grab him as he passed down the line of cells on his way to use the phone every two weeks.

"Me gusta," they would whisper.

They moved him to Leavenworth and the bus arrived in the middle of the night during a summer rainstorm. In the distance, around the tortuous highway at the crack of a lightning bolt Bobby could see the spire and walls of Leavenworth.

And he knew in that flash what the United States is all about. The whole thing is just so big just to scare you.

The bus stopped at the base of the hundred steps up to the main prison.

A trusty prisoner placed a used Army jacket over the shoulders of each prisoner as they stepped out of the bus with their handcuffs in front of them and their ankles shackled.

The prisoners squinted up through the rain and lightning at the spire of Leavenworth stabbing the soft cloud bottoms.

They shuffled twice to each Leavenworth step as they struggled up the cliffs of hell.

Inside the prisoners were told to face the wall in a straight line. A young Indian saw the fear in Bobby Ford's eyes.

"Yeah, you're here," he said.

And they both stared at the trophy case ten inches from their faces filled with color photos of the families of the

President, attorney general, director of the B.O.P., and the Leavenworth warden, and the hearts and testicles and fingers and teeth of former prisoners.

In the basement intake dungeon, Bobby and the inmates with tattoos covering their backs sat in faded pink boxer underwear waiting for the gargoyle Leavenworth guards to shine giant flashlights up their asses and hand them fresh old clothes. A cluster of griffin guards hunched upon the stone clump desk scrutinized the crumbling brick-and-dirt-walled holding cells.

Each guard wore a string of prisoner fingers around his neck.

In the morning the in-transit unit rose for breakfast at five in the colossal dining area, room enough for a soccer stadium and the sun.

Bobby got in line for his eggs and pancakes and hash browns, and toast, and gawked around at the square tables where Bugsy Siegal and Leonard Peltier and the Birdman of Alcatraz and Horace Tschetter the Mennonite mass murdering machinist had once eaten eggs and pancakes and hash browns, and toast.

On his bus holiday Bobby Ford also went to El Reno federal prison in Oklahoma, where he witnessed federal officers kick an inmate to death and then flood outside to jack off by shooting their shotguns into the air.

Bobby Ford left prison and checked himself into the mental institution in Cherokee, Iowa. He had received directions from the prison psychiatrist, who was from Iowa. The MHI is three city blocks wide and long, a Gothic red brick with clay tile roofs.

The new crazy person enters upon a rose-patterned marble floor the length of a small town main drag.

Bobby was taken up the elevator and around the bend, then up a half stair to the locked ward.

Just like he imagined: the wide, vanilla halls and long,

quiet rooms where he could sit and rock. He loved it, being institutionalized, being special, having a condition.

He read "One Flew Over The Cuckoo's Nest" in the dusty rays of a south window and got well enough to walk to McDonald's, the way the doctors measured wellness for non-insurance patients.

An uncle from the colony met Bobby at the entrance hall and drove him to the closest city. That was all the farther Bobby could go. He said thanks and the uncle went home because it was time to slaughter pigs.

He couldn't stay, or he would have, he said.

In Sioux City Bobby rented a room above the movie house on Third Street.

He slept for eighteen hours, then inhaled a breakfast of hash browns, eggs and gravy, and toast at the down-home café around the corner.

He returned to his room to put on his tie, then walked to the Ford dealership where he talked his way into a sales position in the used lot.

At the staff Christmas party at the Holiday Inn on Hamilton Street, the owner, Sammy Sindelar, caught his 15-year-old daughter skinny-dipping with Bobby in the hotel pool while attached at the hips.

Bobby was handcuffed behind his back, face-down and naked by the side of the pool with his rose and barbed wire tattoo on his ankle fully exposed, while the rest of the sales staff leaned on the balcony railing and watched, sipping bourbon from clear plastic cups.

During spring graduation practice Martha Pontiac talked to her friend from the industrial technology building. He would see what he had in his workroom.

Elana wrestled the bed frame from Martha's back room, gouging the door jam. At the top of the basement steps she let it go.

"Ooops."

Elana set the mattress on the floor and opened the window. She went to Martha's room to try on hats and sunglasses. Then she went on a walk around her new neighborhood to scout for desk materials.

Elana and Martha walked at night. They smoked Winstons on a park bench next to the trail by the Missouri. They drank Schlitz beer from cans and watched "The Fisher King" with the lights off while eating half-pound hamburgers and broccoli cheese casserole. After midnight they helped each other up the walnut tree to place the antenna. They decorated Elana's room with electrical equipment and painted the logo on white poster board in red and blue letters: KREV.

On a Monday morning, they rose at five, made each other coffee and toast and got ready for the early show.

Elana smiled as she slid behind the desk and scooted her chair up to the microphone. She ran her palms over her desk, careful to watch for slivers. Martha, seated on the sofa, held her coffee cup in front of her face with both hands.

"Five, four, three, one, two," she counted.

"Good morning, friend," Elana began, instantly becoming her confidant radio persona. "This is Radio Free Siouxland, back on the air. We're broadcasting the seeds of the revolution on KREV 92.9 this morning.

Elana recounted the FCC raid two weeks ago.

"I'm coming to you today from Room 306 of that hotel in Memphis. Keep hope alive."

She did an imitation advertising segment for "You Hardly Know It's You" memory blockers. "Look for the little blue pill."

"Now this song goes out to special agent Hargrove. I want to know who the men in the shadows are."

Martha sat on the couch, watching nervously, hoping the jury-rigged equipment would hold, wondering how long they could stay on the air, hoping they wouldn't burn down the house or the beautiful walnut on the first day.

Elana put her feet on the window sill.

Watching a cardinal on the clothesline, she held the microphone in her hand and watched the scant neighborhood traffic.

"I want to thank my friends in the Nebraksa Café, the scene of my next clandestine remote.

"Now, I'm goingk to tell you about old contry. Not Loretta Lynn. Chckaslavokya. My father, Milosh, he was obsessive-compulsive, tried to keep his famly pure. No drink, no smokes, only radio. Radio Free Europe on the dark living room of a Prague apartment on Pariska Street."

Martha walked to the window, cupping her mug in her hands.

"Nineteen and sixty-eight. The Prague Spring.

"The Soviet invasion. Writers forced underground. The truth. Where was the truth. Only the lie. Seek the lie and you will find the truth, he said. He walked at nights, hiding in doorways from the tanks, from all soldiers. He stood on the Charles Bridge. Perhaps he jumped, was he pushed, shot? You could say that. He had nowhere he felt he could go. And so he died."

Elana's voice trailed off, as if she had departed the room to return to Prague. The breeze carried lilac smell into the room. Martha remembered she had rolls baking.

"And so I go out to all you who sit alone with your radio. When the network news theme music comes on at the top of the hour and you say to yourself, this is bullshit, I am here for you, darlinks. This is Olga from Prague wishing you a happy day in America."

Martha returned and set a full plate of gooey pastry covered in a fresh white towel on Elana's desk.

"Here are The New Radicals. It's seven-thirty two in Siouxland. Get up if you're going to work. Either way, I've got news for you after this."

Martha fetched the coffee pot.

"Where do you get your ideas?" she asked, looking at the lists and notes on the legal pad in front of Elana.

"I don't know," said Elana. "I …" The music faded.

"Now, my little papushkas. I have history lesson for you.

"1996 Telecommunications Act, U.S. Radio industry deregulated. Now about seven white guys in a small booth in Denny's owns every radio station in the United States. They decide you like songs A,B, … hmm …. C, and you will sit still for X amount of Z-brand news. And that's what you get in Phoenix, New York and Des Moines and all points in between," Elana said.

"They don't tell you about the billions made by defense contractors to start the wars in Africa and then to supply the major countries to respond. They don't tell you about the Catholic priests going to prison for protesting against the defense contractor's million dollar nuclear weapons, because, guess what. The defense contractor is the same guy who owns the radio stations and the television stations and the movie studios."

A siren cried in the distance and Martha's heart leaped like a frog under a blanket.

"And they own the law enforcement agencies who told you that I was a threat to national security. They don't want me to tell you and so they are looking for me right now in their special tracking equipped minivans," she said.

"The airwaves, my friends. They are the most abominable tool of oppression. They are the first things seized by any tyrant.

"We're gonna git on out of here now. My personal stalker is unzipping his fly again in the bushes. … Some more Jackson Browne to close out your drive. … People die for … the little things. A little corn, a little beans. Special agent Hargrove. Boy, boy, this world is not your toy.

"… Take care my friend. Until we meet again … stop obeying."

EIGHT

"And when the band plays "Hail to the chief,"
ooh they'll point the cannon at you."
— "Fortunate Son," Creedence Clearwater Revival

The next morning a pleasant fresh pastry smell curled around the jagged block corners of the jail. Most prisoners did not attend the morning meal, so Pontiac always ate breakfast. On the way back he talked to Burton. The two had gone to Sioux City North High School together. Burton joked with Mark as he locked him in his cage.

Pontiac strolled into the block smiling.

The mornings were quiet. Most prisoners in the nation slept until lunch, the others thankful for the respite after a long night. Pontiac groaned when he saw Michael Zags sitting at his table.

Pontiac hustled into his cell and pissed.

He lay on his bed for twenty seconds, then strode out and sat across from Zags. They smoked in silence. Down the hall and around the corner they heard the Today Show. They heard guards laughing. Bobby Ford coughed hard, then rolled to his side. Al Arthur cussed the hall light and pulled his grey blanket over his head.

"You don't like George Bush?" Pontiac said.

"Not particularly."

"Why's that?"

"I don't know. I guess I just don't like his face," Zags said.

"What did you say?" Pontiac said. "What made them throw you in here with us?"

"What you get out of asking me that?" Zags said.

Pontiac pushed his pack across the table.

"Free meals for life," he said. "An abundance of good, wholesome companionship."

Michael took the pack and shook out one of the home-made cigarettes.

"It was morning break, 'bout, nine, nine-thirty-two," he said. "We been talking about it the night before. They all know me, where I been. I just said I thought Bush ought to be shot."

"That's it?" Pontiac said.

"Among other things. There coulda been something about Waco, Ruby Ridge, Oklahoma City," said Zags.

Pontiac nodded for him to continue.

"Listen. Bush works with Reagan, the biggest arms dealer in the modern world," said Zags.

He crossed his legs and plucked another hair from his nose, then examined it between his fingertips.

"And there's, umm, no recourse, you could say. They smuggle guns to the contras behind the back of Congress, sanction the killing of American nuns in El Salvador and nobody basically does nothing. Nothing except Bush to replace Reagan when it's time.

"Then Bush implodes Iraq, same as Reagan squished Grenada. Bush jumped Panama and kills thousands of people, who knows how many?

"These are war criminals, Bush and Reagan.

"Hugo Banzer, Augusto Pinochet, Idi Amin, Baby Doc Duvalier, George Bush. They all killed civilians on purpose."

Pontiac held up his palms.

"Sorry I asked."

He reached for the deck of cards on the cell bars, removed the lidless cover and began shuffling. Like a pacifier, the cards calmed him. He settled in for the morning.

"You're the only construction worker in America who knows what a Hugo Banzai is," he said.

Michael grinned.

He told Pontiac who he came to know who Hugo Banzai was. He talked about growing up on a farm, one of seventeen Irish kids in three upstairs bedrooms. His father's grandfather had come to the United States from Cork, Ireland, evicted by the landlord, spending ninety days on a damp ship, losing a daughter to a clandestine sea burial.

Michael went to the seminary, one of the best and brightest, reared by God and the church for stardom. He opted for law school and took his bar exam at McFadden's Lounge.

He became involved in the Catholic Worker movement, spending time rocking babies at the shelter and arguing through the night with bomb-throwers. He worked construction and hitchhiked to Oregon to cook on a fishing boat. He left a girlfriend at a midnight keg party in the woods celebrating his birthday in Coos Bay to return to the Midwest because he wanted to.

They talked until after "The Price is Right" and didn't notice Bobby Ford turning the channel to "Love Boat."

Bill Mourning Dove climbed the three chipped steps to the shower holding a towel around his waist. He put a foot inside the rotting box to push the knob to start the water. He let out a yell when the cold water caught him.

Pontiac told Michael about being a regular in the county jail.

"Everybody knows me," he said. "Like on Cheers," he smiled.

Mark said he had never been in a real prison.

"You don't want to go," said Zags.

"Why?" said Pontiac. "Why do you give a shit about what

a George Bush does? None of that is about us. It's a different world, man. The United States. The United States isn't
even us.

"Kennedy? The shuttle 'splosion thing. Stealth Bomber?
Shit.

"It's just on TV.

"It ain't real. Trust me.

"What has it got to do with us? Go try to find somebody
to complain to and you'll find out how much. We don't live
in the United States, man. It's not our country.

"This is our country."

He waved his hands above his head like a circus ring
master trying to draw the attention of the crowd to the
opening act.

He stood in the middle of the room and raised his hands
to the ceiling.

"Ladies ... and gentlemen!

"Welcome ... to the greatest show on earth.

"Poor men locked up for trying to get their share from
the rich men."

He let his hands fall against his sides.

"And we call the poor me the criminals! Incredible sleight
of hand!"

He swept his hand and bowed to the cement floor.

Faint clapping came from one of the cells.

"Thank you."

Getting into the role, Pontiac took long strides to the end
of the block to stand in Baltimore and Mumford's cell.

"Here we have — stand back! — two young black men.

"Stand back!"

Pontiac bent his knees and showed the palms of his
hands to his fantasy audience, his eyes wide with terror.

"One came to the circus from North Omaha, the off-
spring of a Black Panther. Please! Stand back!

"The other joins us from darkest Haiti. He was raised by a
voodoo doll and can speak only at night.

"Stand … the fuck … back!"

Baltimore and Mumford sat on their beds and stared at Pontiac with tilted heads.

Pontiac put his hands down and walked slowly back to the table.

"This is our world."

He sat down and stuck an unlit cigarette in his mouth.

"Burt is our mayor, our president, our garbage collector. The girls at the front desk, they're our cops. Keep out the riff-raff."

Michael picked up the homemade ashtray of quilted gum wrappers and emptied it in the toilet in his cell. He set the clean ashtray on the table and sat down.

"I don't know," Zags said. "What would it take? To make us part of that country?" He pointed to the television screen.

"Being able to vote," Pontiac said. "Like making some damn difference. Having somebody notice you. They laugh at us. They laugh at us out there because we don't have no country. We wander around. We sit in the library, beg change to sit in McDonald's and drink one cup of coffee all morning and just try to be warm or cool or dry. And then we got to move along because we really aren't members.

"Wait."

Zags put up both hands to say, no, it's okay, go ahead.

"In here they can't see us, can't laugh," Pontiac plowed through. "And they're scared of us, would rather puke screwdrivers than come in here 'cause it's not their country. Our country, ain't got no army, no navy, but we got laws and we got … procedures."

"I know that, but," Zags said.

"We survive. Like Lakotas on the reservation, like Kurds in fuckin' I-rack. We survive, beneath the dominant culture, waiting for our time," Pontiac said while sitting down.

"Uh, huh." Zags held up both hands.

"Right. Night."

He walked into his cell and hopped up to lie down.

The next morning Michael Zags sat at the table after he returned from breakfast. He began to puff. Officer Burton stopped and talked before returning to his rounds. He asked if Zags wanted the television turned on.

"No, thanks. I like the quiet."

Zags heard snoring from Pontiac's cell. He turned his head to see Al scowl over the top of his covers then roll to his side and fold the thin plastic pillow, making a pita pocket around his head.

Mourning Dove's house was quiet as one minute before a midnight attack. Mendez stood in his white underwear to pee, wandered out to the dayroom squinting his eyes, then shuffled back to his bed, still asleep.

The grey lump that Baltimore called "Mount Rushford," stuck up in the middle of Ford's bed.

Martin Mumford perched on the edge of his bed rubbing his eyes. He held up his lit cigarette to Stephan Baltimore as Baltimore passed out of the room. Baltimore, light as café latte, looked white compared to Mumford's pitch tint. He used the butt to light his own.

He eased in across from Zags, to the left. He stretched his legs out under the table.

"Pinochet," Baltimore, half-awake, groaned from deep in his throat. Oh, brother, thought Zags.

"You want me to kill Pinochet?" he asked.

Baltimore pulled a torn clipping from his jumpsuit pocket. The headline and story said that Chilean general Augusto Pinochet had been detained in England, accused of killing and torturing people in his own country after a coup in 1969.

"You see this?" asked Baltimore.

"I've been hearing about it, yes," Zags said.

"I heard you talking about Banzer and Duvalier. My mother is in Haiti. My name is Lebot. I escaped and took the name on the city buses.

"Nixon helped Pinochet kill Allende, of course you know.

"You will help me kill Duvalier, Baby Doc? He hurt lots of people. I will kill him. You will help me?" Baltimore annunciated rapidly now, with French spice.

"I will not help you with that," said Zags, "but if you ever want to sweep this dayroom, I'll be with you shoulder to shoulder."

He swept cigarette ashes from the table into this hands and shook them over the tinfoil ashtray. He rose, intending to leave.

Baltimore circled his hand around Zags' arm like a blood pressure wrap and motioned with his head to sit the fuck down.

Zags sat.

He folded his hands in his lap and looked across the table.

Baltimore slid over to be directly across from Zags.

"There are many bad men that should be dead," Baltimore said. "I will make a list."

"Yeah. Make a list," Zags said. "We'll form a committee," he said under his breath.

Baltimore strode to his cell. Mumford was back in bed, snoring, his back to the cell door.

Baltimore regained his spot at the orange table.

He laid down a white pad and with his fingernail peeled back the end of a yellow pencil.

"POL POT," he said, then wrote in capital letters on the top line. He put a dash then wrote in caps again. DEAD.

He continued down the left side of the page: Idi Amin, Saudi Arabia; Baby Doc, southern France; Alfredo Stroessner, Brazil; George Bush, Texas.

"I hear he lives in Minnesota," Zags said. "Just a rumour. Nobody knows about it, I know it sounds crazy, but Minnesota's pretty cool, I've been there."

Baltimore looked up as if he did not believe it.

He stared at "Texas" on the page, refusing to change it.

Baltimore double-checked his list, then rapped his knuckles twice on the table.

"Thanks, man," he said and sauntered triumphantly back to his cell carrying his list.

Michael Zags joggled his head and decided to go back to bed.

Mark and Michael slurped coffee at the Sundowner Grill & Bar on Fourth Street.

That's what Mark called the jail cafeteria.

The long overhead light flickered strong enough for Mark to read.

He sang softly, flipping the pages of the Sioux City Journal.

Michael waved off a refill from Ford, who was acting trusty for the day.

"I'll have another handful of those creamers when you get time, sugar," Mark said.

Ford flipped him the bird.

Mark offered Michael a cigarette and lit both with one match.

"Nothing in here about you," Mark said.

Michael pretended not to notice.

"You are a strange man, Zags. But you've got a point with some of your shit."

"Like what?" Michael said. "You do all the talking."

"Like how we should kill the rich to even it out. Charlie Manson woulda loved you."

"Never said anything about killing anybody," Zags said. "Not really."

"Just checkin', " Mark said. "You do know you're goin' to prison. They won't let it go."

Mark flipped his ash into his soup bowl.

"I think they will," Michael said. "That's the whole point. Nothin' makes any difference. Nobody cares. News is entertainment and come get the new Disney toy at McDonald's."

"Whatever," Mark said. "You're in denial 'cause you can't

afford to think about it. You can't imagine sitting here with me drinking coffee very morning till judgment day and you're wondering what your family is doing this very minute. You sort of wish you never done it."

Zags sucked on the cigarette and observed four stone-faced young Hispanic men promenading down the hall, carrying new jail bags.

"I did it for them," he said.

"Maybe," Pontiac said. "But you'd like to walk outa here and go order a frosty mug Coors Light at the Legion Club, slap a few back, shake some hands."

"Maybe," Zags said.

"And them spics would just as soon cut you up for carp bait as tie your balls to a bus bumper," Pontiac said.

"They don't know about you. They never will know about you and if they did, they would think you were a chump.

"They respect power. Just as everybody else does.

"The others don't care about you either. Sorry.

"The only way they would see you is from television and then you're just another kook. This is not Czechoslovakia 1968.

"These people do not read.

"They care about blowin' … shit … up, Jackson.

"You ever been to a summer movie?"

Michael shook the paper, tried to fold it, then crunched it into a ball and threw it under the table.

"You are public enemy numero uno, Huck," he said. "If anybody gave a shit, that is. Why would any John or Jerry grilling steaks give a hoot about you?

"What is there to revolt against for him?

"Golf league and gas prices. That's what they're talkin' 'bout."

"I guess I'm trying to be on the other side of that," Michael said. "Maybe dump hot coals down Jerry's pink Bermuda shorts, as it were."

"You got some repressed anger to deal with," Mark said.

"We can talk about that later. However, what I'm saying is you have no constituency, governor. Nobody cares about you. It's Titanic time. The ship is going down and every motherfucker is grabbing all the shit he can carry.

"And the Virgin Mary has a night club act at the Starlight every Tuesday. Ha! Everyone has thrown in the towel. I'm tellin' ya. Even the Lutherans, my man. Even the sorry ass Lutherans. It's a sad situation, I'm tellin' ya."

"Doesn't matter," Michael Zags said. "It's still right. I don't have to succeed. I just have to try."

"That's fucking bogus Catholic talk," Mark said.

He poured a plastic container into a new cup of coffee.

"You say you are fighting the government. Son, Sitting Bull didn't get bitch-slapped this bad."

Mark whispered.

His eyes bulged from leaning over and trying to look up at Michael.

He leaned back out of breath, took a drag on his cigarette and a drink of coffee. He leaned forward.

"You are such a measly gnat, the one you're fighting doesn't even know you're out here buzzing your tight little ass off. I know how you feel," Mark said.

He stuffed out a cigarette on his plate.

"Get a grip. This is new for you. You are doing, something."

"I do think about it," Michael said. "I think about the wrist bracelets kids bring home from Sunday school. W.W.J.D.

"What Would Jesus Do? Would he say to make sure your own light bill gets paid and don't worry about them unless you have a little bit left over? Would he say to invest for a good rate of return when there is a baby with no shoes sitting on the walk in front of your house?"

"He'd say do what you can," Mark said. "You're not the only one. To think you are is wrong."

"The Okies of today are from Oaxaca," Michael said.

He tilted his chair back onto the back legs.

"In the '20s the people with something didn't see the others driving past them with mattresses tied to the roof. Same way with us now," Michael said.

"We can help them, but it will cost us."

"When you go trying to change the world with one move, it's like giving up," Mark said. "It's committing suicide because you can't take the daily grind and expecting the rest of us to canonize you for it."

"I don't care. They shouldn't put people away for doing this kind of stuff. Some day they'll figure it out," Michael said.

"All right, then. We got to do something," Mark said.

"We?" Walt said.

"I ain't doin' nothing special the next couple days," Mark said. "I could help you with your campaign, as it were, senator. You got any money? We could use some more cigarettes."

"Let's walk," Mark said.

"Thanks, sugar doll," he called to Ford as they got up to stand in line. "You keep the change for yourself."

The next morning Zags sat in the dayroom after breakfast.

Bobby Ford came out of his cell. He asked Burton if he had received any money on his books. Burton said he would check. Ford sat down across from Zags and asked for the loan of a cigarette.

Burton stood by watching the TV through the bars. Ford picked up his cigarette and went back to his cell.

"You know," Burton said. "Even dental hygienists get the blues, sometimes."

NINE

"THIS IS THE WORLD WE LIVE IN.
THESE ARE THE HANDS WE'RE GIVEN."
— Phil Collins

Pontiac sat at the table.

"How's breakfast?" Zags wandered out rubbing his stomach under his T-shirt.

"S'okay. Grits. Ever had grits?" Pontiac looked up.

"Nnh, hnh," Zags said as he put one leg over the bench to sit sideways. He leaned and elbow on the table and reached for one of the home-made smokes sitting in a neat row in front of the yellow legal pad in front of Pontiac.

"Mind?"

"Go ahead," Pontiac did not look up.

"Whatcha doing?" Zags asked.

"Nothing," Pontiac said.

Zags tried to read upside down from Pontiac's paper. He had a heading in capitals, then a line of words down the left side.

"I suppose you can tell a lot about somebody by the plans they make, huh?" Zags said.

"Yeah, I s'pose," Pontiac said. "Or by lack of plans. What you gonna be when you grow up?"" Zags swung a leg over and faced off.

"You mean after I kill Mendez' wife's boss and Baltimore's Haiti dictator? Death row resident. You?"

Pontiac twirled the pad to face Zags.

- Jack Ruby, Ruby Ridge
- Cowboy poets
- There should be

Zags looked up. Pontiac swirled the pad back.

"I thought you gave that up," said Zags.

"I don't know why a guy would," said Pontiac.

"Jack Ruby? Ruby Ridge?" Zags winced as if the words made his eyes hurt.

"Ever think about it?" said Pontiac. "Right. Nobody has. I'm on to something."

"Cowboy poets?" Zags said.

"Oh, forget that," said Pontiac, "but somewhere there should be some guy writing in the window of some old house in Missouri with a banana nut candle burning while a big storm begins outside and he's got his new Guy Clark tape playing and he's trying to write about us, about jail, about prisoners, telling the truth about America.

"There's nobody, but there should be."

"Another enigmatic list," Zags said. "Must be all these Type-A's in here."

Zags reached for the pad.

"Mind?"

He picked up the pencil.

"Just for something to do."

He began to make a list. He wrote down Baltimore's list, Mrs. Mendez' boss, and "the FBIs."

At the bottom of the list he put "George Bush."

"Hey, wait a minute," said Pontiac, grabbing the paper. "Don't put Bush's name on a list like this. We could get nailed.

"Put ... uh, umm."

"KGB," Zags said. "Kill George Bush. He was the head of the CIA once, you know, KGB, all spies and shit."

"Killing George Bush. Hmm," Pontiac hummed like a new engine. "Aaa-ight."

"KGB," Zags said.

He erased "George Bush" and wrote over it, turned the page sideways to make sure you couldn't still see the name, turned it to show to Pontiac.

They both smiled, like the co-creators of some fucking Greek art or some shit.

"Don't they say on those magazine television shows that prison is a school for criminals?" Zags said. "That's us. We need to start learning something."

Zags rose.

He carried his metal coffee cup with him and ran it down the cell block, dragging it on the bars. He walked back again.

"Get up! Get ... the-fuck up.

"All criminals in the dayroom, on the double. All you dirty, no-good, lazy fucking lawbreakers get your asses out of bed. Now! There is work to be done."

Ford peaked over his blanket and then ducked back down.

"Alcatraz," Pontiac smiled. He walked into each cell and threw off the covers of each of the men.

"C'mon you convicts. Like the man said. Get ... the-fuck ... up."

"Shh," Zags put a finger to his mouth trying to squelch a giggle. "Burt'll hear." Baltimore and Mumford stood in the door of their cell, eyes closed, hands by their sides. Al Arthur staggered out in bare fee and white underwear. Ford stood below the television with his arms folded, looking up, then reached up to try the knob.

"Can we get this turned on?" he hollered down the hall.

Pontiac leaped into Ford's face. "Shut the fuck-up," he hissed. "This is a meetin'. We don't need no fuck'n tel-e-vi-sion."

Mendez and Mourning Dove ran brown, tattooed fingers through long black hair and wandered out, looking for a clock to see what the damn time it was.

Baltimore, then Mumford ventured a little farther out into the dayroom light, like hyenas testing the glow of a campfire.

Mumford lit a smoke and gave it to Baltimore for a torch. They moved together toward the table.

Michael Zags sat with Pontiac. Zags noted the tired, mad faces around him and pretended to make important notes with his bare fingers in the hard tabletop.

Pontiac folded over the first page on his pad. He traced a pencil mark on the top line.

"Everybody got a smoke?" Zags asked, checking the glares around the circle. Mumford let smoke into Zags' face.

Mourning Dove and Mendez stared at the stupid white men at the table.

Bobby Ford plunged a hand past Al Arthur and accepted one of Pontiac's Finest, then a book of matches. When nobody asked for the matches back he slid them down into his breast pocket.

"All right," Zags said.

He looked over his shoulder down the hall.

Mendez moved toward the bars to say he had it. Zags looked back.

"You guys seem to think I'm a killer. Sorry. I'm not. I'm a construction worker with too much education. I'm just somebody who for some odd reason thinks he knows where he lives."

He scratched an itch on his forehead.

"I can't do any more than you."

Mourning Dove made a move toward his cell.

"However."

Zags put a finger in the air and immediately yanked it down. "I don't think we need to forget about that world just because it's not our world right now. We need to prepare ourselves for the day we are released. We need to educate ourselves."

Mourning Dove stuck his hands down the front of his underwear.

"We need to start reading the paper, taking an interest in things," Zags said.

"The definition of boredom is forcing yourself to do something when you would rather be doing something else.

"We ... need ... to ... want ... to do ... this ... time."

The circle mumbled and grumbled and sent Zags to hell.

"Now, just let me go," Zags said, putting a hand in the air like an objecting counselor for the defense. "You men been wanting me to talk, so I'm talking. If you don't like what I say, then at least I won't have to talk anymore."

Pontiac watched the circle and handed a cigarette to anyone who needed it.

"Not that some of you aren't doing that already," Zags said. "I just think we need to stop looking at that television as though we are watching shots from the moon."

"Fuck you," Mourning Dove said while turning to go back to his bunk.

"And we need to make a list," Pontiac said as Mourning Dove plopped hard onto his back.

"If you're going to kill people, first you make a list," said Zags. "Ain't that right, chief?"

"Fuck you, punk," came the voice from Mourning Dove's cave.

"There are plenty of folks who need killing. We could start making our contribution by figuring out who they are," said Pontiac.

Baltimore moved up and pressed his stomach into the table.

"You for real?" he stared at Zags.

"Yessir," Zags said, holding up his arm and pinching it.

Baltimore looked at Pontiac, then back to Zags.

Baltimore pulled a folded piece of paper from his pocket. He tossed it on the table.

"I want them on the list."

Zags unfolded the paper and pushed it to Pontiac.

"Put these men on the list," Zags said.

Pontiac began to number down the page.

"I don't want nothing to do with this," Bobby Ford said.

"Me-neither," Arthur said.

"You-all crazy," Mumford said. He waved his hands to dismiss them and walked back to his cell, shaking his head.

The next day Zags followed Pontiac through the chow line, taking a tray and spoon, then accepting a plate of noodles chow mein from the trusty, then a small dish of ice cream from another prisoner. The ice cream would melt before you would get to it, but not to take it was to not get all that was coming to you.

The felony tank ate alone.

They carried their trays into the lunchroom.

Zags and Pontiac sat at one of the six round tables along with Mumford and Baltimore.

Mendez and Mourning Dove sat by themselves. Al Arthur and Bobby Ford sat at another.

Burton rested his tray on the card table holding the coffee pot. He ate quietly in the silent, tinkling room. The white floor shined bright enough that you might not need lights, he wondered, knowing that it better or he would hear about it.

Along one wall inmates had been allowed to draw a mural of a rural scene.

The lane to the farmhouse started at the bottom of the wall and lead to the top concrete block course where the white Victorian sat with a wrap-around porch facing out.

A woman in a white apron pinned clothes to the line as children played in the yard.

A puff of dust trailed a red pickup jaunting up the lane, a man coming home from work, his arm on the window ledge, his right hand draped over the top of the steering wheel.

The artist had been able to sneak his signature at the bottom.

Mark Pontiac.

The men hunched low over the tables like eagles dissecting rabbits with their beaks and talons, but not really hungry.

Mourning Dove walked slowly to get his coffee.

He and Burton stood together in silence as the coffee level rose in the cup like a slow flood.

"Hey, Pontiac," Mourning Dove called out.

The room echoed like an empty machine shed.

Zags thought he jumped and hoped nobody noticed.

"That your old lady?" the Indian said, pointing with his cup to the picture.

"Nope," Pontiac said. He brushed noodles from his mustache. "It's your mamma, your mamma-squaw. That's me in the pickup. That little girl with the football and black hair? That's you. You're the black sheep of the family."

"Baaaa," said Arthur.

Soon the whole room was bleating.

"Hey, Burt!" shouted Bobby Ford.

"We get to play baaaa-sketball this afternoon, huh?"

"Buuurt. Buuurrrrtttttooooonnnnn."

Burton scooped a last plastic spoon of noodles into his mouth, then shoved his tray into the scullery window.

"Line up!" he said.

"D-Block!"

He stood at the door.

Those not finished grumbled before walking to the window and piling their trays where the trusties could collect and count the spoons, dump the uneaten food in the garbage and rinse the plates before putting them in the dishwasher. Burton counted the men, then walked down the hall. They followed, around the corner, past the laundry turned left again to walk past C-Block, one of the two misdemeanor sections.

The felony prisoners stared hard at the silent, stiff ring of boys in blond hair and bleedy tattoos around the chipped table in the middle of the day room like a Kafka diorama, raised above the hall floor by two inches.

The boys stared down at their cards, trying to appear dangerous, hoping not to be noticed. An old man sat on the edge of his bed in the corner cell, his hair sticking up like pointed mashed potato mounds, his beard fresh-shaved, his toes showing through his socks. He watched the men from D-Block marching by, lifted his buttocks toward the hall and passed gas loudly.

Burton counted to himself as they walked past him into the cellblock.

"Three, five, two, seven," Mourning Dove recited as he walked by Burton with his lips moving. Burton smiled to himself and told the front desk that D-Block was secure.

Pontiac hunched over the table and dealt four hands of spades. Zags, Baltimore, and Mendez sat down and scooped up the cards.

"Four."

"Five."

"Six."

"Take it, partner. I can help you about anywhere," said Baltimore to Zags.

"Table talk," said Mendez.

"Hey, don't slouch," he told Baltimore. "Sit up straight."

"Table talk," Pontiac said.

Mendez reached for a cigarette from Pontiac's neat pile. Pontiac covered them with his hand.

"You was giving them out before," Mendez said.

"That was a meetin'," Pontiac said. "I can't be the supplier every damn time we play."

"I need a smoke," Mendez said. "I always smoke after I eat. I'm callin' a meeting."

He reached for a cigarette, keeping his eyes on Pontiac.

Pontiac pulled his hand away from the cigarette pyramid

he had rolled that morning. He reached below the table for his legal pad and reached the pencil off the bars. He crossed his legs and looked at Zags.

Zags pushed up, then walked down the row of cells, stopping at each door then moving on. Each man came out to the table, zombies to the ram's horn.

Arthur, Mumford and Mourning Dove stood back with arms folded.

"We need a name for our group," Zags said.

"How 'bout the Cub Scouts," Mourning Dove said.

"The Cubs," Mumford said.

"Pack 127," Arthur smiled.

Zags grinned.

"D-Block Revolutionary Front," he said.

"Sounds Communist," Pontiac said.

"Prisonistas," Baltimore said.

"Chain Gang," Bobby Ford said.

"We need a website," Arthur said. "www.con."

"Shee-it," Mumford said.

He waved his hands at the groups and walked to his cell. He climbed between his grey blanket and green sheet, pulled his knees to his chest and closed his eyes.

Arthur and Mourning Dove split to stand in front and behind the table.

"I figger the name can wait," Zags looked at Baltimore, then Mendez, then Baltimore.

"What do we need a meeting for," Baltimore said.

"Is this a club?" asked Ford.

"We got to have dues. All club's got dues."

"You're paying your damn dues," Pontiac said.

"I heard that," Ford pointed a finger at Pontiac.

"We're making a list," Pontiac said. "Here's how it damn goes. We are a club, a group, a gang, a brotherhood. I don't care what you damn call it.

"We are taking the law into our own hands. They don't know what to do with it. Burton? Brisco? You kidding me?

Them's the good guys? We can do better than that."

He puffed, ashed, blew out smoke.

"Read the damn newspaper, read them books they damn bring us. Things ain't the way they should be. Maybe we can't get out there to do any good, but we can try. They want to kill us."

He looked over his shoulder toward Mumford.

"There's plenty of them out there needs killin' too."

He twirled the pad around and showed the names from Baltimore's list.

Pol Pot.

Idi Amin. Baby Doc Duvalier.

Alfredo Stroessner.

George Bush.

"Pol Pot's dead," Arthur leaned in and put a finger on the paper.

"That's right," Baltimore said. "That one's already-dead."

Pontiac put a neat line through Pol Pot.

"All right. That ones' dead," Pontiac echoed, like a school teacher correcting papers.

Mendez fingered the list.

"How do I get a name on the list?"

Zags looked at Pontiac.

"You nominate them," Zags said. "Then we vote on 'em."

"And if they get on the list we kill them?" Mendez said.

"That's the idea," Zags said.

"We never voted on them on that paper," Mourning Dove said.

"They been nominated, not approved," Arthur said. Zags looked at Pontiac.

"Mr. Baltimore, you wanna explain to the group why you want these guys popped?" Pontiac said.

Baltimore took the list and looked down.

"I know nothing of these men. Only what I hear. Even Baby-Doc. Never saw him, only saw what he done. The others I have read about, just as you have.

"Umm. I think we should kill them. So that we can cross them off the list. Cross them off like this Pol Pot. Cross them off the list and move on."

"That's no explanation," Arthur said.

"Put the FBI down," Mourning Dove and Al Arthur said at the same time.

"Why the FBI?" Zags said. "The whole FBI?"

"Reasons," Arthur said.

"Yep," Mourning Dove said.

"Why George Bush?" Mourning Dove said. "Why you want to be killing George Bush?"

"China," Zags said in a hoarse whisper.

"After Tienanmen Square he sent his boy, that Brent Scowcroft dude to talk to the Chinese leaders telling them it was all right, the U.S. was cool with it all, no problem."

Zags puffed and crunched his eyes at the smoke.

"Panama. He went in there to take Noriega and gassed thousands of Panamanians. We watched it that night like a made for TV movie. Just Cause. We went down there and killed people, just 'cause.

Zags took another drag on his cigarette and ashed in his pants cuff.

"El Salvador. Nicaragua. Him and Reagan. Willie and Waylon and the boys, they killed and killed and killed just to keep communism out of there, or more to the point, to keep the rich folks in concert clothes and boutonnieres.

"The Cold War. After Russia folded shop, George Bush and his men, they all ran to the toilet to stick their heads down the john and puke. How was they going to keep their buddies in business making bombers and F-16s and magic motion missiles if we didn't have any enemy.

"Well, they recovered.

"Gulf War. Old rich men killing young men for oil, tying a yellow ribbon around their necks and stringing 'em up.

"Omaha. North Omaha. Nigger town. Bunch of shacks. Poverty isn't the problem. It's the solution."

Alford made his voice deep.

"The drug war," he said. "Fuck'n guys doing eighteen years for first-offense marijuana possession. Fuck'n people goin' crazy in prison, committin' suicides in prison. Fuck'n families busted up because of too much prison."

He backed up a step and looked at the floor.

Baltimore looked at Mumford sleeping.

Zags paused to give Alford's statement respect.

"I finally got it. Finally learned my lesson," Zags said. "Followed the golden rule path of my history, my math, my science and this is where it led me."

"We need to meet every week," Al Arthur leaned in.

"We each get to nominate somebody and we have to make a speech just like you did. Then we vote, just like you said."

"Hide that motherfucking list," Mourning Dove stared hard at Pontiac.

Pontiac nodded slowly. One time up, then down.

The men returned to their cells.

Mourning Dove grabbed a towel from the bars and walked to the shower. Bobby Ford hollered down the hall for someone to turn the television on.

Burton sucked his gut to breathe, then waited to the count of ten before he came around the corner.

"What do you want?" he hollered at Ford.

"Can we get this turned on?" Ford said. "I get anything?"

"I can check," Burton said.

"'preciate that," Ford said.

"You won't kill me if'n I don't?" Burton grinned.

Pontiac stopped in the middle of shuffling. He looked at Zags without moving his head. Zags tried to act casual and froze-up. Al Arthur turned his trunk in the middle of a piss and looked at Burton.

Burton swaggered down the hall, his head up, his keys jinglin' Dixie, his hips swinging back and forth like a cop elephant's ass.

Martha Pontiac's Choices In Neuroses group stood outside her front door. Paul Novotny pushed three times on
the doorbell. He turned and giggled. Someone put a hand
over the bell. Two faced toward the street. Martha appeared. She tried to push the door open.

Paul and the others had to back down two steps to make
room.

"Come in. Come in."

Martha stood to one side, greeting her class. The group,
herded into the living room, stood in the middle like sheep
looking for a hole in the wire.

Martha began collecting coats and motioned toward the
chairs.

She pinched Paul's elbow. They both brought out cups
of tea for the others. Martha set a plate of cookies atop the
magazine stack on the coffee table.

"Thank you for agreeing to meet here today," Martha
began.

"You all fit in Paul's car then?"

They nodded slowly.

"I wanted you to greet a former member of our group.
You all remember Elana. Elana?"

Elana entered from the back room, her arms across her
chest, hands tuck in the opposite sleeve of the white sweater she had borrowed from Martha. She stood by the door.
The group members swiveled their heads. Paul stared, his
eyes narrowing. Elana met him. He looked away. A Lou
Reed song played through the back room door.

"This is the age of Video Violence."

Elana returned to the room and closed the door.

"Well," Martha said. "We'll be talking to Elana again, I'm
sure. Why don't we begin."

She reached out to hold the hands of those nearby. The
rest followed, holding limp hands, fingertips, almost touching hands.

Martha asked Paul to lead the group in reciting the De-
siderata.

"Go plaaacidly," they monotoned together.

In her room Elana caressed the microphone and watched
the light rain.

"And that's what's killing me this morning, my friend,"
she said. "You take care."

"She never talks."

Paul helped Martha with the dishes after the meeting.

"Who?"

"Elana, the one in the door on the radio. I'll bet she's got a
good voice."

"She does," Martha said. "Here."

She dropped her towel on the counter.

Elana whisked through the living room sporting a floppy
black hat and sunglasses, with a Morningside letter jacket.

"She does," Martha said.

"I'll show you, sometime."

She touched Paul's arm on her way to catch Elana.

TEN

"IF YOU GIVE A MAN A FISH HE WILL FISH FOR A DAY, BUT
IF YOU TEACH HIM TO FISH HE WILL FISH FOR A LIFETIME."
— DAN QUAYLE

H ey! Anybody down there!"
Brigita Householder peeled her coat and
dropped it on a hook.
She pushed the door closed.

"Hey, Mickey? Richard? You guys down there?"

Brigita reached to where she knew the railing would be
and stepped off into the darkness with her right foot. She
strengthened her grip and stepped again, down, down.

She descended into the basement.

With her fingers on the wooden railing she felt with her
knuckles the plywood that Michaela's father had tacked up
in the heat of last summer.

He was sure it would keep the house cooler in the summer and warmer in the winter.

That had been Ita and Mickey's playful mantra for
months: Cooler in the summer, warmer in the winter,
workers of the world unite.

As Brigita found the carpeted floor she located the light
ahead.

She let the railing go and stepped into the void.

The couch would be on her right and the wall with the
plaques and the half bathroom on the left.

The blank television screen shined in the corner.

"Buddha Sony."

The light from the room down the hall glowed under a closed door.

She heard voices.

She called out and the voices stopped.

That's weird, she thought.

Brigita extended her arms and felt her way down the corridor. Her palms hit the nothingness-never-was-never-would-be of the open bedroom and the laundry.

She found the walls again, placing one foot suspiciously ahead of the other, sliding the open hands along the smooth plywood panels then finding the ridge breaks then the smooth space.

The door flung open. Light assaulted the corridor. Brigita shielded her face with her hands. She saw the silhouette of a tallish being with covering over its head and protuberances where its ears might be.

"Mon Dieu, mon ami. Where you been?"

Richard Hall flicked on the hall light and looked at his watch. He slid the earphones down to his shoulders over his backward Cleveland Indians ball cap. He grabbed Brigita by the shoulders.

Brigita stopped.

Richard looked into her eyes. She smelled pepperoni.

"Contact," he said.

"No!" She knocked his hands off like a defensive lineman shedding a block and surged past him.

"Well, we're close," he said, "this close." He followed close after, shoving the pizza crust into his mouth.

In The Command Center Mickey perched in front of one of the three computers.

She stared into the screen while her hand guided the mouse. Her left hand reached to the pizza box between the machines, which occupied most of two heavy metal desks laid end to end.

The room was prepared in off-white concrete block bunker motif.

Brigita pushed back the top of the pizza box and peeled off another Canadian bacon and pineapple slice. Richard took another and stood behind Mick holding two pieces of his favorite foreign food.

"H'lo." Mickcy acknowledged Brigita's presence while staring into the computer.

"Colonel Perkins is giving an online interview to Tom Brokaw," Richard whispered.

Mickey scrolled down the screen, then clicked the mouse twice, then leaned back in the swivel chair and looked at Brigita, seated in front of the computer.

"Brokaw doesn't know the first thing about the JFK case," Mickey said. "Going all over old shit. This is no breakthrough."

"He's part of the coverup," said Brigita.

Brigita moved the mouse on her machine and the screen was reborn.

"Anything on Bigfoot?"

"No time," said Richard. "We were waiting for you. You said you'd be here at seven."

Brigita examined the white clock on the wall above the work stations. The unique design showed the most famous frame of the Patterson-Gimlin film of Bigfoot of 1967, with the animal mooning like Marilyn Monroe.

The two long arms were the hands of the clock. Right now the left arm was on the four and the right one on the seven, making the Yeti look like a maitre d' inviting you to sit down.

Brigita, Mickey and Richard considered themselves the main cogs of the "Nature Lovers Group." They used the computers and a mailing list to track Bigfoot, UFOs and new developments in the Kennedy assassinations. The third computer, on the table with an unopened software box on top, would be dedicated to the animal rights issue.

Brigita leaned back and lowered her feet onto the desk like Barney Fife before a brainstorm.

"Mom had me ironing."

Richard pulled up another chair on wheels and leaned over the backrest, positioning himself between the two women.

"I want to do some field work," he said.

"Here we go," said Mickey.

"Buy a farm," Brigita said.

He tore off a bite of one slice and stuffed it with his tongue into the left side of his mouth and then ripped into the slice in his other hand and stored it in his other cheek.

They waited for him to chew.

Brigita tickled his cheeks.

"You look like a chipmunk."

"Pair of testicles," Mickey said.

"Let me scratch your nuts," Brigita leaned toward him. Richard bolted.

"This is all fine," he said, stretching his palms and arms to encompass the machines, the grey file cabinet against the wall, the poster of Oliver Stone, the gold-framed plaque showing a spaceship shining a beam of light to the ground, the map of the world on the north wall with multi-colored tacks.

"But we need to go out … there!" He did a Saturday Night Fever move. He looked at the floor and stuck his right hand into the air, pointing to the ninety-degree angle between the ceiling and wall.

"We have to go in search of, no matter how much fun it is sitting down here in the dark at three in the morning and telling ghost stories. If we're really serious."

He regarded Brigita, then Mickey. "We need to move on."

"Where are we going to look?" said Mickey.

She flicked her eyes back to the screen. With an instinctual motion of her thumb and pinky she called up the Northern Exposure fan website.

"You want to move to Oregon? Fine, but I am needed here. Without me there would be dozens of folks wandering around Pamida toting their shit forever."

"Dante's Department Store," said Richard.

Brigita smiled and slid her feet down. She shoved her butt and found the backrest of the chair with her tailbone.

She stared at Richard.

"All right. I've got yer grassy knoll right here."

She scratched her private parts.

"No, really. The day we find something is the day I'm gone.

This shit gives me the willies."

She walked to the refrigerator in the corner. She stared at the newest calendar of events stuck to it before she opened the door and pulled out a pop can. She peeled it open and stood behind her empty chair.

"But it would be pretty cool," she said, looking at Richard. He reached for another pizza slab. "You know, to know the truth and shit."

The back screen door shut like a cap gun firing. The kids heard the sound of feet stomping and muffled voices.

"Mickey, you down there?"

"Yeah, dad.

"Ssshhh," she said to Richard and Brigita.

Verlin McDonald pushed on the light and the basement came alive. He hung his camouflaged coat on a hanger and left his orange cap cocked on his head.

Mickey's heart leaped with each clomp of waterproofed boots hitting the steps.

She waited for the crowd of boots behind him: clomp-clomp … clomp.

Richard grabbed the plastic bag from the table, lit a match and waved his hands in the air.

"I had the lights off, da-ad," Mickey crawled her chair to the door and gripped the door jam with both hands to fling her head into the hall.

"We don't want to fall over one of your mamma's porcelain duckies," Verlin said.

His chin wagged long as he talked. His wisp of red mustache flirted with his upper lip and nose, the hair around his chin a matted "V," the hair on the left side of his mouth flat where he set the stock of his shotgun.

Verlin marched down the steps into the rec room.

Above the big screen television hung a deer's head. A row of silver and gold snowmobile racing trophies sat on the mantel above the fireplace to the left of the TV.

He guided Rod and Rodger Tipple on a tour of the fresh paint job on the wainscoting.

Verlin walked behind the bar to the refrigerator and pulled out three non-alcoholic beers. He held the three in his left hand for Rod and Rodger to grab. They turned their tops and flipped them onto the bar.

Rod and Rodger wore tan snowmobile coveralls and purple Vikings stocking caps. The twins came to Verlin's shoulders, but they didn't know it. They thought they were as tall and as fast as wildebeests.

They lived together in the home place on their parents' farm. Their folks moved into the new brick place on the other side of the drive the year the twins graduated high school.

When they weren't at Verlin's they watched Red Green at home and drank Moosehead beer from green bottles. They chewed Skoal and spit into the first empty, Rod in the recliner and Rodger with his legs stretched out on the couch.

Verlin had quit drinking late last year. The twins went along with the routine so's not to suffer the steps sermon again.

To Verlin the world was alcoholic, most notably those who did not drink.

Mickey listened to them swallowing their beers without talking, then their rubber boots swishing through the new shag carpet like bush grass.

She could feel them outside the door when Verlin's boot appeared in the open door, then his left hand fingertips, the scarred, dirty knuckles, then his giant head, two feet from ear to ear, smiling, reaching behind the door to grab Richard without looking.

Verlin sniffed the air like a deer edging into an open cornfield in late afternoon.

"You been burning candles again. Lemme guess. Storm Watch. Smells like rain. I like it."

ELEVEN

Burton walked past each block asking if anyone wanted to go to church, which meant it was ten-thirty.

"I been working with my hands longer than you been alive," Zags said.

He crouched over the table with Martin Mumford.

"I was gonna be a bricklayer 'for I got busted," Mumford said. "My uncle got a comp'ny."

"Yeah?" said Zags.

"You can't just come in here and 'spect to be one a the boys," said Mumford.

"You have a meetin' and makin' lists. You ain't one a us. Can't be," he said. He swept a pile of nails through the bar into the hall. "You mixed mud? See your hands."

Zags laid his palms on either side of Mumford's.

Mumford's black hands shone. A pink scar ran the width of the soft pads of his left palm. Zags' palms were calloused, with dirty permanently scratched into the joints.

"I was an arc welder for Noah, son," Zags said.

Zags rolled his hands onto Mumford's. He wrapped his fingers into Mumford's and began a gradual python squeeze. Mumford let his hands go limp and tried to pull back. He looked around the cell and tilted his head at Zags.

114

He yanked back, then tried to stand. Zags' hands held him in place like a steel pin set in concrete.

They sat there holding hands across the dayroom table.

Zags let loose and resumed his rolling practice.

"Don't get into a pissin' contest with a fire hose, friend," he said. "I'll remember the same. Actually, I feel downright honored to be among you men. I don't consider myself one of you. I don't consider myself one of them out there. That makes me homeless, right? Perfect."

He spoke with his head down, watching his fingers learn their new trade.

"The only reason I led that meeting was guys were coming up expecting me to be more than I am. I thought we ought to talk about it out in the open. Might be fun, something to do. A real American pastime, you know?"

Mumford leaned forward. His white bulbs bulged, with red and blue stripes and lines.

"This ain't no game," Mumford hissed like a snake. "We ain't playin'. You see any fool here playin' games?"

He leaned forward, stretched his neck and extended his arms like the ten-thirty preacher.

Mumford straightened up and stared at Zags.

He turned and walked to his cell.

Mark Pontiac stopped in the doorway of Al Arthur's house. He stuck one foot inside, kicking a dustball out of the way.

"You got cigarettes?"

Arthur rolled over, away from the wall. He tossed the cover and sat up.

"Yeah," he yawned. He reached to the end of the mattress and brought back a crunched pack of Marlboros with the matches hunchbacked in the cellophane. He stood and handed the pack to Pontiac.

Pontiac put up a hand.

"No, I'm good. Just wonderin'."

"How's the eye?" Pontiac pointed to his own eye.

Arthur touched his eye.

"It's okay. Thanks."

"I'm sorry," Pontiac said. "Sometimes I get … ."

He stared with glazed eyes at the cement floor, dark grey trowel swirls sloping toward the walls.

"I shouldn't a got in your face like that," Arthur said. "You remind me of my dad."

"He have a mustache?"

"No. He led with his left and kicked hard, too. 'Cept he had pointed toes on his caboy boots." He rubbed his stomach and sat. "No wonder I ain't got no appetite."

Pontiac sat on the opposite bunk.

"Mind?"

"G'head."

Pontiac offered his Marlboro pack of perfectly rolled Buglers.

Arthur licked the end in a twirl and clenched it between his thumb and third finger. He took a long drag, tilting his head and scrunching is eyes. He sucked two more quick with puckered lips without touching the cigarette.

"You got an old man?" Arthur said. "You know, somebody on the outside."

"No," Pontiac said. "My dad's right here. That old guy in C-Block?"

"Him?" Arthur said, squinting his eyes and flicking his ash in the toilet.

"Hmm, mmm. I don't think he recognizes me anymore. I offer him smokes. He just stares me down."

"That's sad," Arthur said. "It is, man. That's straight-up bullshit."

"Nothing nobody can do," Pontiac said. "It be that way, sometimes."

He got up to leave, leaning forward as he rose to miss the top bunk. Arthur put out his clenched fist and held it.

Pontiac tapped and accepted Arthur's return.

TWELVE

"Is this your meal, Jackie Brown?
I've seen people throw more than this out."
— John Mellencamp

Baltimore looked in the mirror in his cell.
He moved his head around trying to find a clear view.
He patted the top and sides of his hair.
As always, Pontiac and Zags were seated at the table.
Zags nodded toward Baltimore.
Pontiac hunched in closer. Zags scooted up.
Pontiac started the story.

Stefan Lebot grew up in the dirt of Sun City, Port au Prince, Haiti.
He hung around the medical clinic run by the nuns.
One of the American lay workers took a special interest in Stefan. She had little choice. Anytime she managed a rest, there he was, sitting on her knee, silent, like a bird.
The woman was from Sitka, Minnesota.
Her parents worked with a group at the Catholic convent. Each month they loaded up syringes and masks and gauze and wheelchairs for shipment to Haiti to supply the mission. The woman told them about the child who had adopted her. He seemed to have no parents, brothers or sisters.
The boy asked the woman from Minnesota who he was and where did he come from.

117

With tears in her eyes that he collected on the tip of his finger as they slid down her cheek, in Creole she told Stefan Lebot, whose name she grabbed from a brand of French candy bars donated to the mission, that he was the most recent descendent of Toussaint L'Overture, the Haitian revolutionary who freed the island from the rule of the Spanish and the French.

"In 1798," he said. "Did they know about me?"

"Yes. Oh, yes," she said. "They knew about you. They have been expecting you. And they are so glad you have finally come. We are all so proud."

Stefan grew up at the mission. The Sitka group decided they wished to sponsor him. They wanted to bring him to the United States and send him to college.

He and the mission woman sat on the cement stoop his last night in town. They smoked American cigarettes and sipped French wine from Dixie cups. In the morning she paid for his cab to the airport.

In order to get a cheaper rate, his flight went by way of Baltimore. Stefan got off the plane to have a drink in the airport lounge. He spent four hours drinking martinis with the money the mission group had sent him. He missed his connecting flight and rode the bus to Minnesota on what was left.

He decided on his twenty-hour bus journey to change his name to Stephan Baltimore in honor of the evening in the Baltimore airport lounge, when he first came to America, to impress his benefactors that he would change his life around, that he had learned his lesson once and for all.

The mission group decided against sending him to the private college in the Twin Cities. He would spend two years at Morningside College in Sioux City first, to see how it went before spending the big bucks.

In the winter of his second year Stephan became involved with the forty-seven-year-old wife of his graduate student economics professor. The instructor caught them in bed one afternoon in the married student housing building and Stephan was charged with burglary.

He pleaded guilty after his advisor promised he could stay in school after the charges were taken care of.

Martha sat in her living room, her feet resting atop the magazines on the coffee table. Her cup balanced on her chest.

As soon as the front door swung open she was out of her chair. She snatched Elana's hand and rifled the pockets of her jacket.

"What's this?" she held a vial of pills in front of Elana's face.

"Nothing," said Elana. She took one step around Martha. Martha cut her off.

"I didn't do it, okay?" Elana growled.

She bared her teeth.

"I never do it. Never will. It just keeps going and going. It will never stop."

Martha took Elana's arms.

"Your father was not brave to kill himself, if that's what he did," she said. "Revolutionaries don't kill themselves. They fight and sometimes they die and sometimes they win, but they don't quit."

"Is this ... how," Elana dropped her head and sobbed.

The Twins cap fell to the wood floor.

"We show our kids what we do in the face of tyranny? That's what it is, you know? You can't see it, but it's the same. No tanks, but it's the same."

"Yes."

Martha squeezed Elana's arms.

"You keep going. You speak."

"Speak?"

Elana threw off Martha's hands.

"What good is that? What good is talk? What good is work, mowing the lawn, paying taxes? What!"

Martha gently put her hands on Elana's shoulders.

"Do you know how many people like you there are in this country?"

A tear dribbled down the side of Elana's nose.

"Nobody," said Martha. "There is no one like you. There are thousands of Dan Rathers or the trained seals at KZOO."

Elana licked the tear when it reached her mouth.

"And that's why you have those pills. They put them in your hand. It's not paranoia. They have to make you take yourself out. It's much messier if they have to do it."

"Like with King?" Elana wiped her eye.

"Yes," Martha put her hands down.

"Little piddly-ass Sioux City has Elana Usak speaking the truth and it doesn't know how lucky it is. There's no way it possibly could."

Martha took one step back from Elana.

"Like a child does not know how lucky it is to be well cared for. How could it? But it is still lucky. And mothers do not quit caring because they don't get roses with their coffee."

"But, my," Elana said.

"Your father is not you."

Martha turned to sit down.

"You have a radio show to do. I have to go to work."

She drank her coffee with closed eyes.

Agents Don Hargrove and Jeffry Fry sat in their car outside the Nebraksa Café.

"That should be Nebra-ska," Fry said.

Hargrove watched the street.

He checked himself in the mirror and saw Sheriff Jeremiah Williger pull up.

Hargrove rose to greet Williger, who scrambled to grab his hat to meet Hargrove halfway. They crunched each other's hands. Fry came up with his hands in his windbreaker pockets.

"She was in there."

Hargrove motioned with his head toward the café.

Fry looked at the café letters. Williger nodded.

"She's long gone by now," Fry said, looking back. His stomach rumbled.

"We need to sit on this place," Hargrove said.

He wore black leather gloves and a brush jacket. Williger noticed the GAP blue jeans.

"I suppose I could," Williger said.

"But …"

"You need to do that," Hargrove said.

"She's back on the air. We have two teams out with tracking equipment. It won't take long, but she'll bolt and she might return here."

"Sure thing," Williger said, turning back to his car.

Fry and Hargrove waited for traffic and walked to the café, stepping over a pair of muddy robins-egg blue women's underwear to reach the curb.

"You white ducks killed Bobby Kennedy and don't put a cap in that fool?"

Martin Mumford watched Dan Rather on the evening news.

Pontiac sat at the table making notes.

Bobby Ford sat next to Pontiac, his back to the television.

"Tells a lot about a man, the kinds of plans he makes," Ford said. "Whatcha writin'?"

"I guess that'd be none of your damn business," Pontiac said without looking up.

"Here, lemme see," Ford reached for the pad.

Pontiac grabbed Ford's wrist and twisted it so that Bobby was staring at his own middle knuckle.

"Man! Let go. Shit. Geezuz!"

Ford stood and massaged his wrist.

"You got to locate your sense of humor. My God, man!"

Ford walked to the corner of the block and stuck his head into the bars, straining to see down the hall.

Mumford wagged his head at the floor. He looked up and put his raised hands up like a preacher. He walked to the screen and flipped channels.

"Howdy Doody and the Bobbsy Twins. Will you look at this? These are all the same, man. You know what I'm talking about? Shit."

He sat down, put his elbows on the tabletop and stretched out his legs.

"C'mere," Pontiac said.

"Hey, sales-man. Lookit. Look at my list and tell my fortune ... motherfucker."

Ford walked back. He tucked his T-shirt into his jumpsuit, the top rolled down to his waist. He sat next to Pontiac, who pushed the pad over.

Ford read down the line.

"We started this thing just in time," Mumford said.

He looked over his shoulder to Pontiac.

"They's crazy. Sheet."

He pointed at the television.

"Get one of those?" he pointed to Pontiac's smokes. Pontiac nodded and Mumford put a cigarette in his mouth. He cupped a hand around a lit match and brought it to his mouth.

"Look at that!" he pointed again at the television.

"Ho, come on over here, mamma."

Ford pushed back the list.

"All right," he said and walked off.

He walked the four steps to the front door of Zags and Arthur's house.

Zags lay on the top bunk with his back against the far wall. The light burned as always in the middle of the ceiling, inside a wire-mesh cage.

Arthur slept, his face to the wall, a thin rough cover over his head.

"Hey," Ford said.

"Whatcha readin'?"

Zags held a legal pad against his thigh, his right leg crossed over his left.

"Huh?" he said.

"Oh, you're writin', " Ford said. "Everybody's writin'. Catfish is writing, you're writin'. Whatcha writin'?"

"Letter."

"Oh. Wife?" Ford asked.

Zags shook his head.

"Kids? You got kids?" Ford said.

"Hnh, uh. Judge," Zags said.

"I wouldn't do that. They do not like to be contacted directly by the accused," Ford said. "Noo-ooo, sir."

Zags looked up and stopped writing.

"Cigarette?" he asked.

Ford accepted and leaned against the opposite bunk.

"Break time," he smiled, holding out the cigarette as a toast.

"Everybody deserves a break," Zags said.

He put his pad down and sat up, dangling his legs over the bedside.

"Blow the whistle. Prisoners can quit being prisoners, for fifteen minutes. Bring in the people, open the windows, turn on some music."

"Let us hold our kids," Ford said.

"You got kids?" Zags said.

"Yeah. Two boys, three," Ford said. "They live with their mom. They was supposed to come visit."

He puffed and twisted his neck to blow the smoke behind.

"You know," Ford said.

He held up the cigarette to make his point.

"When I worked in the automobile industry, I used to hate coffee breaks. I was a worker, a salesman, no order-taker. I don't mind saying, I was good."

He blew smoke again.

"I hated that break room, though."

"'Cause you wanted to keep working?" Zags said.

Ford peered up from staring at the floor.

"Huh? No. No. I don't know. I … I didn't know how to coffee. I know it sounds crazy. You know? You sit down, shoot the shit. How's the wife. How's the team? How's the weather? Nice tie. What'd you do this weekend?"

He considered whether to continue.

"Questions like that every morning of every day for-fucking-ever. Doesn't that scare you?" Ford said.

"Scares me," Zags said.

"You ever wonder what it's like when you die? Even when you go to heaven. It's for-fucking-ever. Like one of those Twilight Zones. It never, ever stops. It gets me dizzy. It scares me," Ford said. "I actually had a panic attack one night thinking about that. I never told anyone. Jesus H. Christ. Who-ah."

"Store!" The night guard pushed a cart down the hall.

"Store!" Ford said.

"Break time's over," Zags' cigarette sizzled in the toilet and he pushed off the bed, landing flat on the concrete. He held onto the bar until the tingles evaporated.

On the gun metal grey cart waited rows and stacks of blue Bugler tobacco, Marlboros, Snickers, shampoo, card packs, packs of coffee, tea, orange juice, Afro cream — a lemonade stand in hell.

Ford stood behind the rest.

Mendez, Mourning Dove, and Pontiac got in line in front of the guard. She studied her sheet.

"Mark Pontiac. Three Bugler, two Marlboros, six Snickers, two stamps."

The guard stacked each named item in the bars.

Pontiac waited until she finished to collect his goods. He stopped past Baltimore's cell and tossed him a pack of Marlboros.

"Even?" he said.

Then the Catfish walked past Bobby Ford and put a packet of Bugler in Ford's gut without looking.

Ford considered the gift and immediately sat down at the table to seize a level spot for rolling.

Zags accepted his ten packs of Marlboros and three packs of matches. The guard did a double take.

"You're that terrorist, right?" she said.

"Excuse me?" Zags said.

"That nut whose going to kill the pres'dent, right? That's you. No 'fense."

Zags walked to his cell to store his tobacco in a line down the left side of his bunk where the mattress was not wide enough to fill the space.

"Catfish, you here again?" the guard said.

"By God, I think you're right," Pontiac said.

He roamed his head around the ceiling, walls and floor. He strolled out of his cell smoking a factory cigarette, one hand deep in his jumpsuit pocket, like a tycoon exiting Delmonico's.

"Let's go," Baltimore said. "You get half this pack. You can't sleep all the damn day."

"I sleep during the day's all," Mumford said.

His grey cover formed a bubble around his face. He spoke out an opening through which he could see the floor.

"At night I read, do pushups, sit ups. Three hundred, three hundred."

"That's a punk's move," Baltimore said. "You ain't afraid. You got to get out there and show them you ain't afraid."

"I ain't afraid, they're just stupid. People's stupid, or hain't you noticed?" Mumford said.

He turned the cover back and looked up at Baltimore looming overhead.

Mumford eyed Baltimore.

"You always want to be everybody's friend. Why? Haven't you seen enough of people to know better?" Mumford said.

Baltimore sat on the edge of the opposite bed. He leaned forward.

"I've seen enough of people to know that they can surprise you, in good ways and bad. I've seen bof."

He got up and walked out to the table.

He stood in front of the television and looked up.

Arthur Mendez sat on the bunk across from Mourning Dove in Mourning Dove's cell.

Mendez began again on a story he had started before groceries arrived. The story about how he had come from El Salvador by himself, made his way to Del Rio, then north.

Mourning Dove leaped into a narrow opening in Mendez' soliloquy and told about a plaque outside the high school in his town with the name of his brother who had played basketball and gotten run down on main street by a drunk driver.

Zags wandered into Pontiac's cell carrying a piece of the Sioux City Journal. The paper got passed around the blocks each morning. They weren't supposed to keep any souvenirs, but it often appeared with rectangle holes.

Zags read the article to Pontiac about some people getting their throats cut in Kosovo.

Zags asked Pontiac if he could see killing somebody to keep them from killing somebody else.

Pontiac said he could.

Zags asked him how 'bout the death pen'lty.

Pontiac said most definitely, he could throw the switch.

Pontiac told Zags about the time he got out from doing ninety days and joined a softball team with a bunch of his high school buddies. Pontiac said he couldn't understand a word they said, so he found a way to get back into jail.

Bobby Ford sat at the yellow table with Al Arthur.

Arthur was teaching Ford how to make a rolling machine out of the tinfoil inside a Bugler pack.

"Eliminate poverty?" Arthur glanced up at the TV.

"They don't get it."

He stared at Bobby.

"Eliminate poverty."

Al put out his hand.

"How much you got what you don't need? Put the shit in my hand."

He looked down to roll.

"They don't get it."

He pointed at the TV.

"So we don't get it."

He nodded at his hand.

The guard chugged back pushing the white cart, breathing heavy. She stopped in the hall, next to Ford and Al Arthur. She read from a list on a clipboard.

"Meds!" she shouted.

On the table sat a waggly line of white pill cups.

"Meds!" Ford shouted and stood, reaching one hand through the bars.

"Robert Ford," Ford said.

She looked at him, then the list, then handed him a cup and a cup of water. He swallowed both, then opened his mouth so she could peer in. He raised his tongue and handed back the paper cups. With rubber-gloved hands she pitched them into the basket attached to the cart.

"Doin' the Thorazine shuffle tonight, Ford?" Arthur said.

"No. Cold medicine," said Ford.

"Yeah, yeah, same-ol same-ol," Arthur said.

Zags walked up to the bars.

"Michael Zags," he said.

She placed a cup with one cream and green pill at the bottom. He swallowed it and the water and showed her his tongue.

He turned to walk away.

"Prozac," the guard said while marking Zags' name on her list. Zags stopped and turned to stare at her.

"You ain't killin' nobody, Mr. Prozac," she looked at him, then back to her list.

Zags pursed his lips, then dropped his head, then walked into his cell.

Baltimore stopped by the table on his way to the shower. His cut arms and chest above the white towel drew Zags' attention. He tried not to stare. Baltimore bee-bopped, singing into his shampoo bottle.

On his way back, Baltimore stopped at the table, now holding Mendez, Mourning Dove and Pontiac along with Zags.

"The United Nations Security Council. Looks to me like a meetin' could break out at any minute around here. You looka here, brothers. These here white boys cain't hep you, but they can damn-sure hurt you. You think about dat and den you remember it."

He began a rap.

"The ruling coalition and the main opposition. You gotcher ruling coalition then the main opposition."

He sang into his shampoo bottle and imitated one of Mourning Dove's war whoops.

"Baby, baby, bitch, mothafucka hooo," he played the shampoo bottle like an electric guitar. "Heh, heh, heh, Shiiit."

In the cell he ripped off the towel and flicked it at Mumford's ass under the covers. Mumford sat up and hit his head on the thin metal frame of the bed above him.

Baltimore stood naked with his legs spread around the toilet to see into the mirror to pick at his hair.

"The black devil is right," Mendez said.

"In my country we used to get all these church people coming down. They couldn't do nothing. They wanted to share our pain for three days or seven days or two years, then whoosh."

He flattened his hand and slid it on the table like an airplane taking off.

"They're gone."

Zags stared at Mendez.

"What you think I'm stupid?" Mendez said.

"Even you," Mourning Dove said to Zags. "You can't."

Zags put up one hand.

"Pretend I'm not here."

"But those gringos killed lots of my people," Mendez said.

"They only way they help is to stay away," Mourning Dove said.

"I can't go back," Zags said. "The tracks are filled in, over-grown."

"This is a time whose idea has come," Pontiac said to himself. "You can't manipulate history. You just take what it gives you."

"Say what?" Mourning Dove said.

"You can't make this be 1968. However, we have the prison issue," Pontiac thought out loud.

"We got it big time, I'd say," Mourning Dove said.

"You're a smart Indian, chief," Pontiac said.

"You ever hear Paul Harvey on the radio at home?"

He looked at Bill Mourning Dove.

"Every day at noon. My grandfather listened," Bill said.

"Ever wonder if it's really him?"

Pontiac smiled and licked a new cigarette.

"You know, like those Soviet premiers who they say are fine and then you find out they were dead a month already. What if Paul Harvey is dead and they've got some guy in Indianapolis suburb broadcasting, just so the government doesn't lose that voice."

Mendez whistled a Gloria Estefan tune toward the hall.

"You ever think about the joys reserved just for the rich?" he flipped back.

Mourning Dove glared at him and pulled his head back to bring Mendez into focus.

"The stuff we can't do. There are certain good things reserved for the rich. I can't think of any right this minute, but they are there, you know, theeengs," Mendez said.

Baltimore nudged Pontiac so he could sit down.

"Now we got a meeting," Baltimore said. "Now the brothers is represented we got us a quorum, a representative body, you understand what ah'm sayin'?"

"We understand what you're saying," Pontiac said.

"I think that was a rhetorical question," Mourning Dove said.

Zags put his hand in front of his mouth and tried not to smile.

Baltimore wagged his head and the splatters rained on everyone.

"You fuckin' dog," Pontiac said, scooping up his rolling papers.

"Why don't you go shake somewhere else?"

"Heh, heh," Baltimore snickered. "I'm feeling good. I go to court this week. Just found out. My lawyer wrote me a letter. First one I ever got. I'm going home."

"Wherever that is," Mourning Dove said.

"Ain't it a bitch?" Baltimore looked at Mourning Dove. "And then you die, right, homes?"

"Gotcher home right here, Zulu."

Mourning Dove stood and cupped a hand around his crotch.

"Pull out that sorry ass list a yours," Baltimore said.

"Anybody got any bad guys they wants to nominate? Then we vote, right? C'mon, roll 'em dice, wack us some mothafuckas."

The next day at lunch Don Burton leaned the Kool-Aid cooler down to drain the last bits into his cup while keeping his eyes on the men at the tables.

He set his tray in the window and told the cook to keep an eye out, he'd be right back.

Pontiac watched Burton round the corner.

He stared in the tray hole and saw "Puff Daddy" Pfister gawking out like a Holstein counting blue Chevy's, wiping his fat hands in his stained apron, chewing on a weary straw.

Burton pinned his keys against his leg and swung just his left arm. He turned left again and stared into the dead eyes of C-Block. The boys froze while scooping their cards.

The old man in the last cell rose from sitting on his bed when he saw the officer hurrying past. He met Burton in the corner and stuck his hands between the bars.

"Hey there, Burt," he said. "Give this to my son, how 'bout it?"

Burton stopped and looked at the coverless paperback, cradled as an offering, as if it were infected with malaria.

Keeping his hands pinned to his sides he stared at the book, then looked at the man. Burton tilted his head to the left and pinched his left eye to tell the old man he was crazy.

Burton stepped back a half step to avoid touching the book or the man, then pivoted to continue his mission, shaking his head, watching the endless treadmill floor scroll underneath.

Burton reached for the key that would open the block.

He stretched it on the bungee cord connected to his belt and inserted it softly.

He slid the door to the right and stepped inside the sally port, through the second door.

He tippy-toed into Baltimore and Mumford's cell.

Where would they put it? he wondered.

Who would have it?

Ford. The fuck.

He walked quietly into Ford's cell.

He put his black shoe tentatively on the toilet to look over Zags' bunk. He lifted the mattress and ran his hand down the top, around the sides. He knelt on the floor to check the bottom of the frame.

He checked the open bunks used for shelf space.

Nothing.

He searched under the table in the shower, stood on the table to check inside the vent.

Pontiac. The writer.

Burton strode into Pontiac's house, first pausing at the door.

A yellow legal pad lay atop the rough grey blanket.

Burton took on long step and snatched it up.

He flipped inside and found the page with the list of names.

He scanned down then ripped the page free and tossed the pad on the bed.

He hurried out of the block and locked the doors behind.

The prisoners walked past C-block.

Mumford and Baltimore stared hard at the frightened bunch at the table.

"Hey, fish, gimme your 'bacco," Mumford said to a nineteen-year-old with his back to the bars.

Mumford stopped.

"I know you got tobacco. Lemme have some."

The boy rose from the table without looking and walked into his cell.

"Let's go!" Burton hollered.

"D-Block, inside! Let's go."

"I got business I'm conducting," Mumford said.

"Let's go. Now! Burton demanded.

Mumford moved off.

The boy stayed in his cell. He sat down on his bed and stared at the floor.

The old man in the last cell sat on the edge of his bed reading from an old paperback as D-Block tromped past.

By the time Mumford walked past Burton complaining about what was he in such a hurry for, Mark Pontiac was sitting with his legs crossed under the dayroom table, thumbing through the pages in his yellow legal pad.

Around him he had displayed the necessary accouterments for an enjoyable afternoon: cards, ashtray, matches, tobacco. He leafed through the pad, then back again, then page by page.

He looked across at Zags taking his accustomed seat.

Pontiac walked back into his room and searched his Marlboro-carton cabinets and bureau.

As he sat back down and aimed a glance at Zags, a Burton apparition appeared over Zags' shoulder.

"Anything else you men need 'for I go nurse maid the rest?

"Huh?"

He eyed Pontiac, whose countenance for an instant froze Burton in position while his hands, heart and body raced to battle stations.

Pontiac's eyes moved for an instant to the bulge in Don Burton's shirt pocket.

"You all right, De-troit?" Burton said to Pontiac.

"You ain't comin' down with something? Get you a Ty-le-naw?"

Pontiac did not answer.

"Well, boys, if there's anything I can ever do," Burton said while moving off, "just give me a holler."

He waved back over his head with his right hand as he waddled down the hall. His shadow rode the concrete wall as he hit the light from the C-Block dayroom.

"The list is gone," Pontiac hissed at Zags.

Baltimore, Al Arthur, Bill Mourning Dove and Miguel Mendez circled the table. Mumford laughed to himself as he pulled the covers over his shoulders for afternoon naptime.

Bobby Ford eased his bare buttocks down on the cool steel and shot up like a burnt Pop Tart when he felt the dirt track.

"Jesus!" Who's been in here? Goin' through my stuff!"

He noticed his rumpled bed. He pulled up his jumpsuit and buttoned it around his waist. He stormed into the dayroom to take his prey.

"Bobby Freak Ford," Mourning Dove turned toward Ford's cell.

"Who, the-fuck, was in my," Ford said.

Mourning Dove walked to stand in his way.

"Somebody turned the list in to the man," he said. "You wouldn't know who that would be?"

Ford pushed past him and squeezed between Baltimore and Arthur to put both hands on the table in front of Zags.

"Somebody was crawling around in my house. There's footprints on the toilet," Ford said.

They followed Ford into his cell.

Al Arthur climbed to one top bunk, Baltimore to the other.

Mourning Dove, Pontiac, Zags, and Mendez squeezed between the two lower bunks and bent over to examine Ford's steel toilet seat.

Mendez peeled off his right shoe and held it bottom-up close to the track. The narrow half-moon ridge pattern of the blue boat shoe did not match the horizontal stripes in the faint dirt track.

The men walked flowed silently back to the table and resumed their stage positions.

"Burton left chow hall. I seen him," Pontiac said. "He had something in his pocket. He came back in here and shook us down."

"Why?" Mourning Dove said.

He stared down at Ford who avoided eye contact.

"Why would he even know there's a list, or what's on it?"

Ford picked up his arms and folded them across his chest.

"You know he listens, fuckin' pig. 'Course he heard you guys talking about offin' Bush and them."

"Uh-huh," Mourning Dove looked around the group.

Ford put his shoulders down and pushed through. He pulled down the toilet paper roll from the opposite top bunk in his cell, slid his left hand inside and rolled off a handful.

He wiped the track from the seat, unbuttoned his suit and sat.

He reached toward the pillow for the magazine he said his daughter had sent him. He opened it and stuck it in front of his face, while his short, round dick peered out from underneath at the men at the table like an angry turtle.

Burton took a deep breath and nodded at the officer in the control room to be buzzed in after break.

He pulled on the steel door and for a moment the sound of laughter rushed into the jail from the lobby like air into a vacuum. On his right he stared into the pocked window of the empty visiting room. Thick lasagna odor squeezed under the locked kitchen door on his left.

Don Burton trudged into the maze of corridors to make his last count.

The buzz hit him in the stomach.

He was entering jail, a foreign country. He had to be on guard. He was hated. Don't think right now about pushing a daughter on a swing or a mother in the nursing home. He walked past B-Block, the long misdemeanor cell. He counted as best he could. The card games and taunts diminished a level as he passed and he could not help but listen for any whisper directed his way. He turned left around the locked library, then left again down to the D-Block and C-Block hallway.

When he felt tired he couldn't do a good job.

He couldn't talk and joke like he could in the morning. He hated them and it made them hate him more, he thought.

Geezuz, he tugged on his pants with one hand. That's it. I'm buying that Slim Fast Crap on the way home. We can too afford it.

The hallway dungeon spread before him as a railroad track headed out of town. If he could only get outside, out of this basement with no air and everything locked and everything chipped and stained and mean and ugly.

Ugly floors no matter how often you buffed them, ugly people, lower class people. They breed downward, affixing themselves to what they could find and afford.

Ugliness.

He reached the end of the hall, the four isolation cells, empty now.

This morning they held a string of four drunken college boys, laying in their own puke to push against the wall to kick on the doors, crying to be let out.

Another left, then a right past the kitchen.

He traded taunts with the kitchen supervisor out seeking two trusties to help him put out the next meal.

Burton opened his locker for his jacket, not reading the quote taped to his door.

"If at the bottom of law and order there is only a man armed to the teeth, a man without a heart, without a conscience, then law and order are meaningless." Henry Miller, The Air-Conditioned Nightmare.

Well, he did the best he could.

Burton pushed through the double glass doors in the lobby.

"G'night," he waved over his head.

He walked past the steps and boarded the elevator. He dug his Braves stocking cap out of his coat pocket and pulled it over his ears, then ripped the hat off and stuffed it back into his pocket.

The door opened.

He walked into the main floor, the cafeteria for courthouse employees and visitors, the information counter. Two Hispanic women sat stoically on the vinyl chairs in the horseshoe waiting area.

Burton had no trouble avoiding eye contact.

He hunched his shoulders as he pushed through the first outside door.

He felt the slobbery day on the wet floor, then leaned into the outer door. He touched each ear with the palms of his hands and then shoved his pockets in the slits on either side of his black coat.

Burton waddled leaning forward down the sidewalk headed for the street.

He stopped in front of an oncoming van, stood straight, staring ahead. After the traffic passed, Burton moved across the street, still not glancing either way.

His car waited alone in the middle of the parking lot. Burton began to search for the keys. He glowed, now within its penumbra. He unlocked it, opened the door and checked behind the back seat.

He had bought the black and white '57 Chevy in high school.

The radio still worked, which was what his wife's relatives wanted to know each Thanksgiving before anything else. He backed up carefully and pulled to the street. He glanced at the odometer: 67,090.

This would be the year he'd hit sixty seven-five. Or not, if he took it easy.

He lovingly gripped the Hurst shifter as he pulled into the street, moving up to speed, sliding into second, the gear works felt like leather-gloved hands linking.

Each year Alie got him new fuzzy dice.

Last Christmas was red and white.

They swayed from the rear view mirror as he adjusted it slightly. All four of the Burton children had been conceived in the back seat.

Alyssa liked to go out in the car on warm summer mornings before the kids or the neighborhood mowers had awakened. She would nudge him with two steaming cups of coffee in her hands, wearing just one of the girls' T-shirts. He would follow out the back door down the side-walk, his head down, arms churning, thighs scraping.

She would have an oldies station playing.

Burton wished he could have been street officer.

He got no respect from them when they brought somebody to the jail, thinking him forever a fat kid too sickly to play outside.

Burton popped in Chopin's Greatest Hits.

He cranked Polonaise in A-Flat Major.

He imagined he was constable Louis Chiraque of the St. Michael's gendarme force. Mrs. Kramer's wiener dog danced on two legs across the street to the music. Jimmy Turner promenaded his Duster through the stoplight. Burton looked at his wristwatch and drove around the lake keeping an eye peeled for timberwolves and bears.

He imagined retiring after his shift with a jelly glass of cognac with his stocking feet stretched in front of a cedar log fire in his cabin in the deep woods behind A&W.

Jimmy Turner hauled his friends in his father's Buick and wished they would be careful.

The pimples on his forehead an Appalachian hollow, his biology teacher called him "zero" because he always got zero-for-whatever on quizzes. His speech teacher, Mr. Guinn, who wore crispy grey suits and red ties, made fun of Jimmy for not being confident.

Once, Jimmy skipped biology and walked out the back door to his car. He drove in the country and tried to understand the lyrics to "Miss American Pie," plunging to the depths. He wished he could keep driving.

Later, somebody would come by and see his meatless skull sitting on the side of the road, holding up some farmer's mailbox. They'd pull up, toss a crumpled Olympia can at his head and say, "Jimmy Turner, what a fuckin' loser."

Cars with engines had replaced plastic toys in the bathtub.

They wanted independence, to be left alone.

They wanted to world to notice them, driving around on Friday nights in main drag wagon ruts, waving their hands over their heads, telling the universe they were something special and new.

They drank beer in bulky used cars bought by their fathers, heavy cars good in an accident, and bayed after annoyed girls like bloodhounds.

At midnight they ate hamburgers and French fries with special sauce at Arctic Circle with the five dollars slipped to them under the supper table by their grandmothers. They wandered home to masturbate into red and grey hunting socks bought by their mothers at Montgomery Ward.

Burton checked his watch again then putsied past the Aime & Shoot Bar.

The sign on the front window said that Alien Autopsy was performing inside. Don's brother Larry would be in there trying to peddle his new line of Kiss My Bass T-shirts.

In front of the American Theatre Burton remembered that tomorrow was his mother's birthday.

He cranked a U-turn. Like a submarine on cruise control he slinked across town, past the bases-empty ball fields, the pregnant mom's housing units and the Kum n' Go on Taylor to the Peaceful Pause nursing home at East Ninth and Sugar.

He nodded to the teenage night staff giggling around the front desk. They scattered, reciting a litany of duties they needed to get back to.

Don slipped off his hat and tiptoed into his mother's room.

He flinched at the urine smell and pulled the sheet up around her shoulders.

By the light of the parking lot lamp shining against the south wall he saw the black and white photo of all the boys, with bare legs stretched out on the lawn, eyes squinting, gathered around Luella perched in her green and white lawn chair.

Merle's shadow extended from the lower ledge of the photo, his finger forever flexed to snap the picture.

Each time Don came to visit she asked him why those strange people were sitting so close to her.

He sat in the light blue recliner, then climbed out to push it away from the wall and from between the bed and the dresser. He sat and flipped the lever for the footrest.

Luella whined.

Don brushed her hair from her face.

She smiled and patted his hand.

It felt like crispy KFC chicken skin.

Burton folded his hand around hers and leaned his head back. An orderly's cleaning cart squeaked in the hall … going away. Don closed his eyes and remembered a basketball game in the driveway. The sun as big and hot as a circus tent in August, lemonade in glass pitcher coming out the door, behind it the smiling face of a woman, her hair, black as clotted blood, pulled back in a waist-length ponytail wearing a happy yellow dress and white apron with a red flower print.

He awoke in a fright, looked at his watch and ran down the hall and out the front door.

At Marlowe Street he turned right at the light down his street, his neighborhood. He rolled the window down, zipped up his coat and cranked CCR.

Alyssa Burton stood in her operatory in the waning daylight. Her black hair stood at attention as she leaned into the mouth of her last patient. The older man, his eyes as far open as he could manage and his mouth the same way gripped the plastic arms of the chair with pink fingers. His toes pointed to the picture of pheasants feeding by the side of a country road.

Alie's lab jacket, an array of buck-toothed gophers brushing each other's teeth with gigantic, primary colored brushes, was spattered in the day's gore.

Her white Nike's displayed matching splotches on the toes. Her hands ached and her butt hurt from pinching it all day trying to get leverage to clean the plaque from the teeth of all these old fools.

"Good night," said Dr. Bluders as he passed her door.

She stepped on the lever to shoot the old man higher.

The receptionist checked the schedule for Monday again. She picked up magazines in the waiting room alphabetized them in the rack and said good night to Dr. Kakowsky as he fell into the front door and the weekend.

Zoe grabbed the frame of the door, balanced on her right foot and stuck her head into Alie's room.

Mr. Zerke was rinsing his mouth in the sink by the chair.

Alie joked with him and eased the chair down, stopping short and laughing when her victim grabbed for the arm rests. She unhooked the chain and bib around his neck.

"You're all set. Start flossing Z. I really had to dig to get at some of that shit."

She showed him the door with a flap of her hand.

Mr. "Z" ran his tongue around his mouth and inched past Zoe, then hurried toward the door.

"Have a good weekend!" Zoe said.

She trailed him to the front door letting him out, locking the door quickly behind.

The dental clinic fit nicely at the corner of La France and Fourth Street. A year 'round Christmas ornament, the green hedges blended just-so with the brick covering of the square building with the puff of smoke departing the chimney. In the front yard a brick sign stood next to the serpentine walkway to the fine wooden door.

The busy intersection featured Alie's corner office, the light in her room emanating through the blinds in the waning light.

The world at that corner looked like an animated Dairy Queen cake with real stop signs and working snow blowers, a bathtub Virgin Mary shrine to the middle class. Alie cleaned her instruments while Zoe stood in the doorway telling about her son's basketball team and her daughter's violin lesson that night.

Alie reached up to flick the overhead on the chair and reached for her coat on the hanger.

"Well, the weekend is here," Alie said.

Zoe backed up. Alie flipped off the room light.

The drivers outside at the stop light shifted their focus from Alie's perfect life to the signal above the intersection and revved their engines. Zoe walked once more through the office, checked the lock on the cash drawer and flicked off the last lamp, making her way in darkness with a hand along the wall to the door.

Alie piloted the van into the driveway. The garage door was closed behind the Chevy.

She stopped even with the back door. She saw Don inside, over the sink.

They had supper with the two kids home.

Afterward Don had a beer then another and showed Alie the piece of paper he had lifted from Pontiac's cell.

"You got it," she said. "Good."

The next day she cleaned Charles Ballantyne's teeth. Ballantyne, the Sioux City American Values Insurance agent and city councilman, had begun using an electric toothbrush.

They both agreed they were anxious to see the results.

Alie remained hopeful of being appointed to the park board after several years of trying. If she got to that first step the dominoes would start to tumble. She fed Charles all the gossip that dribbled out the vulnerable mouths of her patients. She told Ballantyne about the note her husband had wrestled from a group of criminals in the jail.

Ballantyne didn't appear to notice. He walked with his head pitched to the sidewalk on his way to the office. He said h'lo to his secretary, walked into his room and thoughtfully closed the door.

He poured himself a cup of coffee, sat behind his desk, clomped his feet on top and watched a plumber and a cable technician laughing, each with one boot in the mud, while he called the statehouse in Des Moines.

THIRTEEN

"WE HAVE GRASPED THE MYSTERY OF THE ATOM
AND REJECTED THE SERMON ON THE MOUNT."
— GEN. OMAR BRADLEY

Pontiac and Zags sat at the dayroom table after breakfast.

They each rolled smokes.

They sat for a while in silence, sometimes with eyes closed.

Zags leaned across.

"What about Mumford?" he said.

"I don't want to talk," Pontiac said. "I'm tired."

"C'mon, man."

Pontiac shook his head, adjusted himself on the cold steel, lit his smoke, blew it at the ceiling, and began Mumford's story.

Martin Mumford grew up at his grandma's house in North Omaha on Binney Street. His family lived next door to his grandmother and grandfather.

He spent most of his time at his grandma's.

His father was in the penitentiary.

Martin's grandfather lived for a while. Martin remembered him sitting on the front steps his cheeks puffed out, blowing on a harmonica. He taught Martin to blow and suck on the two hole and the three-four-five up and down lick and then he wasn't there the next day.

Martin's mother walked every morning to the bus stop one block away then rode downtown to the federal building with the blue windows where she was a secretary in the United States attorney's office. His grandmother said it was a 'portant job.

His grandmother peeled onions and potatoes in the kitchen and talked through the screen window above the sink while Martin dug for old coins in the flower dirt next to the house.

She kept talking while she heard him scratching in the dirt. She tried to find interesting things to say to keep him digging. When the digging stopped she turned away and cleaned house.

She talked one summer about his dad. She said he was a panther. Martin shook his head in the mid-morning sun and swatted flies. A panther, he thought. And me, ah'm a fuck'n raccoon, a coon diggin' in the fuck'n dirt.

Grandma said Martin's dad was in the North Omaha riots in the 1960s, burning houses and businesses to protest about some king getting shot. Martin wondered why they burned their own places instead of marching downtown or into Dundee or Benson and burning some white houses and shops and shit.

He remembers his father driving past his grandma's in a low long maroon Bonneville with a bunch of his friends. His father waved to him with a pistol and told Martin to be good. That was his last memory of his father.

His mother never let him go to Lincoln to see him.

The buildings in the neighborhood remained blackened and scarred while the houses in Dundee and West Omaha grew corpulent with shrubbery and coats of paint.

His grandmother talked that summer through the screen about a man she called "Senator Ernie," who used to come by the house and sit on the step with Martin's grandfather.

She said the man whom he had never met was one of Martin's best friends.

She said this barber from North Omaha lived in Lincoln, too, and he fought for the black people in North Omaha. Martin wondered if Senator Ernie ever got tired of fighting and if he ever met his father.

Martin remembered the day he sat on the front step talking to his grandmother while his mother was working and his brothers and sisters were off again somewhere. He told her he was going to go fight somebody. Anyone would do, but he was tired of not fighting. Maybe he would find Senator Ernie and learn how.

He remembered the last thing his grandmother said. She said through the screen, "I been around this neighborhood and this city. I get so bored by what I see in the newspaper, on the TV, in the library, I just want to scream," she said.

"Then I see some ol' boy down at the bus stop and he's listening to this friend a his talk on and on about nothing, stories he's told every day for the last thirty years. And that ol' boy nods and grins and just listens. The only interesting thing is kindness, Martin. You come back and see me. I'll be waiting at my window."

She heard the digging stop.

She turned to sit in the living room for just a while.

Martin rode the bus downtown, then jumped another bus out of town.

He didn't know where he was going. He just knew he was gone.

He got off the bus when his money ran out in Sioux City.

He lived on the streets, in the shelter and ate supper each day at the Catholic soup kitchen, vowing every summer to go to Lincoln, asking someone every now and again where it was.

On the day he and his best friend of two weeks were drinking by the river, the police woke him up under the bridge and told him he killed his friend.

Martin couldn't say they were wrong.

Elana sat on the edge of her roller chair and rested her chin on her hands in her window sill and listened to Greg Brown.

Martha knocked and entered. They exchanged waves. Martha took one step and a long reach to place a letter on the desk.

Elana nodded.

She announced another Brown song, picked up the letter and followed Martha to the living room.

"I got this from my son this morning," Martha said. "I thought you might be interested."

Elana read while back-combing with her left hand.

"I have to talk to him," Elana said. "When are visiting days?"

"That would not be such a super idea," Martha said. "Those phones are monitored. Write him a letter."

"They open them, surely," Elana said.

"I didn't know Bush was coming," Elana said. "This is big."

She rushed back to her room. She ran her palms down her legs. She straightened her hair. She blew out between pursed lips.

"George Bush is coming to Siouxland and we need to welcome him," said the deep voice at the microphone.

Martha went to the kitchen to phone Johnathan to tell him to turn on his radio. He might like this. She thought with the phone in her hand, then put the receiver back without dialing.

The fourth stepson of Martha Pontiac ruled an empire.

But his father loved his criminal son more, and so like other boys, instead of shaking his father and asking to be loved he sought to conquer the world, demanding to be noticed.

He stood on the balcony overlooking the acres of copper vats. He closed his eyes and sucked in the earthy smell of the hops. He stuck his hands in his raincoat pockets and leaned as far back as he could until he thought he might fall. Then he leaned farther.

Johnathan Pontiac, the owner and founder of Pig's Style Beer, "made right here in Sioux City by people who drink as much as you do," placed his hands on the brass rails and shouted down to one of his foremen in a yellow hard hat.

"Jeremy, my man! Hey! Who won last night?"

Jeremy put a hand in the hair, then pointed to his ears with both hands and kept walking.

Behind Johnathan Pontiac on the wall, one floor above the brew house, shined a mural of the same color pig drawing that adorned each brown bottle of Pig's Style Beer.

The mural ran farther than Johnathan could, showing the seven laughing pigs seated at an old style wooden bar wearing overalls and flannel shirt, in a business suit, in a Morningside College Athletic Dept. sweatshirt, in police uniform, doctor's scrubs, white T-shirt.

Each pig wore a different color baseball hat, with the team names of various Sioux City high schools and colleges.

At the lower right edge of the drawing was the scrawled signature of Mark Pontiac.

John Pontiac surveyed the scurrying of the worker ants below. He enjoyed observing how they moved quicker while he stood above them.

He liked to step back against the wall where they couldn't see him and then back to the rail, then step back again, and watch them trying to spot him, slowing their walk, then speeding up again.

Sometimes John would play with them on the balcony for a couple of hours after the morning managers meeting like a child with a favorite ant hill and a sack of firecrackers.

"It feels good to hurt you," he gritted his teeth and watched the old men and boys underneath, "to hate you, to let you go down the drain just like me."

John got the idea for the business when his father had showed him an article in the Sioux City Journal about an animal rights protest at IBP.

The photo with the story showed a pig with its throat cut hanging from a chain on the kill floor: This Little Piggy Went to Market, read the caption.

The protesters outside the plant poured buckets of red paint in the driveway for workers to drive through to get to the parking lot. They said that "pigs are sensitive, intelligent animals. Stop eating pigs."

Johnathan scanned the story and also read the Quick Fact chart below that said there were more pigs in the state than people.

He sat on the couch with his brothers, staring at Sesame Street, waiting for their mother to yell to get ready for school. He saw how hungover his father was. Johnathan marveled at how much his father liked beer, to suffer so for the love of it.

He thought his dad was trying to tell him something by guiding him to the article. He made himself believe his father loved him enough to be hinting this to him because he had a plan for him.

Yes!

And what his father was trying to say was that pigs are smart, this is a pig-dominant culture, beer is worth it no matter what. Put it together, son.

He saw the empty bottle of Old Style next to the television under his father's red seed corn cap. Usually his mother had scooped up the bottles and cigarette butts before the kids got up. This one had hid.

Pig's Style! He screamed inside his head and jumped up in the middle of the room with his hands in the air just as his mother said they needed to get a move on.

"See there, you boys should follow John's lead. Take them upstairs, and make sure they brush their teeth this time. For two minutes!" she said.

But his father never took an interest in him or his business, other than to drink the free cases Johnathan carried home.

From the railing, skipper with both feet on the lowest cross piece, John could see the end of the room. The last one hundred yards, barely a year old, had taken a zoning variance with the aid of a bone tossed at the feet of councilman Ballantyne.

In another five years this "micro brewery" would shove Coors and Budweiser into the sludgy shallows of Salt Lake.

Salt Lake.

The name was bitters on his tongue. The Olympic organizing committee had never heard of Pig's Style Bee-ah, they had said.

But couldn't a small brewery be allowed to sponsor the Olympics? He'd pay whatever. They said he doubted he could swim in that deep water.

He'd give them mountain fresh streams. They'd beg for him to shoot Iowa piss in their mouths after this trip from George Bush made Sioux City and him famous.

John stepped down from the rail and ran his hand back and forth over the indentations his gripping had left in the railing.

Fuck the g.d. Olympics, he growled to himself. Fuck 'em aaawwwll. Piss & Pig's Style Bee-ah, that will be the g.d. official Olympic slogan after he was through.

The Choices In Neuroses group had asked to continue meeting at Martha's house.

They liked being able to get out of the chilly FirstStar Bank community room.

They still wore their sweaters at Martha's, but now, for stylin'.

Elana sat with the group during her breaks.

Gradually she decided to trust them, inviting them into the studio during broadcasts.

One morning Paul sat on the weathered sofa. With a frown he scratched a toothpaste spot on his clean sweatpants.

"Good morning, friend," Paul glanced up and watched Elana.

That voice.

It's her.

As he was carrying an armful of coffee cups into the kitchen, Paul cornered Martha putting away butter with her head and shoulders inside the refrigerator.

Paul held the door.

Martha listened with the bright light in her eyes.

She closed her eyes and felt her thighs warming.

"She shouldn't have told the group," Paul said.

Martha stood up and with a terse smile pushed her way out of the refrigerator.

"She who? Told what?"

"Tammy Williger, her father is the sheriff, and Judy Hargrove, her husband is an FBI agent. That's what. I heard them whispering. They'll tell. Fucking bipolar assholes."

"Oh-my-God!" Martha slammed the refrigerator shut.

Cartons and jars and boxes fell over inside.

Paul made a move to open it. She blocked his way with outstretched arms like a protester chained to the post office door.

Martha straightened her hair and hurried into the living room. She helped the others out the door and strode into the studio room.

"Oh my God!" Paul heard through the closed door.

He stood near the front door with his Twins cap in his hands. He looked down and plucked a dollop of white frosting from the dot on the "i" of his red and blue Twins sweatshirt. Paul had his right index finger in his mouth up to the second knuckle as Martha and Elana walked in cradling their elbows in their palms.

"They could be coming right now," Paul offered.

"Thanks a lot," Elana said. "Thank you for your help," said Martha. She moved to open the door.

"I could take you somewhere," Paul said toward Elana, not looking at her.

"What?" Elana said, annoyed.

"Your stuff. It's only the first floor. The ground is still soft," he said.

"What's he talking about?" Elana said to Martha.

"But they'll throw you tapes out again," said Paul. "Maybe you should get it out of here, unless you have unlimited resources, which I don't. Maybe you do. I don't know, but."

Elana put up both hands like a faith healer.

"I get the picture," she said. "He's right."

"Back up your car to the front door," commanded Martha.

"The grass," he said. "Forget the g.d. grass!" she said.

Martha pointed to the studio and followed Elana to the back room. Elana calmed herself and signed off for the morning. She flipped off the power and she and Martha began unplugging and boxing up. They unhooked coaxial cable, the one-watt FM transmitter, the control board, the turntable and CD player. They wrapped newspaper around everything and put the new microphone back in the original box.

They left the antenna in the tree, but covered the lead line with mulch. They met Paul at the front door.

In the meantime he had gone to Casey's for three English Toffee cappuccino and rolls with multi-colored sprinkles.

"Turn off your flashers," Martha said.

They packed the boxes in the trunk and the back seat.

"You have to go, too," Martha said.

"What?" Elana's eyes said, go where?

"Come to the college," Martha said, her arm on Elana's shoulder.

"I'll meet you in the union cafeteria.

"Go! Hurry!"

FOURTEEN

"As swiftly as the cliff sheds the water of the wave,
so does the sunshine turn to grey."
— IN-TRANSIT UNIT GRAFFITI,
TERRE HAUTE FEDERAL PENITENTIARY

The bent frame under Myrtle Mourning Dove squeaked as she threw her weight into turning the steering wheel of the yellow station wagon.

She aimed for the remaining spot in the parking lot by swerving to the left then cranking hard-right. She clenched her butt muscles, punched the middle piece on her glasses and craned her head to see over the wheel and the end of the car.

The wagon slid between the pickup and the rusted Ford like the last puzzle piece.

Myrtle shut off the engine and dove into the purse beside her for change to plug the meter, while keeping her foot pushing down hard on the brake pedal until the engine stopped.

She found Kleenex and rubbed her nose. She turned and threw her legs out of the car, then pulled herself up by the door. She pulled her sweatshirt down around her waist and slung her purse over her shoulder.

She checked her watch, then hurried across the lot toward the jail, carefully watching the ground as she walked. Myrtle stopped at the street and let the traffic from the last light relieve itself down the road.

She scrolled up the county courthouse, at the golden dome and the marble eagle atop, then down to the prisoners in the orange jumpsuits outside on the Indian summer day, using hoses and shovels to scratch the shit from the sidewalk.

When the light at the intersection turned red, Myrtle picked her spot and crossed.

She walked past the prisoners, eyeing them. They scraped and watered, while the deputy in a crisp tan shirt and black tie and down vest joked with them.

Myrtle heard one of the prisoners, a young Indian, say that it was eagle shit they were scraping.

"And that's eagle crap on top of that U.S. eagle," he pointed to the stone bird atop the government building.

"The real thing don't like fakers."

Myrtle smiled and kept walking. She walked through the stone and plant lobby to the elevator. She pushed "basement" and rode down with a white woman and her handchild.

The boy edged into the elevator holding onto his mother.

The mom reached to push the button, though it was already lit, while holding her child's plump paw with the other hand. They held each other in the elevator and walked out clutched together.

The two women stood in line at the desk to sign the visiting sheet, then sat down in the last two metal folding chairs along the wall.

Myrtle let her head rest.

God if only time could pass, she thought. If only time could pass. If she could relax and let the days go things would be a little better.

Reading projects completed, prisoners released, children graduated, babies born. Spring, then summer, picnics, home brew, fresh tomatoes.

She smiled dimly with eyes closed.

And then it all needs doing again.

Her eyes opened and she stared at the wall in front of her.

She shook her head as if at someone in her dreams and the woman pulled her child close.

Get another haircut, new prisoners trucked in, a new stack of books sitting unread. Fall, then winter, no doubt.

That night the phone cart rattled down the hall, next stop D-Block.

Stephan Baltimore proudly commanded the corner of the dayroom, first in line.

William Mourning Dove crouched first on the right side of the north end of the yellow table, second in line. Michael Zags sat on the left side of the north bench. He had thirds. Martin Mumford wiped his eyes with the heels of his hands and wandered in from his cell. He leaned with his back to the phone line, his elbows on the table, feet stretched out, his head inclined toward the television screen.

He was next after Zags then, goddammit.

Baltimore accepted the phone through the bars. He slumped on the floor with his legs crossed with his back to the rest. He twirled the phone line with his fingers like an eighth grade girl on Sunday night. His smiled showed he had fled D-Block.

He laughed loud.

"Oh, now! Oh, shuddup! Oh, you know that's right!"

Mourning Dove stared a hole in Baltimore's back, making sure he did not go overtime. Michael Zags wrote a letter while he waited, hyper-aware that no one be allowed to sit between he and Mourning Dove.

Arthur hunkered on the floor outside his cell, his knees pulled up tight to his chest, the ends of his pants hitting the middle of his calves, the heels of both feet pulled out of the blue slip-on tennis shoes. He held a letter in his fingertips.

With that letter he walked without rising. He squirmed his legs and mouthed the words and ran the fingers of his right hand, then his left, backward through his hair, switching the letter and the hands through the hair along the way.

He slid to his back, crossed his legs and held the letter straight up with both arms.

Miguel Mendez sat on the floor of his cell with his back against the bottom bunk frame. He wove pieces of Juicy Fruit wrappers into a frame for a picture of his wife. He cursed the constant noise of the television. He willed Vanna White's smile to spread across her face until her teeth and gums and tongue screamed for relief, for the blonde's head to explode inside the screen and send those idiots in front of her to the emergency room.

All ... day ... long the set blared and then blasted away inside this head even after it was shut off. On Fridays they were allowed to keep the television on until eleven instead of ten, supposed to be a gift. To him it was the torturous stringing out of an endless day. Each minute noticeable, walked past like a self-obsessed model down the runway, each voice, each mood remembered, like a slow-motion highway accident.

He looked at the floor to the pictures by his knee that they could not see, scowling at the loud Ford commercial and with two ivory crescent fingernails plucked another wrapper from his materials stockpile.

Mark Pontiac lay on his stomach on the top bunk, his head crammed with nothing-to-do. The cap of his skull burned. His lower lip felt numb. He had not eaten lunch or supper, and the thought of food made him sick. He had not slept in two nights. His chest ached. He raised and lowered each arm to check for numbness.

Why he would be depressed, if that's what this was, he couldn't figure. He was more used to this life than any other.

He liked not having to get up hungover at six in the morning to pull on stiff work boots over blistered feet, and limber up his hands and smooth Vaseline over his cuts so the lime wouldn't burn, or stuff a chunk of rock of alum in his pocket to keep his crotch from burning and rubbing from sweat. To get moving and try to forget about the clock, to get through one more stiff, stern day on an angry job site.

His old man would already be on his second cup of coffee, maybe cooking sausage and eggs, going over the work plan for the day in his head, gathering up the empties and putting them in a plastic bag on the porch.

The brothers would be rising for school as the two men backed out of the rutted driveway in the old white pickup, handling the shift stick, steering wheel and plastic coffee mug, one arm on the top of the seat, his head aimed out the back window, over the motley pile of tools in the bed: bent hoe, toolbox jammed open, spade with the handle broken in half, two halves of the sawhorse diametrically opposed in the corners.

They both worked for Wolfe Bros., until Mark's dad got in a fistfight with one of the bros. They knocked down four courses of new block work and rolled over the footings for fifteen minutes.

Mark went along with his dad to Scotty's afterward, where they laid out plans on a napkin for their new company: Pontiac & Son.

They drank together: Pontiac & Son.

They left the pickup and tools parked out front, out of gas.

Mark's dad traded it weeks later for a pickup's worth of cigarettes.

Mark tucked his right elbow and rolled to his back, He lifted and grabbed the pillow from the other end and folded it under his head. He reached with his left hand without looking to pull out the letter from his mother.

He crossed his left leg over his right and unfolded the letter from behind the cover, using his leg as a desk.

Tues. nite

Dear Mark,

I have just returned from night class. Have freshman intro to soc. this semester. Hope you are well. Miss you. Say hello to your father. Am sure he is there. Have not seen him around.

Something struck me tonight as I was standing in front of all these wide-eyed young women and men. If they only knew. If they only knew the terrible things they are capable of, the slaughter, the dismemberment, the eating of their own progeny over a spit, with barbecue sauce. Any terror imaginable has been taste-tested by the human race time and again.

Need these young people discover that on their own? Should I tell them?

Do they need to know or should they be allowed to return to their dormitories to burn frozen pizzas and watch Gilligan and Star Trek re-runs, smiling, undisturbed.

Shouldn't I let them in on the bad news along with some of the adult attempts at correction?

I chose to discuss suburban circles of commerce.

Long live Gilligan.

You are my beautiful seed, though I know you hate that metaphor. Buried deep below the city.

You will bloom.

Must sleep now. Love you.

There is somebody I want you to meet.

As always, Martha.

Mark worked with his father while this woman raised four hooligan babies and trooped off to the college for night class.

She made him.

Pontiac forced himself up.

He put one foot onto the steel toilet top and let himself down.

He pushed the water button and leaned over to drink. He filled his hands and splashed his face as he straightened his back and saw himself in the mirror.

Jail mirrors, he thought, always cracked and cloudy.

These guys are good.

Evil, but good.

He saw enough of his face to recall Jack Abbott's book. Pontiac had a jailin' face. Sunken eyes, thousand-mile stare, straight lips. He looked like the driver's license of a corpse.

In the belly of the beast.

Mark put one foot on the seat and leaned over the sink.

His breath fogged the mirror. He had seen men like him come through the county jail. Men who wouldn't know what it was like to be scared of jail. Who sat down at the card table as naturally as if they were meeting siblings for lunch at Applebee's. Men who had done years in lonely bedrooms and juvenile facilities and penitentiaries.

He felt comfortable with them and now he cringed.

Mark closed his eyes.

He tried to conjure his real mother's face ... or a smile that was not deadly or perverse ... or the colors, red or purple or mauve.

What the hell is mauve?

Abbott talked about sensory deprivation.

How a sudden glimpse of color or the feel or texture can drive a man to an afternoon of weeping.

Pontiac saw the men in the mirror.

A second grade class tour, the kids allowed to sit on the men's laps, or a pet kitten or dog would bring these hard men to their knees. They were always that close to not making it. They knew it and they gritted their teeth to hide it and that's why they hated anything nice or gentle, in themselves or others.

Pontiac boosted himself to the top bunk.

For a while he studied the Dakota Dunes dog track schedule for the next day, marking his bets. He had made thousands of fantasy dollars on the dogs and had never been inside the front gate.

He let the paper float to the floor, in ablution of his own cleanliness rules.

He stared at the flat paint ceiling and allowed his body to soar above the city, to look down upon the jail from the outside, the free world, to see the smoke from the chimneys of the real people.

Real tears raced down his cheeks and he flew.

He flew and at last he slept.

Michael Zags hadn't been to prison.

Now he faced Leavenworth, Terre Haute, Lewisburg, Atlanta, all face-on, looking straight up at walls a thousand feet high, all at once, all by himself.

He wrote a letter to his sister in Minneapolis.

She had graduated from Saint Catherine's with a music degree and now lived at the Catholic Worker House on Portland Avenue, considering joining the Franciscans.

Sister Mary Ann, he wrote.

Got your letter. Thanks.

Came today with supper. Mail call always comes with the evening meal, which commences at four-thirty p.m. Jumpsuits button up required. We dine stylishly early.

How's everybody? I haven't heard much.

Not too much else to say from what I wrote last.

I'll be going to court soon. Then to prison maybe.

Prison.

What a word. I dream about the word.

Everybody fears it even if they don't know it, from the day they figure out there is such a thing.

I think of living forever in a very small room, made with claustrophobia, scared beyond description. Which maybe isn't too far from the truth. I hope not, though.

I don't think there is any way you can prepare yourself,

except maybe to have been born black or Indian or Mexican. I wonder if they are scared of prison too.

You getting along?

When I first came in here, walking past the long row of bars, the dayroom, I felt I was being let into a cage of monkeys, orangutans, gorillas. I wanted to tell the guard, no, wait, I don't belong in there.

But now they don't seem like animals anymore at all, or else I'm just one too.

They all have names and personalities, down here in the cellar behind the canning jars and the sewer pipes and the storm drains.

I'll write when I have more to say. I'm in line now waiting to call you, so you'll get this after we talk.

Bobby Ford usually watched television after supper. Each day he would take his spot on the front bench to lean backward and gape up. Usually he put his pillow on his spot before supper. This day he had somehow forgotten. He glared out at Martin Mumford with his elbows all up and then leaning over in a paroxysm of Black Laughter and considered killing him.

Bobby Ford thought about killing Martin Mumford in all his deep blackness, his loud, no socks, threatening blackness. Bobby Ford walked to his toilet to pee, unbuttoned his crotch buttons and watched Mumford in his mirror.

If he strangled the fucking nigger or broke this window and grabbed one of the shards and shoved it into his neck he would never get out of prison. That fucking coon would have done that to him by taking his place in front of the television.

Bobby Ford's kids — there could be some out there — would come to prison, for the rest of their lives. They would for sure never get over it, never forget it. They would be hurt by that loud, lazy black spider sitting in his spot in the dayroom.

If he didn't sit on the bench and watch television what would he do now? He couldn't pace and show that he was flustered, scared. He shot his eyes around like disco lights in the bowling alley. He could try to sleep, but he was too upset.

That goddamn pillow!

He should have set it out. Why didn't he? He was too upset over the footprint on his toilet seat. He watched television at this time of the day! Then he would turn around to join the card game and smoke. That was the way it was. Now his whole night was ruined. His whole life.

Tomorrow he would have his pillow out first thing in the morning and that g.d. vine swinger, the black snake from some crack house in some neighborhood where they don't scoop the sidewalks, where they just pour the garbage out the windows on to the lawn, would not ruin his life.

Ain't no way.

Ain't happenin'.

Not in this lifetime, Jack.

Huh, uh.

NO, sir.

Just when Bill Mourning Dove realized he was more than just another man in line for food outside The Master's Table he couldn't have said. He had been dealing with the whole grace through sacrifice concept lately. And he realized that his brother had let loose a spirit spray, and that he had been slimed.

He had been considering becoming a self-esteem instructor in the elementary school. He could take classes at the community college. Or he could start his own radio station. None of that standard Sioux City crap. This would be real music and he would be the disc jockey, like that one dude on Northern Exposure.

Though Mourning Dove walked with his head high back to his cell after his call, his stomach hurt way deep down.

He and Myrtle had talked about the regular stuff. Neither was over his brother. He had lived with Bill and Myrtle, off and on.

But talking about the list, the list D-Block had put together, that was something to laugh about. Myrtle said she would ask her friends for some ideas. They'd probably volunteer to bring potluck and help with the shooting, too, she laughed.

The television show changed. Mumford looked around the room, then walked into his cell and pulled the covers to his shoulders, scrunching his knees to his chest.

The card game droned on, the same talk from the same game of the night before and before that, thought Mendez. He had one corner to go on his frame. He put the project up on the top bunk, then got to his knees and made the sign of the cross.

The woman guard walked down, the static talk on the walkie-talkie meant bedtime.

"Nighty night," she said as she walked down the row, shining a light in each bunk.

"You okay, Martin?"

"Yeah," he said.

"Communist, you okay?" she smiled at Michael Zags.

"Okay here, boss," shouted Mourning Dove.

"Piss here, boss?" said Arthur.

"Piss boy," she said.

"Lockdown!" she shouted and spoke into her hand machine.

The cell doors closed. The sally port doors charged open. The guard cackled into her machine and walked in, down the rows, stopping at each cell to say a word.

She walked out, spoke into the machine again and the two sally port doors shut behind her. The lights in the dayroom snuffled off and the cell lights dimmed, making the hall lights bright.

"Night John Boy," sang Mourning Dove.

"Night Little Buffalo Dick," said Pontiac.

"Night Maaaarty," said a voice in the dark.

"Shut the fuck-up motherfucker!" shouted Mumford.

"Na-nite, Marty," said someone else.

"Fuck you all," said Mumford.

Baltimore stuck his head out the side of his bottom bunk to read a two-year-old Sports Illustrated from the library cart by the hallway light. Pontiac lay in his underwear on top of his covers on the top bunk. He liked to alternate beds. He finished off a cigarette with a wince and fired it down into the toilet. It sizzled for a split instant like steak on a backyard grill. His bed creaked as he sat up to roll another.

Zags and Arthur visited in baritones.

Mourning Dove lay on his back with his hands on his stomach, staring at the ceiling inches from his head.

Mendez lay on his stomach under the thin cover, snoring.

Bobby Ford crept around to the corner of his cell in his underwear.

He stuck his nose out the last opening.

"Niiigght, Martin," he sang in a high voice.

"Shut the fuck up-Ford," Pontiac said.

Ford sprang back to his bed and pulled the covers up.

At one a.m. the night guard clicked down the hall. His flashlight moved with his right leg. He talked into his walkie-talkie, not bothering to be quiet for the sleeping prisoners. The doors of the sally port clanged open. The guard stalked in, click, click, down the row, shining a light into each cell, counting to himself.

"Mornin', Gary," Pontiac said.

"Mornin'," said the guard, walking past.

He strode back without speaking.

Pontiac sat on the top bunk, his big bare feet hanging over the side. He rolled another cigarette. Gary glanced at Mumford doing pushups. The doors clanged shut.

Gary and Pontiac repeated the scene at two and three.

At the four o'clock count Pontiac was asleep.

As the night guard checked the blocks each hour and talked to the street cops who brought in prisoners and the woman who worked the front desk, while the lights at the corner clicked from green to yellow to red and the kids drove past, the men in D-Block dreamed like summer campers.

They dreamed of being twenty feet to the north.

What could that possibly be like?

They had never been there before.

They had each been born in jail.

They had never seen their mothers or held their children. They had always known Burton, always known his name. He had always been there in the morning, telling them when to eat, to read, to watch television.

They dreamed of really blue sky, flying up through the clouds, falling down into clouds and bouncing lightly.

They dreamed of playing softball and baseball.

Their dogs licked their faces as they slept. They made love to fairy princesses. They told their fathers they loved them and helped their mothers peel apples for pie.

They laughed.

And they smiled, wide, a wonder their faces did not crack and clatter to the floor like old pottery during a change in the weather.

They cried as it came near the time they had to leave their loved ones and blindly wiped real tears from their cheeks. They reached out their arms and could not reach out because of the top bunk or the ceiling.

They moaned and they jerked and they sobbed some more.

They grabbed themselves, not wanting to walk down the cold upstairs hall to pee.

Teetering on the precipice of their dreams they heard the school custodian's whistle down the hall. They heard the jingling of a little brother's toys in the living room. They heard someone reaching for keys to start a truck.

They clinched their teeth at the click of hard shoes on smooth, shiny concrete.

They heard the metallic-tasting language of a machine.

They opened their eyes and saw their mothers had flipped on their bedroom light against their wishes.

They felt the coarse blanket on their shoulders, heard the growl of Burton, "Brrr-ekfst!"

And the mechanical opening of their cages.

They opened their eyes, squinting, then rolled to their backs and shut their eyes, trying to retrieve their dreams, remembering they were in prison.

FIFTEEN

"THERE'S A JOKE HERE SOMEWHERE, AND IT'S ON ME."
— JOHN MELLENCAMP

L uke Pontiac downshifted into Saint Sysyphus, Minnesota.

He searched for last summer's tornado damage. Took out a neighborhood and a private college, they say. He chugged down the main drag.

On the west side of town he pulled into a truck stop convenience store. He left the motor running and pulled his mother's letter from his front shirt pocket. He pushed back his cap, adjusted his glasses, and held the letter out the window to arm's length.

"Your grandmother said he was a shady character," he read.

"It's true that he does not prefer the sun, honey. But I feel he probably needs us. You come home. I've got supper on."

Luke folded the letter and returned it to his pocket.

Them two had always went their own way.

They preferred jail.

They didn't want to be out having to make a living.

He sighed and ground the transmission. He turned the wheel and headed back, up main.

The air brakes on the purple Kenworth exhaled in relief as Luke parked across the street from Martha's home.

He marked in his log, put the clipboard back into the

rubber band around the visor, flipped the visor, and pushed at the door. He jumped down and felt six inches of concrete through the two-inch sole of his cowboy boots, all the way up his spine.

Luke placed the tips of his first two fingers under the bill of his pinkish cap and pushed it until his forehead turned white.

Inside, Martha fingered the soft cushion of her chair with the muscles of her buttocks and heard the bark of heels on the front steps.

She sat still and waited for the knock.

Then smiled when she saw the face in the door window and the screen pull away.

The wooden door whooshed in across the carpet.

"Hey, hey!" she smiled wide, rising with her arms to give him his hug.

"Good to see you, darling," she testified in close.

She let go and with a sweep of her hand admitted the presence of others.

Verlin McDonald, Rod and Rodger Tipple pushed out from deep in their too soft chairs and extended their hands up to Luke.

Luke grabbed hold and the men fell back.

Martha hurried to the kitchen for the coffee pot and another cup as Luke accepted the leather recliner in front of the big window.

The chairs and blue sofa formed a circle in the living room. In the middle sat a wooden coffee table mounded with months of Time magazines. Each outside magazine threatened to slide to the floor. Each person shot occasional nervous glances at the magazine nearest them, ready to reach out should the inevitable avalanche commence.

In front of each chair was a worn, flowered hassock. They all crossed their legs. Then red-faced and out of breath, Rodger released his handgrip on his leg and rested his brown work boots on his personal blue footrest.

"Thanks, Mom," Luke cupped the steaming white lather mug his father had lifted from a Sioux City barbershop, and set it on the lamp stand beside him.

"Whatta you guys doing here?" he looked at Verlin, then Rod, then Rodger.

They each pushed their cup to their mouths with both hands.

"Saw your mom at Food City," Verlin said. "She said you was coming in. We asked to be here."

"They've got some things to discuss with you," Martha said. "How was your trip?"

"Good," Luke said. "Whatsup?"

Luke wore his new brown insulated vest over a brown plaid flannel shirt.

Verlin and the twins had kept on their jackets. Each sat with one hand in a coat pocket with the other now gripping the ear of a white mug.

Martha wore a red knit pullover sweater over a used, clean grey sweatshirt.

"Well," Verlin began, nodding at Rod and Rodger, then to Martha, then Luke.

"Last night, couple a nights ago, one of our novitiates was running a routine email check. We do it, you know, on a routine basis, just to ... well, it gets kind of complicated."

"And illegal I would imagine," Luke said.

The twins nodded together.

"Hmm, that could be," said Verlin. "I'll have to check on that ... anyway, he found a message from a Myrtle Mourning Dove to her sister in Rapid City ... South Dakota.

"We got the return message," Rod corrected.

"Not the original to the lower Dakota," said Rodger.

"Yeah," said Verlin. He put both feet on his hassock, then dropped one to the floor.

"Comes back, the sister's message. You know, where it repeats the original message below the response?"

Luke stared at him in silence.

"Anyway," Verlin continued. "The just of it is that some inmates in the Sioux City jail are planning ... are you ready for this?"

Luke stared.

"To ... kill the fomer president of the United States."

In punctuation Verlin dropped his boot to the floor and shot his coffee cup to his mouth with both hands, peering out over the top at Luke.

The twins switched pocket hands.

Martha set her own cup on the floor and hurried to get the glass pot for refills.

"And ...?" Luke said.

Martha set the pot on the floor and took her seat.

"And we are on red-fucking alert, twenty-four hours," Verlin said. "Sorry," he nodded to Martha, who stared without acknowledging.

"It's just like before," Rod Tipple scooted to the edge of his chair and leaned forward.

Luke sat and gave Rod his attention while sniffing around the corner into the kitchen for the warm banana bread he knew Martha would pull out after these nuts left.

"Well," began Verlin, "as journalists, as researchers, we don't feel we should alter the course of history. We thought we'd catch 'em in the act and get it on film."

"Zapruder City," smiled Rod.

"Patterson-Gimlinesque," said Rodger.

"Tell me," said Luke. "Is Don Burton and his hygienist wacko wife going dental again?"

"Could be," said Verlin. "We haven't heard anything about that as of yet. Good point. Write that down," he said to Rod who was scribbling in pencil on a Motel 6 note pad that had materialized in his hand.

"There won't be no doubt about this one," said Verlin. He stood and thanked Martha with a handshake. The twins followed him out.

Out the door window Luke watched them scrap for the

window seat. Martha brought out the bread, now laced with melted butter. She set the board atop the magazine peak and sat down.

"Here, baby, eat," she said.

Elana and Paul sat in the front seat of his car.

Paul raced the dial up and down the radio, then snapped the knob.

Elana slumped with her eyes just above the window. Paul spread his hand, then closed it, then again, trying to get the feeling back after sitting on it for several minutes.

A light rain dotted the windshield. Afraid to run his battery down, Paul left the engine off. A line of buses pulled up to the front curb, yellow elephants each gripping the tail of the one ahead.

Other parents pulled up to the circle drive. The prime spots long taken, the newcomers were forced to parallel park or shoot in angles toward the curb while the others watched with penitentiary faces. Africa may burn and you will surely die, but my son will not walk farther than he must, not on this day.

Finally, the children emerged from the school building.

They walked out slowly, dragging backpacks and paper mache bunny skulls, their straight lines disintegrating in the sun.

The little boys and girls in primary colors, droopy hair bows and socks that had given up the fight, resembled rock stars confronting excited fans after yet another day's work. They regarded the grinning heads in the car windows as they might a cold lump of mashed potatoes on their lunch tray.

The choreographed car doors swung open. The parents approached the objects of their obsession with open arms, wiping chin slobber. No matter what drivel the grumpy kids would mumble would be taken during these few magic moments as tablets of gold by these bored house moms and dads who had spent the morning and afternoon

scrubbing counters and perusing photo albums and Special
Forces magazines.

Elana had stayed with Paul a lengthy week.

She slept in his room surrounded by stacks of Star
Wars magazines and posters of Don Gullett, the former
left-handed pitcher for the Cincinnati Reds. Paul slept
on the pullout couch until early afternoon each day after
watching cable television through the night.

Hargrove, Williger, and Fry had visited Martha twice and
searched her house.

Two FBI agents and three telephone company employees
had spent half of one morning taking down the antenna
from the tree.

Martha had been told not to leave the area.

Sheriff Williger conducted a six-hour Saturday workshop
at the Civic Auditorium with eighty-one percent of the two
thousand licensed gun owners in Woodbury County in
case of rioting.

This was Paul's weekend to get his kids.

With his hand on the steering wheel he stared without
blinking past Elana at the school front door. At last a boy
and a girl emerged holding hands and wearing Twins caps,
sweatshirts and sweatpants with Hulk Hogan and Princess
Sabrina backpacks.

Paul kicked his door open, ran around the car and rushed
the children. They looked up on him with horror, then
grinned wide as he approached, leaping into his arms,
knocking him backward. The three rolled on the sidewalk,
apparently unable to get up.

Elana laughed and rolled the window down.

"Who's that?" the boy pointed and rose to one knee.

"Daddy's new friend," Paul said, dusting himself off. He
walked to the car holding his children's doll hands. He let
them in the back door.

They sat in the backseat silently, staring at Elana's short
hair and cornstalk earrings.

Flooring the pedal he started the engine. He jerked the transmission into gear and lurched away.

Back at the house, while the kids sat in front of the television eating Cheetos and drinking chocolate milk, Elana and Paul sat on the front step. Elana wore a hooded sweatshirt and men's tan coveralls.

"I need to get back on the air," she said.

She wrapped her arms around her folded legs. Paul held a warm liter of Coke between his legs.

"Yeah. We need to get that stuff out of the basement. You could, well, they'd just bust you again."

He ground a rock into the sidewalk with his shoe.

He set his hand on the cement between them, hoping she'd take it.

Elana looked at the stubby paw, the grizzled fingernails. She smiled at him. A rapper car passed.

"We could broadcast from your car!" she said.

She grabbed his hand and squeezed it in both of hers.

"What do you say?" she said.

Paul said it would probably be all right, except when he had doctor's appointments.

"How do you do it?" he said.

Elana assured him she knew how to hook up her equipment by connecting to the existing wiring and antenna, taking out the back seat backrest and using the cushion as a desk, she would kneel on the floor.

"We just drive around town and they never get a true reading on us. Oh-my-God!" she whooped. "And we'll be able to reach places we never could before. The college campus, downtown drive time again, South Sioux, North Sioux. The mobile revolution!"

She hugged Paul's shoulders, making his eyes pop wide.

His pop spilled onto the sidewalk. She let him go to charge into the house.

He put his hand to his chest to catch his breath.

SIXTEEN

"Bless prison, for being in my life. For there, lying upon
the rotting prison straw, I came to realize that the object
of life is not prosperity, as we are made to believe, but the
maturity of the human soul."
— ALEXANDER SOLZHENITSYN

D on't go there," Martha Pontiac said mat-
ter-of-factly.
Francis Pontiac jerked his hand back.
They snuggled on the sofa watching the television reports
of the United States attack on Iraq.

"Not that." She searched for his hand and pulled it back to
her breast.

"Don't talk about Luke. I don't want to discuss it. I can't
stand to be like that, not ever again. I can't do this if we talk
about it all the time."

The Pontiacs sat amid a collapsed avalanche of yellow
ribbons.

Martha had gone to True Value that morning and bought
out their new stock.

She wrapped ribbons around the mailbox, two oak trees
on the front terrace the antenna of Fran's pickup, the toast-
er, each leg of the television set, the lamp shade, and the
graduation photo of Luke that now sat on a special table in
the corner of the living room.

Luke and the Sioux City National Guard unit had left a

month ago for the Middle East. But she couldn't deal with the possibilities, the troop movements, the daily mention of it at the grocery store.

Luke hadn't thought he would be going since the unit was a transportation specialty. He drove a tractor-trailer. But they were called up and were now supposedly stationed in Kuwait in the staging area for the ground war that would follow the air attack that the Pontiacs were watching on television.

For months the attack had been imminent.

But even with the warning, when it did happen, it delivered a stolid blow.

The news flashed as they were washing the supper dishes.

The TV was always on those days. The "Special Report" box and pictures of United States bombs hitting Baghdad put an end to the dishes for that night.

The young reporter from the Journal who had been following the families of the Sioux City guardsmen called and asked if he could come over. He took a photo of Francis and Martha watching television with the "Desert Storm" text on the screen. The reporter sat down and visited for a few minutes and then was off to the next leg of his adventure.

But for Francis and Martha there was no excitement.

Luke Pontiac ground the key, rrrr, rrr, rrr.

Nothing.

The C-130 Hercules transport had just off-loaded four Kenworth 18-wheelers to haul support supplies for the ground attack.

Now the trucks would not start.

"Morphodite son of a bitch," he said.

He slapped the steering wheel and jumped to the ground.

"Got the 130s, too," said Tiny Gooden.

"Nothing works right out here. I hate sand, always have. Hate its guts."

Luke chugged through the thick waves to the command

post, a shanty forged from cases of Pennzoil, two-by-fours from packing boxes and canvas tarps, looking for someone who might know what the fuck was what around here.

The men slapped at the heat and the bugs.

They dug in the sand and the sand filled in, leaving no sign of their work. The wind picked up, then blew hard, then roared. The telephone in the makeshift command post rang and rang. The National Guard outfit from Sioux City worked on their trucks, smoked, and watched the F-16s fly over, headed north.

"This is like Red Badge of Courage," Luke told Tony.

"A book."

They sat in the cab of the truck that would not start.

"My dad made me read it.

"I told him I did, but I didn't.

"Then later I did anyway."

Tiny nodded and looked around.

"That kid was looking at going into the Battle of Shiloh, and he's worrying if the others are worried too.

"He doesn't want to die, but he's curious as hell what glory is like.

"He doesn't feel good about killing, but wonders why the others don't seem to mind."

"Don't worry about me," Tiny said. "I'm scared shitless. I can't believe we are here, in the middle of a damn desert. Fuck this shit."

He puffed his cigarette and looked all around.

In the town of An Nasinya, in southern Iraq, on the Euphrates River, Rafi Abaal sat at the table and helped his father plan the wheat planting.

His father tossed nervous glances at the television as he scribbled on his pad.

After the flooding season, the two would harvest, and already he worried about the next fall planting season.

The face of Sadaam Hussein filled the screen.

He told the Iraqi people to be proud of this chance to resist the "hoarde United States."

Hussein likened the Americans to locusts.

"And like locusts they will dry up and blow away," he said. "Poof."

He made a feminine wave of his hand and smiled along with the canned laughter in the background.

Rafi's father screwed up his face trying to understand the American music now playing on the television.

"Come and knock on our door, we've been waiting for you."

Hussein's face grew larger and larger going to the edges of the screen and beyond, then morphing into an Iraqi flag slapping in a stiff wind. Rafi's mothers and sisters huddled around the radio, looking out the front window. No one moved outside.

"The calm before the storm," Rafi's mother whispered.

Rafi had hopes of helping his father put in the year's crops, then working in the jute factory down the highway to save money to attend the University of Iowa State in Ames where he would study agriculture. He would then return home and solve his father's problems.

President George Bush allowed his wife to comb his hair.

They stood in the dressing room just off the Oval Office, being prepped for Bush's national broadcast. He would tell the country what they already knew, that hundreds of U.S. fighters and bombers had attacked Iraq, and that the battleship Tecumseh had been lobbing cruise missiles into Baghdad for three hours.

The lights blasted.

George Bush sat washed about in a sea of lights, sitting straight, staring hard into the camera.

Martha and Francis Pontiac saw the graphic "Special Report: Desert Storm."

"My fellow Americans."

Bush looked calmly, wearily into the red light as if he

were the nice next door neighbor come to the front door with unfortunate news.

"Today, young Americans are again in harm's way, protecting our country and our world from the forces of tyranny."

Bush gave reasons for the attack, when it began, and told Americans that they were prepared to accept the challenge of a protracted effort.

Martha and Francis moved even closer to each other on the couch, her legs wrapped around his, staring ahead, unable to move.

After a full night sleeping in the cab of their truck, sweating heads against the closed windows keeping out the bugs, listening to the flight of aircraft right over their heads, Luke and Tiny awoke to the sound of their commander hollering for them to get ready to move.

A mechanic slammed the hood of the truck and pronounced it "good to go."

The commander, the manager of the Video Warehouse in Sioux City, put his right hand into the air and spun it around like he was making cotton candy at the Woodbury County Fair.

"Let's ride!" Luke and Tiny yelled together, smiling.

Their faces swimming in sweat, they rolled their windows down and stuck their heads out, shouting to the others in their unit.

"Head 'em up, move 'em out!" shouted Tiny.

"Rawhide!" added Luke.

The tractor-trailer National Guard unit from Sioux City moved into single file and headed down the makeshift road. Over the radio Luke and Tiny heard singing.

"Hell bent for leather, we'll be together!"

They joined along, high-fiving, yelling and waving out their windows.

After ten miles and forty minutes they reached a hard-surfaced road, constructed by Exxon in the '70s for

the transport of petroleum. It looked like an Arizona highway, coming from nowhere, headed to the horizon, and
nothing everywhere.

"Civilization!" shouted Tiny.

They moved north, bringing up the tail of the ground
assault that had begun in the night.

Rafi sat at the table, across from his father, still writing.

The women occupied the window in the dark front room.
One sister had made popcorn.

The girls giggled.

Rafi saw the urgent look on his mother's face as she
tracked each path of light, missile or plane or anti-aircraft
tracers.

They were far away, like the stars.

They were real, but not very real.

Rafi also wrote.

His father expected his son to help. That meant Rafi following in whatever activity his father was engaged in. Rafi
wrote a poem, covering it with his hand and arm while he
wrote.

What I Hate

What I hate are old people
And farmers.
So slow.
So stupid.
They keep others from important places.
They get in the way, hard to get around.
Impossible to move.
I dream.
Of old people and farmers.
Crowding the roads, the shops,
the house doors.
Nowhere can I go without

running into them.
They keep me from where I want to go.
I see only the backs of their heads and I hate
the backs of their heads.
Move! I scream.
Get out of my way. Can't you see
I have important things on my mind?
Then, because I cannot move forward,
I turn around.
And there are more old people,
hunched and shuffling.
And farmers with their thick,
dirty hands
and slow speech.
For the first time I see their faces.
Kind faces.
I look again.
One smiles.
I turn away. Another smiles
and hands me a candy.
I am now running, trying to get
through the crowd.
They are all smiling and holding out their
crooked old hands.
When I awake my arms are full of candy
 and trinkets.
I smile.
No more do I have to hurry.
I will also go slow.
I will live.
And then die.
And then go to heaven.
With the old people.
And the farmers.

Rafi's father looked up just as Rafi finished his poem.

He wore a wide smile.

He pointed to his own paper and twirled it so Rafi could see.

Rafi's mother pointed to the sun, now coming up over the ridge toward them.

She almost grinned.

Rafi slid the poem onto his lap and studied his father's work.

His mother howled and framed her face in her hands. The sisters, in black robes, scrambled, dropping the popcorn crock onto the floor. It scattered over the floor in a hundred pieces … a hundred yards apart … as a cruise missile screamed into the kitchen of the house across the street.

That afternoon Luke Pontiac and Tiny Gooden reached the outskirts of An Nasinya.

The convoy slowed, then stopped. Luke and Tiny surveyed Rafi's neighborhood, piles of Stone-Age rubble.

Luke braked and opened the door.

"We're still moving!" said Tiny, reaching for the brake with his foot. "Jesus! Okay, I'll keep it running then."

Luke walked through Rafi's front yard.

Tiny stayed, shouting out his window to the truck behind to go fuck themselves then why don't they.

Luke walked up behind a woman in a black robe, shawl and headdress. She lay on her side in the remains of a wall. A man rested beside her. A man with flies on his lips.

She had her arm over his chest. She chased the flies and wailed, not noticing anything else around her. A handmade table stood in what could have been a family's kitchen.

A heavy black stove squatted across the table, still smoldering. A younger man lay on his back on the other side of the table. The woman handled the one tragedy for now.

The young man with a faint beard and dark eyebrows looked up to the blue sky without blinking.

Luke reached down and pulled his eyelids closed.

The young man's hand clutched a sheet of paper, tight.

Luke pulled the hand with the paper to the chest and covered the hand with the other in a prayerful pose.

Over his head Luke pulled a metal cross and chain and pressed it into the boy's hand.

These guys pray, don't they?

"C'mon man!"

Tiny shouted out Luke's window. Their truck blocked the narrow road from both ways.

"You're holdin' up the freakin' war!"

Luke stared at Tiny and the line of semis behind his truck, along with Jeeps and personnel carriers. It looked like a National Guard unit stopped at a 7-Eleven on the way to a weekend at Camp Ripley.

Luke laid the table down to block the view of the young man from the weeping woman in case she started looking around.

He stepped gingerly through the broken home as if he might disturb something.

Luke climbed into the truck and the line moved north.

The phone rang at the Pontiac's. Martha put down her knife and ran to it the way a fireman rushes toward a flame.

Her lips quivered when she heard the voice.

On main street two cars full of teenagers drove up and down honking at each other.

The newspaper reporter frantically worked the phone and his note pad.

Yellow ribbons adorned each parking meter.

The clerk at 7-Eleven triumphantly waited on the long line of construction workers waiting to buy pop for break.

"Kicked us a little towel-head butt," said one man.

"Yes we did," smiled the clerk. "That'll be eighty-seven cents."

"Here, I got the nickel."

SEVENTEEN

"HE MAY LOOK DUMB, BUT THAT'S JUST A DISGUISE. HE'S
A MASTERMIND IN THE WAYS OF ESPIONAGE."
— Charlie Daniels Band, "Uneasy Rider"

Brigita Householder, Mickey McDonald and Richard Dakota-Hall sat in the command center.
The Bigfoot hands said one-thirty.

The three sat in a line along the table, each in front of a computer. Hamburger bags and French fry boxes littered the tables.

The door to the room was locked and closed.

Verlin demanded it whenever he let the kids do night shift.

Mickey scanned the UFO sightings around the world that night while Brigita monitored a live Bigfoot chat line from Salem, Oregon.

Richard searched the world press for reports of a PETA action at the National Hog Congress in Des Moines.

Photos of a pork processing plant in action had been handed out to busloads of school children attending the congress as part of a statewide FFA convention.

Richard wore the club T-shirt, two Bigfoots playing Frisbee with a UFO on the Grassy Knoll.

The faded blue shirt had a tear beginning near the collar.

He had taken over the animal rights division of the group. He hoped to find a way to hit Pig's Style for their disregard of the swine community.

Mickey liked to keep the ham radio on scan whenever she worked nights. The dial monitored the conversation of twenty night-owl English-speaking ham operators in California, Texas, New Jersey, North Dakota, New Delhi, Amsterdam, Reykjavik, Baghdad and Moscow.

Richard stuck a handful of fries in his mouth and turned to Mickey.

He pointed to his mouth to say he wanted to talk as soon as he was done chewing.

Brigita put her face yet closer to the monitor.

Someone had just sighted a male Bigfoot crossing the wooden bridge into Mill City.

Richard swallowed. Mickey turned her head at the size of his Adam's Apple.

"We need a slogan," he said. "A motto. Words to live by."

"Miller Time," Brigita whispered without taking her eyes off the screen.

"I won't say a word," said Mickey. "You don't even want me to comment."

Richard nodded yes, put his finger in the air and took a long swig of warm Coke.

"Yes."

He stood and wiped his hand across the air, revealing the slogan.

"Free The Pigs. Free The People."

Mickey turned her chair back to her computer.

"No, listen," he said. "We have all these hog confinements out there. All these millions of who knows how intelligent pigs living in three square feet of space, then being trucked to have their throats slit and their skin ripped off their backs. It's barbaric."

Mickey slowly turned her chair toward him.

"And if that doesn't subconsciously affect the human population of Iowa, I'm the king of the Bigfeet," he shouted.

"There is no plural of Bigfoot!" Brigita shouted. "We've discussed this I don't know how many times."

"We need to break our brother swine free from their enslavement!" Richard clenched his fist and held it up over his head practicing his Malcolm X.

He reached into the plastic garbage barrel near the door and pulled out a slimy Pig's Style bottle. He smashed the bottle against the wall.

"Free The Pigs. Free The People," he said.

He turned back. Brigita and Mickey exchanged looks.

Brigita got up and slammed him in the stomach with her fist and walked back to her computer station. Richard doubled over and lay on the floor in the fetal position. Mickey walked down the hall and brought back a broom and a dustpan, which she set down on the floor next to Richard's head. Brigita plopped into her seat and put her hands over her face.

The next day Verlin called a meeting. Trying to smoosh the membership of The Nature Lover's Group into the Command Center caused Verlin McDonald to blush.

So that Richard could get the door closed, Verlin was pushed into Brigita Householder's chest. He hadn't realized until now how she had grown.

He pictured she and Mickey still in third grade, taking two hours to walk home from school as they ambushed the boys, stalking them like British soldiers, pelting them with a meteorite snowball shower from behind every tree along the way.

Mickey would be shoving off to college and leaving the Command Center and maybe never coming back.

He would be stuck here in this musty basement with the twins.

There would be no use for the ham radio scanner. As soon as the breasts of Brigita Householder poofed another eighth of an inch it would be time to claymore the operation. He'd have to keep his eye on Brigita.

Verlin felt Brigita's breasts growing. He grinned down at her smiling up at him and stepped back into Richard.

"Hey! Hey, big-fella," Richard said. "Just a minute there."
Richard closed the door and put his hands into the air.
"If I could just have your attention."

"Shove it, dickwad," said Mickey. "It's us."

The twins slumped at two of the computer stations and
Mickey sat at the other. Verlin sidestepped Brigita and
Richard hunched on the floor with his back to the door.

Verlin turned to face the club members.

He got the twins to shut off their monitors.

He covered what he thought would be an attempt on the
life of the former president of the United States.

"George Washington?" Brigita asked, chomping her gum
and batting her eyes.

"George Bush," said Verlin. "George Herbert, George W.,
George V. Bush."

He outlined their responsibilities as he saw them and
listed the options he thought they should consider.

"What if it's just nothing?" said Richard.

"Then we have nothing to lose by not saying anything,"
said Rod.

"But what if the president, former pres'dent, right? Gets
shot and we didn't do anything about it?" Rodger said.
"You ready to have the McDonald Commission convened
in the Civic Auditorium?"

"Fat lot of good it would do," said Mickey.

Brigita had been sitting on the work table with her legs
dangling. She rose and peeled her red sweater over her
head. She tucked her T-shirt deep into her jeans, using
both hands as if she were drawing a pair of six-shooters
from her underwear.

"I think we just hang out," she said.

Verlin moved to stand behind the file cabinet.

"Just sit there videotaping whatever happens," Brigita
said.

"We pay attention to this Myrtle Bird chick and we find
out where it's going down and we're there. Beyond that,

what can we do, anyway? Call the cops? Right. Like they'd believe us."

"We document the motherfucker," whispered Mickey. "Yeah. This time there won't be no screw-ups, no hiding, we find out the truth about America and we find it out now. Whoever is behind this had been behind the whole goddamn shooting match. This is it. I say we videotape."

"This isn't it," Richard said.

He hung his head and draped his long arms over his bent knees.

His tennis shoes were scruffed with fresh oil from the highway. He had passed an armor coating crew from the state highway department on a ten-mile vision quest walk that morning.

"It's the millennium cockroach. Just strange shit that's really not so strange. People wanting to be something they're not just to show off to some macho girlfriends," Richard said with his head down.

"I say we vote," said Brigita.

Mickey put her hand in the air.

"All for videotape and not telling anyone."

All hands shot in the air, except for Richard, who had his head resting on his arms folded across his knees.

EIGHTEEN

"He lifted her, carried her into the house, and
with her arms about his neck she
forgot about Main Street."
— Sinclair Lewis

P aul sat at the light.
His dashboard digital clock showed seven thir-
ty-nine.
The downtown streets were clogged with traffic. The freeway was filling with cars and trucks and delivery vans. The
incoming lanes from the small towns around Sioux City
were being fed by the lonely avenues and dirt roads from
a seventy-one-mile radius. The Catholic school principals
were now just getting their coffee after a night of fasting.

Interstate 29 south to Council Bluffs and north to Sioux
Falls shoved into high gear, the does in the ditches began to
draw flies and the eyes of crows.

Paul leaned his arm in his open window, picked a scab on
his elbow and smiled at the driver to his left.

Elana knelt in the back seat trying to get the hang of her
new office.

She hollered at Paul to quit banging her around.

He asked where she wanted to go.

She said to just drive and leave her alone.

Some of their squabbling got out over the air.

"I'm sorry," she reached up and touched him.

"I'm just nervous, I guess."

He smiled and turned the wrong way down a one-way and had to dive into an alley to avoid two oncoming Subarus.

Martha sat in her office with the door locked and shades closed, a boombox on her desk, scanning the dials.

"Good morning, friend," came the weak, scratchy voice, like it was coming from Jap submarine sailors at the bottom of the Missouri.

"Yes!"

Martha shot her fists over her head.

"This is Elana Usak at 99.8 and moving, KROLL, broadcasting the seeds of the revolution from everywhere and anywhere."

She sang something in Czech, a ditty, a swear word, an oath, even she did not quite know what it was.

Then her voice became the delicious baritone that made Paul squirm.

"This is Radio Free Siouxland, my friend, coming to you live and kicking from wherever a free breath can be drawn. Here's … who else? Jackson Browne.

"They sell us the President the same way they sell us our clothes and our cars. They sell us everything from youth to religion, they same time they sell us our wars.

"Back in a few."

Elana told Paul to find a parking lot. He jerked to a stop.

She flopped against the car door and pulled out a cigarette, handing the pack up to Paul.

"How's it going?" he asked.

She wiped sweat from her forehead with her wrist and smiled.

"Better than outdoor sex," she moaned.

"This is the best, Pauly. The best ever. My God, what a thrill, thank you, thank you, thank you."

She stretched her legs out on the backseat floor.

He turned and watched the traffic on the overpass.

He flicked his ash out the window, closed his eyes and took a deep breath.

He glanced back at her and saw her hand signal as she prepared to ease back into the flow after the song.

He put the car in gear and concentrated on pulling away smoothly.

"It's fourth and fifty time in America, friends," Elana began in a hum.

"There is hope. We have pirate radio stations in Berkeley, Seattle, Omaha, Ames, New York, Birmingham. There is Radio Free Chiapas and Free Radio Beijing. Keep listening. The drums of freedom beat loud in our chests."

She rustled crumpled papers in front of her microphone.

"Here's a local note. We've been talking about President George Bush, former president, and his visit to Siouxland to deliver us a brand new killing machine. Turns out his welcome has not been of whole cloth."

She went into commercial for the "Handy Andy" company, bringing mid-morning sex to Siouxland housewives since 1939. "You want a mailman, cable hookup guy, newly-ordained priest, just call "Handy Andy."

Now back to the news, she said, taking on a British BBC accent.

"The prisoners at the Woodbury County lockup, though not members of the Chambah, have made plans for a special welcome for the Prez' of their own. More on that latah."

She rubbed two cassettes together.

"Here's a little Lou Reed as we guide you into the eight o'clock hour. If you haven't gotten up yet, just forget it.

"Stop obeying.

"There's nothing out there that you can't get at home, chil'. You know I'm right. It comes from the heart.

"Now here's the king. Prominent men tell prominent stories. Prominent men tell prominent lies. Ye-es, and the prominent men will tear our your eyes.

"Back in a few."

KGB

Martin Mumford was going to kill Bobby Ford.

Mark tried to decide whether to watch or try to sleep.

"I am American by virtue of birth only!"

Martin pointed his finger in Bobby Ford's frozen face.

"My daddy had uncles who were Black Panthers. My great-grandmother knew somebody who ran a stop on the Underground Railroad motherfucker.

"Now what do you think of that, freak?"

Mumford stuck his chin into Ford's face.

Ford sat at the table, peering up at the television past Mumford's penitentiary face.

"I only said you're no different than the rest of us," Ford said. "I'd think you'd like that. Geezuz, lay down."

Ford gripped the bench tight with both hands, tighter than he knew he was doing. The toes on each foot curled to the point of breaking. The muscles in his neck strained taut as shore cable on a stolen ocean liner.

Mumford wagged his head and smiled, because Bobby Ford just couldn't get it.

Ford stood, reached up to turn off the TV, realized he could not and spun back towards Martin.

In an instant he grabbed Mumford around the throat.

He flung Mumford against the bars in his cell.

"I don't get it! I don't get it?" Ford screamed.

"You sit here in my fucking seat! My mother-fucking seat talking to the fucking television, putting everyone down! You talk to the fucking television!"

Ford's face gleamed rose-red, his head shaking like a blender on maniac setting.

"And instead of taking the time to put you on a list and take a vote, I'm going to take your black ass out now, my own-self!" Ford yelled.

Mendez and Mourning Dove walked to opposite ends of the front bars to listen down both halls.

Ford let loose of Mumford's throat, but pinned him with hands on shoulders.

Mumford threw his arms up, knocking Ford's hands from his shoulders.

Mumford smacked Ford with a straight right hand, a straight left and then missed with a left uppercut.

He stood over Ford, plopped in the corner under the TV set.

"Get up, freak. You fucking freak, stand up."

He didn't holler.

He spoke calmly.

Pontiac jumped off his bed and arrived with Zags and Baltimore.

They got between the two.

Baltimore walked Mumford back to his cell. Pontiac helped Ford and hurried him into his bed. Zags jumped to turn the television up.

At the feet of Miguel Mendez lay a small sheet of white paper. He slumped with his orange jumpsuit around his ankles and leaned over to see the writing.

He smiled.

The paper, bordered in hand-made geometric designs, was a letter written in spanish from his sister in San Salvador, sent to a cousin in Del Rio and forwarded.

Juanita talked of a recent earthquake that was not too bad. The Mendez family lived in the poorest section of the city. Juanita attended a Jesuit school, the same that Miguel had gone to before he decided to leave the country. Juanita lived with their uncle and aunt. Their parents had been killed in the 1980s.

The aunt and uncle told them about Archbishop Oscar Romero and Father John Sobrin, who had been massacred by the death squads organized by the rich and the United States corporations to keep the poor coffee workers from doing anything but slave work.

"It is poverty that causes revolutions," Miguel's uncle had told him as Miguel was leaving that night to travel through the mountains to Chiapas and hopefully to Texas. "There are not revolutions in America because there are no poor people there, mi sobrino."

The uncle's family had worked in the coffee plantations of the twenty families. Miguel's father had been a lay minister at the Church of San Miguel in Morazan.

He and his wife had begun to pray in groups with social workers, talking about the rich families who ran the country along with the government.

And then their parents disappeared.

Juanita stayed because the military was not kidnapping girls.

Miguel was to find an uncle across the border in Del Rio, Texas.

Mendez found the uncle and went to high school. He learned English and kicked extra points.

He got married, had a son and continued to live with his aunt and uncle.

When the uncle and his family decided to go north for the strawberry pick in Minnesota, Miguel could either come along or find his own way.

Along the way the van was stopped on Interstate 29 and the family taken into custody by the INS.

All but Miguel were legal. He was taken to Sioux City by the feds to hold for a deportation hearing. His wife stayed on in Sioux City.

Bobby Ford sat with his back to Pontiac, watching "The Price Is Right."

When Bob Barker waved goodbye with his arm around the waist of one of the hostesses, Bobby Ford turned around. He began telling a story. Mark didn't stop him. If it was a good story, what did it matter.

"The residents of Manidoka, Minnesota all wore skates. They all wore skates, but not always, you know."

"Skates," said Pontiac.

"Yeah, skates," said Ford. "Like I said. It's my story, right? Am I right?"

Pontiac let Ford talk.

They passed cigarettes back and forth on the table while maintaining eye contact.

Pontiac felt the looks of the other guys, but kept his attention on Ford's tale.

He nodded, blew smoke at the ceiling, crossed his legs and gently turned down Ford's offer of peppermint candy.

"Thin ice," said Ford. "Something about thin ice. Cracks me up."

NINETEEN

Billy Mourning Dove, his grandmother called him Billy, lay on the top bunk of his cell.

His "rec room" he called it.

He tossed two socks folded into each other into the air practicing his jump shot, trying to come as close as he could to the ceiling without touching it. This was how he meditated.

He laughed to himself.

He could pray in the middle of the day while the television blared, a card game going on and a guard outside hollering for someone to get ready for court or a visitor.

He knew some of the other guys prayed. They never said, but he knew they tried. And they had to have complete silence, which came for about ten minutes between four and five in the morning and sometimes not at all and they would be the ones getting up looking tired and pissed. But he prayed while he tossed his socks into the air.

Old Indian trick, he grinned.

But still, the old thoughts gathered in the doorway, shoving shoulders inside.

He remembered working at the Bennett County Booster in Martin, South Dakota. He was the custodian for the

white couple who ran the paper. After cleaning the job
press machines and sweeping up around the web press
on printing days, Bill joined the Sioux across the street,
sitting on the brick ledge around the courthouse, waiting
for court, waiting for checks, watching the world go by in
pickup trucks.

On Thursday after the Booster was printed and taken to
the post office, Bill walked over to the courthouse ledge.
Anthony New Deer's beagle met him in the middle of the
road and walked with him.

Bill and Anthony sat on the ledge with a handful of elders
who talked some days about the two Wounded Knees and
the shootout with the FBIs at Oglala on Jumping Bull's
place.

Since William Mourning Dove had been there as a child
he was a celebrity and enjoyed sitting in the middle of the
group, on the sidewalk, with his back against the warm red
bricks and listening to the talk.

Eventually someone would say, "You were there, weren't
you, Bill?"

And he would say that he was. And they would ask him
who killed the FBIs and he would say he could not tell
because he did not know.

"But you were right there, in the weeds, c'mon."

And he could not tell them. He could only remember
crawling through the weeds, past the goons and the FBI
cars on the highway and up the pine ridge as fast as he
could go.

Anthony New Deer and Bill would often sit by the courthouse until after dark, listening to the word of happenings
around Martin and Bennett County, of who had their teeth
cleaned that day and who had the special at the Ranch
House Diner across from the Days Inn on the highway.

Bill called Anthony "Near-Beer."

"Whenever Tony gets near beer he has to drink it."

For one summer New Deer was the lifeguard at the

Bennett County Country Club. He still had a key. The two would sometimes walk over through the park to the club and take an after-hours swim.

Bill Mourning Dove and Myrtle Moon Shadow met at the pool.

She was visiting from Ontario one summer. She and her cousin followed Bill and Anthony to the pool, and told them if they didn't let them in they would tell on them.

Myrtle and Bill were married in a traditional ceremony in Pine Ridge and drove off in Bill's red Chevy pickup toward Sioux City.

They were going to be city Indians, they said. They didn't want their children to spend their lives sitting on the court-house ledge.

One year after they arrived in Sioux City, while studying for a test in communication arts, Bill answered the phone and found out that his brother had been killed crossing the wide main street in Martin from the Hoosegow Bar to the courthouse to take care of a traffic ticket that Bill had not paid, so that Bill would not be arrested and brought back to South Dakota where he didn't want to be.

Bill's brother stood in the middle of the crowned street when a pickup full of high school football players in their game jerseys blared their horn for the Indian to move.

Bill's brother stood in the road and gave them the finger with both hands as they ran him over and kept on going. He lay there bent and bleeding and dying as the football players stormed away, blowing their horn, giving each other high-fives.

On the way back to Sioux City from the funeral week, Bill and Myrtle stopped at a pay phone booth when they both saw a pair of eagles swooping loop-de-loop in the sky above the pickup. They found out that Bill's grandmother had passed away as well.

Myrtle would later say that she thought Billy had an American-style panic attack right about then.

He drove fast, not slowing for stop signs or watching out
for deer.

Wearing a white T-shirt with George Custer full of
arrows, with "A Good Day To Die," printed in red cursive
below, Bill walked into the Sioux City Iowa State Bank.

He wanted to hurt that bank, Myrtle said.

He wanted to do something to the white people so they
would feel it in their chest when they tried to fall asleep at
night.

Bill used his counter checks from the Martin bank.

He signed the name of William Janklow and wrote a
check for five thousand.

They gave him the money and arrested him in the parking lot, chest in a puddle, hands cuffed in the middle of his
back, as Myrtle watched, in tears.

"I saw a man driving a car, hand over the seat, leaning
into the back seat, smiling. I thought, 'what has that fool
got to smile about?' Then I saw the blond head of a child in
the back window. 'Ohhh.'"

Mark Pontiac smoked while he talked softly to Burton
one morning after breakfast.

Burton jiggled away and Pontiac snuggled up to his legal
pad and cigarettes.

In the letter he was asking his mother if she still had
his motocross trophies anywhere. He might like to get an
apartment when he got out this time and maybe put them
up on a card table.

Al lay on his bed.

He stretched his legs out and put his hands by his sides.

He closed his eyes and pretended he was standing, then
he convinced himself his feet were pointing toward the
ceiling. He could do that. If he didn't open his eyes he
could sort of forget which way he was lying. With practiced
lack of expression he let himself remember home.

Alford Arthur had never taken denominations seriously.

His mother was a huge Catholic. A rabid pope fan and large enough to make a front-end loader back up down a narrow alley.

Al's father was on the board of directors at the United Methodist Church. Alford couldn't get excited about any of the various church teams in town. He hung out in the back row of the balcony at Saint Benedict's on alternating Sundays and played in the bell choir at UMC twice a month until he got out of high school.

Alford Arthur's big shot family helped to found Sioux City.

His grandfather arrived from County Dunphee in the late 18th century. The McArthurs were the lone English tenant farmers in the county. When they were forced off the land and into the fetid hold of the ship "Jefferson" and sent to America, grandfather McArthur changed the family name. He changed it in his own mind and that was that.

He barely paused in New York for coffee, kept walking, wanting to get as far from Ireland as possible. When he reached the Midwest of America he stopped, began to pile the rocks from a field and then plowed.

Al joined his father in the front office of the mill. He tried cooking in the café and running the scale in the elevator. Next his father tried him out selling seed corn.

Once in Don Wickes' old chicken shed he found Don and half the Christian Academy's graduating class of eight boys cooking methamphetamine. Alford decided to stick around for a few minutes and stayed for three weeks.

In his absence, Alford's Down Syndrome brother Timmy had a birthday party at the group home.

He had his own bedroom, decorated in football curtains and lampshades and three-feet-wide basketballs on the bed quilt.

Tim's thirteenth birthday was the first one Alford ever missed.

"I'm a teenager," Tim told everyone at the party, in the center kitchen, with streamers and a "TIMMY 13" banner across one wall. Every five minutes Tim would go to search for Alford in his bedroom, kneeling on the floor to look under his bed.

Then he would walk in his off-balance gait to the front door to peek outside.

"Al's late," he tugged on his mother's arm. "Al's gonna surprise me," he turned to his father.

When Alford returned to the mill unshaven and unshowered, he announced he had become a partner in a local business.

His father turned, shook his head and walked away, and bumped into his wife, headed the other way to give Alford a hug.

She sent him home to clean up and the three of them went to the Food Court at the mall to celebrate.

Alford told his parents he and his new friends from the Christian Academy were starting a farrowing operation at Don Wickes' parents' place.

And they did that.

Along with the methamphetamine factory in the mud room.

The hog manure stench hid the meth-baking odor.

His father nominated Al for a national Jaycees award. A reporter from the Sioux City Journal arranged for an interview.

The Wickes brothers had found a way on the Internet to make the drug, and one of the boys was taking an organic chemistry class at the community college.

Alford turned out to be an organizational whiz, using the pig shed as a factory and hiring runners to market product around the region.

In one year the methamphetamine business made just over a hundred thousand dollars.

The six dozen piglets sold for $250 each.

Alford and the other managers began to use the drug after the first year. R& D, they called it.

They began to promote their line as a way to get repressed memories to resurface as a means of facilitating therapy.

They said their clients had increased feelings of empathy for others and found it easier to live in the present, "the now."

They began to see themselves as providing a service and became less paranoid, less careful. Not really felons.

One day while Alford worked in the shed by himself in his overalls, cap and boots, in front of a computer with a spreadsheet, his proud father walked through the door with thirty members of the Sioux City Chamber of Commerce, there to surprise the boy pig farmers with a morning Coffee after their first year of successful operation.

The room was filled with cardboard boxes of clear bags of white crystalline powder, half with a reddish tint, half without. The boxes were chalked with the towns of their destination for delivery that evening.

Al's father drove him to jail.

Alford faced up to fifty years in federal prison for distribution.

TWENTY

"Truth is always the first casualty of war."
— Hiram Johnson

B ut what does KGB mean?"
     Zoe stood at the coffee pot and tossed her words
     over her shoulder.

Alyssa Burton sat at the folding table in the break room, running her finger around the rim of her cup.

"Pol Pot, dead already," she repeated.

Then she went down the list of names on the sheet of paper her husband had brought home from work.

"Do you have the list?" asked Zoe.

"No. Burt snuck it back. He's got copies. Slipped the original in where he found it. He can be mean. Says it will drive those boys absolutely insane wondering where it was.

"They got it coming, though, committing crimes and such. You un'erstan' what ah'm talkin' 'bout?"

"Oh, I dooo," said Zoe. She sat down and reached a donut from the box on the table and broke it in half, then into quarters.

"It sounds Russian," she said, dreamily shoving a quarter donut into her mouth and following with coffee.

"Cold-War like. Out in the cold, almost, that one movie?"

"They were probably just doodling to pass the time," said Alyssa. "Poor dears."

Zoe pinched the remaining half and dropped it into her coffee. When it bobbed up she put the cup to her lips and drank back the rest of the coffee and the soggy donut. She ran her tongue around her mouth.

"They might just be fucking with your husband's head," she said, wiping her lips with the back of her hand.

"Yes, I suppose you're right," said Alyssa.

She crossed her legs under the table, put her coffee cup down and licked dried blood from the tip of her ring finger.

Charles Ballantyne leaned back and twirled his chair to face the window. The lower right side of his face had dropped off the planet. He had an itch on his jaw and no matter how hard he scratched, the itch could not go away.

He opened his desk drawer and grabbed a paper clip. He opened it and dug it into his cheek. He leaned back to face the window and put his feet on the ledge.

The right side of Ballantyne's face drooped, he just knew. He could audition for a horror movie. He would stay in the office until the Novocain wore off, then he'd stop off at Stone's Throw for his hamburger and a beer before the council meeting.

The phone rang.

He let his secretary get it.

She stuck her head in his door and said it was "Des Moines."

He waved thanks and smiled with the left side of his face. He said, hello and put the receiver next to his right cheek.

It didn't feel right.

He switched it.

He pushed hard with his shoulder to pin the phone against his left jaw.

He searched around the desk for a pen, listening to Matthew Pontiac cough into the phone.

"Sorry, Charles, I've got this cold. What more do you know about our friends in your jail?"

"Not a thing."

Ballantyne pushed back from his desk and turned to the window.

He got up with the phone and walked the few steps the open the blind a bit more.

"Just that we have this list that could be something, but probably isn't anything. Anyway, it's just a piece of paper."

Ballantyne seated himself again and pushed the phone into his ear. He heard breathing. Matthew Pontiac's voice changed. He spoke slowly and forcefully, not friend to friend, but ruler to subject.

"Except for the fact that my brother and father are in that jail. The list is not a coincidence. Your faxed copy is not clear at all, something huge is going on."

"What about Michael Zags as well. Are you calling that a coincidence? What do your fellow council members think about all this?"

"They don't know yet," Ballantyne said as he stood.

"They should, tonight," said Matthew Pontiac. "You will have to get this all worked out beforehand. Do you understand, Charles?"

"Yes."

The phone turned silent.

Charles dropped his pen and pushed the receiver into his ear with his left hand. He heard a dial tone. He hung up the phone, swiveled toward the window and put his feet on the ledge. In the windowpane he watched his hand touch his cheek.

TWENTY-ONE

"Our twelve blue sneakers squeaked, like the stiff black
dress shoes of a high school FFA club on
the marble rotunda hall on a field trip to the Capitol."
— First-time drug offender upon entering
Leavenworth Federal Penitentiary to begin
an 18-year, no-parole, no good-time sentence

Bill Mourning Dove sat at the table with Michael Zags and Mark Pontiac.

"What you doing up already, M.D.?" asked Michael.

"Can't sleep," said Bill.

"You're sweating. You warriors go flat-out when you wrestle with your conscience," Pontiac said.

"Old Indian saying," Mourning Dove said, "says fuck you, white boy."

"That's one catchy line," Pontiac said.

"Gotta love that lore," said Zags.

"Old Germanic saying," said Pontiac, beginning to roll a cigarette, "says eat me."

"Shut the fuck-up!" Al Arthur yelled. He wrapped his pillow around his head and huddled to the cold wall in his cell.

"I hear the list is back," said Mourning Dove. "Where do you think it flew off to, cuckoo?" He nodded toward Ford's cell.

"Burton," said Pontiac.

Michael Zags glanced at them both and returned to his paperback.

"He'll tell. We got to get rid of it, then," said Bill.

"He just likes to fuck with me," said Pontiac. "If we make something of it, then he gets his kicks. If we just keep still, we beat him."

And if he calls in the Secret Service we take a B.O.P. mini-van to Leavenworth," said Zags.

"What if we did it?" said Mourning Dove.

"Yeah. He's right," said Zags.

He put the book face down on the table.

"Just flush it."

Mourning Dove cupped his hair and pulled it out from inside his jumpsuit. He smoothed it and let if fall onto his shoulders and back.

"Me and Mendez was talking last night. We're all going down anyway. Why don't we just kill George Bush? Do something good for once."

Pontiac slid a cigarette to Zags, then one to Mourning Dove.

"He was telling me about where he came from," Mourning Dove said. "He said you guys were like his mom and dad and the people they hung with. He called them base communities of resistance. He said that's what this is.

"We could say we don't go along. We don't accept gettin' shit on, being at the bottom of the totem pole. We resist. We don't go out to Custer's fucking parade and run after the candy he throws.

"We kill Custer."

They all looked at each other.

"It worked once," said Mourning Dove.

A toilet flushed in C-Block.

"First," Zags touched the ends of his thumbs together and pointed his fingers to the ceiling.

"I ain't nobody's mom and dad. Pontiac can be whatever he wants.

"Second. Bush comes here," Zags said. He put both hands flat on the table, his elbows crushing his book.

"He flies in, gives a speech, drives past the jail. Kids waving American flags. Yellow ribbons tied to the lamp posts. What's wrong with this picture?"

"No dead Indians," Pontiac said.

"No. No motherfuckers in orange jammies," said Zags. He leaned forward.

"Really, c'mon. How we gonna be there in the first place? All this is talk. When it comes down to it, we're not going anywhere. Except to another jail.

"Nobody is getting out of here before George Bush comes to town. We might as well forget about it. Burton can shove that list up his ass, don't know why he's so interested anyway."

Pontiac twisted the end of a new Bugler masterpiece creation.

"I'm getting' out," he said.

They gawked at him.

"What are you in here for, anyway?" said Zags.

Pontiac licked the cigarette and lit it.

He told them how he'd been coming to D-Block for thirty years. How he was in this time on another misdemeanor doing ninety days and would get out the morning that George Bush was to come to Sioux City.

"If what the paper says is right," he said.

Zags tore a match from the pack on the table and marked his spot.

"Whatever happened to Mendez' parents?" Zags asked.

"They died," said Mourning Dove.

Elana and Paul shot up Inkapduta Drive doing sixty-five.

Behind them sparks shot from under a black and white cruiser as it bounced over an intersection. The police cars lights flashed red to orange and around and around.

Elana spoke rapidly into the mic.

Keeping his eyes straight ahead, Paul searched down the cushion of the passenger's seat for his billfold. He stuffed a Cheetos curl into his mouth and pulled a string of hair through the gap in his teeth.

The sirens whined.

Paul jammed on the brakes at the red light.

Elana slammed into the seat, using her knees and hands and chest to keep the equipment from crashing forward.

"What the freak is going on?" Elana screamed over the air.

"Oh-my-God!" Martha stared into her radio with wide-open eyes and mouth. She reached for the trashcan with her feet just in case she had to vomit.

Paul rolled down his window in time to see the police car flash past.

All four tires came off the ground as it soared over the intersection. The arms of the officers flew up. The front tires hit, the frame smashed the pavement, then the hindquarters lit in silent slow motion like a bloodhound clearing a fence in a morning cartoon.

It disappeared down the hill.

The light changed.

The driver behind Paul leaned into his horn. Paul swung around and saw the F-150 pickup filled with four large men. He waved and signaled a turn into the right lane, causing a Ryder rental truck to screech to a stop.

Paul continued waving to everyone, turned right against the light and pulled into the first parking spot against the curb.

Paul popped the clutch and leaned his head back. Elana frantically checked connections and picked up tapes and notes. She kept her head down and continued with her morning show. Without looking Paul pulled a box of Twinkies from the dashboard and finished his breakfast.

"Okay. Just some special effects we're testing for Lucas-Films, one of our sponsors," said Elana.

She stretched out on the floor holding the microphone with both hands on her lap. She closed her eyes.

"It's seven-twenty-nine, for those who can't tell time," she said. "And also time for our weekly group session. Come in, take a seat. The coffee and sugar cubes are in the corner.

"Any dictionary readers in the group today? Go ahead. Admit it. Everyone here this morning has something wrong with them.

"We're all defectives, tossed out by the sorters.

"Hey, you ever see a picture of Otto Von Bismarck. Really. Now there's a guy, a career military man, with the jowls and mustache and vacant stare.

"He and Norman Schwarzkopf so blessed happy they let them play with guns and they get to be statues and dictionary pictures, too.

"Look at these two guys now group. If they weren't professional killers, what would they be? Right. Swooshing a mop down at Saint Angelo's after funerals, maybe bowling afterward, pointing a channel-changer the rest of the night.

"Here's a little BTO for you grey-haired ladies we all know and love. Takin' care of business. Be right back y'all."

Back in her office Martha cranked the radio and danced around the room, lifting her floor-length Guatemalan red dress to her knees and swinging her grey ponytail like an airplane propeller.

"You want I should move?" said Paul.

"No, this is fine," said Elana.

"You got any more of these?"

She pointed at the Twinkies box.

He turned it upside down. Three empty wrappers fell out.

She watched clouds out her window.

Paul counted blue Chevy's.

"Now, quickly, we've got a punch list of things to cover today, group, and we haven't much time.

"For you who plan to go job hunting today. Don't. Disobey the Nazi work ethic. Be a violator. An asocial.

"Ever come to a small town and see the elevators from like twenty miles away? You have . It looks like Oz. And that's how we see small towns. Perfect. But it's not like that, once you get closer and closer and closer, then too close. A friend of mine once told me there are no good guys, not really, only crushed squirrels in the street and kids with cigarette ashes in their cereal. I'm afraid that's much closer to the truth than we want to admit, group. Group?"

She changed position, trying to stretch her legs.

"Yes, there, Amanda? Which came first, the conservative populace or conservative media?

"Now, group, it's time for you to go. Get on out of here. We have seen the promised land. I might not get there with you, but deep down, we never really liked each other anyway, right?

"Salvation is possible, group. It's easy. It's right there. Feed the poor. Stop war. It's right there behind the curtain. We're just too super-afraid. Throw out your medication group, and take that first step.

"Okay. Gotta go. It's seven-fifty-eight on your Wednesday, the middle of your workweek, as they say. You be good. This is Elana.

"Over and out."

Paul stomped on the pedal and turned the key.

He stopped, counted to twenty by thousands and tried again.

"It's flooded," Elana said.

"Just wait."

Elana began packing her equipment to slide into her trunk. She heard brakes squeal and car doors slam and stretched her neck to see who had broken whose tail lights.

Out the back window she saw two deputies in brown uniforms pointing shotguns. Two more crouched in front of the car pointing guns at Paul, who had his hands in the air. A tow truck driver with his red lights flashing backed up behind the front deputies.

KGB

Agents Hargrove and Fry wore dark blue windbreakers with FCC in white letters and white shirts with black ties. Blues Brothers, thought Paul. Hargrove stood at the driver's door and began to open it with one hand while keeping a pistol pointed with the other.

Agent Fry opened the front passenger door and slid in, holding a hand gun to Paul's head. In his left hand Fry held his photo ID. He put it in front of Paul's eyes then Elana's.

Elana held her hands up and tried to kick her program notes under the back seat. She quick pulled the KREV poster from the trunk and stuck it in the back window in the face of the shooters.

Paul turned his head at the stench of Fry's hairspray and eggs on his breath. Keeping his weapon on Paul, the special agent backed out of the car.

"Get out slowly, keep your hands in the air."

He opened the back door.

Elana tried to push up, lost her balance and grabbed the door. She winced and listened for the shot. She looked up at Fry with wide eyes and put up her hands.

Elana looked around.

Half a dozen brown and white Woodbury County vehicles blocked traffic at all junctures of the intersection.

Sheriff Williger stood in the middle of the road wearing his round brown hat and directing traffic with an egg plant flashlight. The tow truck driver began to hook up to Paul's car. The television vans squealed tires and tried to find a place to park.

The drivers of the cars gawked as they crawled past. Groups of two and three began to form on the sidewalks on both sides of the street, with arms folded around, clad in T-shirts and jeans, watching the capture, pointing at the television reporters they recognized.

Fry handcuffed Elana behind her back and led her to an unmarked car down the hill. Hargrove took Paul up the hill to another waiting vehicle.

The weather ball turned red.

At the Woodbury County Jail Paul and Elana were processed and held in separate holding tanks.

After questioning by Hargrove and Fry, Paul was released just as lunch was being served.

The two questioned Elana as she drank white milk from a carton and ate tuna casserole, carrots and red Jello from a tray. She was then dressed in an orange jail jumpsuit and admitted to the women's unit.

TWENTY-TWO

"… No one suspected, that there had been, from the beginning, a single-minded dictator in the White House, a Lord Protector of the Union by whose will alone the war had been prosecuted."
— GORE VIDAL, Lincoln

Ryan Mahoney, former president George Bush's chief aide, followed Matthew Pontiac into Charles Ballantyne's office.

Ballantyne dropped his feet from the window ledge to the floor and stood.

"What a cool surprise," he reached his hand across his desk.

Pontiac grabbed it and squeezed without shaking.

"This is Mr. Mahoney," he said. "Charles Ballantyne."

"Mr. Ballantyne."

Pontiac received Mahoney's coat and draped it over his on Ballantyne's coat tree. He dragged the comfortable chairs from across the room. Ballantyne crouched behind his desk, thinking that he might have to pee. He leaned back, trying to affect a relaxed look. He uncrossed his legs and rose to move the pencil holder so he could see.

"To what do I owe this surprising, honorific visit?" said Ballantyne. "I would have ordered some better weather if I'd known you were coming. Coffee?"

"Let's cut through the lawns right to the main highway," said Pontiac. "Up to speed."

Ryan Mahoney crossed his legs and straightened the seam in his pants.

He pulled a pen from his inside pocket and opened a note pad that had appeared in his lap.

Ballantyne thought he dressed like a homicidal attorney.

"Are you FBI?" he asked.

Mahoney did not smile.

"No."

"He's with the Bush office. He takes care of the details before every appearance."

"He's actually busier now than when he was in Washington," Mahoney said. "If you can imagine that."

"No," said Ballantyne.

He shot a glance to the photo of he and Johnathan Pontiac turning dirt on the brewery addition.

Mahoney began to run his pen down a list in the notebook.

"We know about the list confiscated in the prison" he said.

"All taken care of, right, Charles?" Matthew Pontiac slid to the edge of his chair. He did not smile. He stared into Ballantyne's eyes all the way to the junior prom, and to the shares of Pig's Style he had accepted from the brewery.

"I can assure you of that," Charles stood, placing his fingertips on his desktop.

"There will be no problems here."

Mahoney put his leg on the floor, his pen in his pocket and made the note pad disappear. He produced a box of cigars in a silver case and offered them around. Pontiac lit the smokes. Ballantyne came around and sat on the end of his desk.

"Now," said Mahoney considering his cigar like a prize stool.

"Tell me how you plan to make me happy. Tell me why I shouldn't worry about bringing former president of the United States George Bush to Sioux City. Tell me why you seem to have the only radical movement in the whole country locked up inside your jailhouse and why I should not worry about that.

"Convince me gentlemen, that you can appreciate a good cigar."

Francis Pontiac sat on his bed in his cell, holding a paperback toward the light in the hall. He gripped the edges of the pages with knotted fingers and twisted his neck. The broken pinky of his right hand had healed bent. He used it to cradle the spine of the book. He squinted his left eye and moved the page closer. A shadow blocked the hall light and he looked up.

"We can get that light fixed," said officer Don Burton. "How's your sink been working? I heard you had some trouble."

"Not much," said the old man. "You gonna get that book to my son that I asked?"

"Can't. Anyway, he gets books."

Burton looked down the hall.

"Never gets enough. That boy always liked to read," said Francis.

"They say good reading habits are the key to a good education," said Burton. "It's comforting to see a father take such an interest."

Burton leaned into the bars and turned his body sideways, making not a whit of difference in the privacy of their talk. The old man tried again to find the light.

"You heard … anything?" asked Burton.

The old man looked quizzically into the air.

"Nooo. What do you hear?"

"About … a list. D-Block. You know, that nutfuck that threatened the pres'dent. Got them all fired up over there."

"Fo'mer pres'dent, is what I hear," said the old man while squinting at the same sentence, moving the book, trying to find focus.

"Yeah, former president," said Burton. "But you did hear, right? What are they up to? C'mon, should I be worried? I got a fam'ly, you know."

Burton shoved his cheeks and stomach into the bars.

"Hey. You wouldn't have anything to do with this?

"Yeah, you'd be the one. I never thought about it.

"Now I know. Shit."

He snapped his fingers.

Burton pivoted to his right and pitched his head to the shiny cement floor. He pumped his arms and slowly picked up speed.

The old man adjusted the angle of his head and the book. The young guys at the yellow table in front of the television slapped cards on the table, flap, flap, flap. A toilet flushed and the tin heating duct in the ceiling quivered.

Francis Pontiac continued trying to see, but with eyes closed. He tested his head against the angle iron.

He saw himself seated in his living room with Verlin McDonald and Martha.

"I know what I'm doing!" Francis yelled.

"Keep … your … voice … down," demanded Martha.

He leaned forward and hissed.

"You don't know anything about this. It's not for me. It's for you and the kids the country, hell, the world."

"You can't just kill the President," she said. "That's crazy."

He stood and loomed down on her.

"Don't call me crazy. Don't ever call me that! You just don't understand. You think you're smart."

He leaned over and leaned close to her face.

"But you can be soooo stupid!"

He stood up and threw his clenched fists toward the floor.

"Go back to your books and your cute little classroom. Leave the real world to us."

The door to the stairs leading to the boys' bedrooms swung open, revealing Mark sitting on the stairs, his mouth open and dark in the chair by the lamp stand.

"I need to get to work."

Francis moved into the kitchen, followed by Verlin Mc-Donald.

"Go. Get ready for school," said Martha. "Everything will be all right. Go on."

The next week Mark's social studies teacher stood in front of the class with tears running down his cheeks as he told them that President John Kennedy had been shot and killed in Texas.

Mark and his father heard the news from a television newscaster in D-Block of the Sioux City jail.

The old man opened his eyes and saw the same jail, same cement floors, now with hills and valleys that only he noticed. The tables were painted different colors and the television was newer, color.

He closed his eyes and pictured his wife, what she would be doing that day, coming home from school, fixing supper for herself and sitting in the living room alone, watching the news. He tried to tell himself he didn't resent her calling the police after the fight that morning.

She didn't tell them what she really thought, but that he had hit her, which maybe he had.

… And he tried to imagine what could have caused his oldest son to get himself arrested, too, just to make sure his dad was all right in this dark, mysterious thing named jail.

And why he continued to come to jail, to keep track of his dad. He pushed his lower lip against his top lip enough to make the dimple in his chin appear.

Martha.

Francis let the book drop to the floor.

It made hardly a noise. He lay back on his bed, in the shadows. He put his feet up and crossed his hands on his chest. He dreamed of laying brick and awoke when the night officer yelled from down the line in clipped military cadence.

"Chooow-time!"

TWENTY-THREE

"Religion is what keeps the poor
from murdering the rich."
—NAPOLEAN BONAPARTE

Blanca Mendez, they called her Sally, waited at the front door for her husband. Jose had an extremely bad habit. He was always late. Sally did not like to be late ever. She did not want tardiness to become known as the trait of the Mendez family.

"We are late," she said as he came along wiping frosting from his mustache.

She waved to the children and told them they would not be long.

"Not late," he said.

"Not late at all. These things never begin on time."

He buttoned his pants and picked up his Bible on the wicker chair by the door.

"In fact, we are a little bit early."

He put his fingers together to signify a pinch.

They walked down the winding hills to the church of San Miguel, named after their son, they kidded each other. The Jesuits operated the school next to the rectory.

The small convent that now housed only two elderly sisters hid on the other side of the rectory, connected by an underground tunnel, a fact which the parishioners like to joke about when not in earshot of any religious.

Sally and Jose had grown up in Morazon, attending the Jesuit school of San Miguel. They had been best friends since elementary school.

They remained that way and the others said they would be married at the altar of San Miguel before another coffee crop was harvested. Sally and Jose both pointed fingers and said the other would for sure become a priest or a nun and they would never be married.

They stood at the altar in the summer of their nineteenth year.

Father Rosario said the Mass and danced with Sally at the reception in the church hall in the basement. Jose had his first drink of alcohol when his friends took him in the back of a pickup bouncing around the country roads passing a bottle of tequila.

During the ride the singing young men came upon a road block of pickups and old cars. They stopped and were confronted by men with guns, men from the city that they had not seen before. They asked if there were any communists in the truck. The young men said, no.

Jose made a joke, saying that they had not seen any communists all night.

"But when we see one we will tell them you are looking for them, senor."

The others kicked and pinched Jose to make him shut up.

The men with the guns made the partyers turn around and shot over their heads to scare them. Jose and the others rode in the back of the pickup flat on their backs all the way back to the church, passing the bottle and raising their heads only to drink.

Jose didn't tell Sally about the road block until a couple of years after they were married. It hadn't seemed important and he didn't remember the details all that well, anyway.

They walked holding hands and stopped several times to talk to friends. They were drawn by the warm glow of the light in the rectory where the liturgy committee was holding its weekly meeting. The group met in the rectory to plan the masses of the week, often around themes highlighting the differences in the living conditions of the rich and poor in El Salvador and pointing out how Jesus talked about the rich and the poor in his parables.

Father Daniel and Father George said Jesus does not want the poor to suffer with smiles on their faces, but to put food into those faces.

"If need be, you must reach for that food wherever it grows," said Father George with a sad look on his young face.

When Jose and Sally tip-toed giggling in the side door, then through the kitchen, they waved at the smiles that greeted them from the circle of wooden and metal chairs in the priest's living room.

Father George, seated at the top of the circle, was talking, his white collar askew. He nodded and smiled and looked at his watch to make a joke on Jose. The Mendez' took the two chairs in the circle reserved for them.

After the talk, the discussion, the note-taking and the delegating of duties, the group broke for juice and cookies. Afterward, they said their goodbyes. Sally and Jose walked out the back door and said, no thank you, to an offer of a ride.

"We don't get that much time to ourselves," said Sally. "This is our chance to be alone."

Jose hugged her and smiled wickedly, making their friends laugh.

On a summer's evening in 1986, Elliot Abrams, George Bush, and Alexander Haig eased into their chairs on the second floor deck of the White House. They each smoked a fat black cigar and lounged on blue and white lawn chairs.

The President came around with a "Tommy Lasorda" commemorative glass of whiskey and Coke for each, then took his seat.

At each cook-out he liked to give his guests something to take home besides a hangover. The four formed a half circle, looking out on the broad lawn and Pennsylvania Avenue and Lafayette Park. Reagan had invited the advisors to the patio for the weekly grilling, he called it.

He liked to make steaks and fry up slices of potatoes mixed with bits of onions. He also wrapped corn on the cob in tinfoil.

Wearing a Dodgers cap and a Beach Boys autographed apron, he proudly told stories while he poured lighter fluid on the briquets and lit the fire with long matches he scratched on the side of the White House.

They had eaten inside to watch Dan Rather's news, then meandered out to enjoy the night air.

Behind Reagan waited a cooler of Old Style on ice for after the traditional one glass of Jack. They accepted putting up with Reagan's homey pretense as part of the job.

For a while no one spoke, each asking the chance to just sit, letting the whiskey find bottom, to feel the breeze and enjoy his incredible position.

A car, two cars moved down the avenue. A couple walked a tall white dog on a leash. A monstrous limousine turned the corner with some difficulty.

"The Polish make it hard, Lord, wherever they may go," Haig said.

Regan told a joke, and another. Bush pushed up to grab an armful of beers and handed them out.

They all knew that the agenda for the evening was El Salvador, and so nothing else of much importance was brought up until Reagan got the ball rolling.

He asked Haig about the communists in El Salvador and Nicaragua.

Abrams gave his report.

Bush, being former head of the Central Intelligence Agency, knew that his words could have a major impact, depending on his timing.

He let the others deliver their pitches until satisfied he had better stuff that night.

"We have to stop it here, Mr. President," Bush said, twisting the cap of his second beer. He reached his left hand back and flipped the cap off the edge of the portico and crossed his legs. The cap whirled out of sight like an errant UFO. He liked to show off his arm in front of deep-voiced Haig, who threw like a girl.

"Colonel Martinez assures us that he can stop the religious movement in his sector. That's where we're getting the most guff."

Bush talked then drank long.

Reagan followed suit and then the others.

"If we proceed, on course, we can stop this thing from going into the mountains. If we don't, it spreads to Honduras, Costa Rica, Mexico."

Haig had met Martinez at the Fort Benning School of the Americas during a weekend training session for Salvadoran officers.

Haig had been asked to speak on Saturday afternoon. Martinez had approached him for an autograph. He took it home as a sign of his importance. Since that time he had deigned to call Haig directly. Haig had complained to Bush and now he was using Martinez as his own.

"No, Mr. President, we can't have this," Bush continued. "Just as you have said, stopping communism in El Salvador is vital to the interests of the American people. The coffee growers have to be able to make a living. Maxwell House and Folgers should not be chased out of prime country by a band of loose nuns and mule skinners."

Colonel Freddy Martinez sat on the top of the front steps of the Church of San Miguel. He wore his fatigues, black boots and green cap. He smoked a Marlboro down to the filter. He watched the members of the liturgy committee walk past. They noticed him, nodding, not smiling.

"Buenos noches, senora," Martinez said. "Have a good evening."

He recognized Jose and Sally.

"Mr. and Mrs. Mendez," he said.

They stopped.

"Senor Martinez," she said.

"Colonel," said Jose.

"You must have a lot of work to do," said the Colonel while looking at his burned out cigarette. "Meetings, comings, goings in the night. It must be important work. It would be intriguing to know what goes on in such meetings."

Jose stared at the colonel. Sally pulled Jose down the street.

"Maybe another time, then," said Martinez while flicking his filter to the ground.

"Hurry home to your children."

Sally gripped Jose's elbow. She walked faster, wanting to run.

Jose looked back over his shoulder and saw the church steps now empty. He grabbed his wife's hand and squeezed softly.

"It is okay," he said.

"He wants to find someone to report to him on the church meetings, that is all. He will try again next week and we will say no. What else can he do?"

"I don't like it," said Sally.

"My hands are like ice and I'm sweating."

She pressed Jose's hand against her forehead.

"We will bring the children from now on," she said.

Sally and Jose hustled around the last corner.

They still saw the lights of their home and shadows in the window. Sally clutched her chest and sighed. Jose grabbed her by both arms and pulled her to the side of the road, out of the way of a speeding vehicle.

The white GMC's brakes squealed like dying swine.

The big machine stopped in front of them, blocking their way.

Another recreational vehicle, this one dusty black, speeded up from behind the couple, skidding to a stop in the dust and dog feces.

Jose put one arm around Sally and held the Bible in the air with the other.

"We are church people!" he said.

"We come from San Miguel! We have done nothing wrong!"

Men with long guns hurried out of the vehicles. Jose was hustled into one and Sally into the other. She cried out to her children, the shadows in the window two houses up the muddy hill.

Then she wished she hadn't.

Jose was thrown into the back of the vehicle and beaten in the testicles and in the face with the butt of an M-16 rifle.

Sally's clothes were torn from her body and she was engulfed by two men not yet in their twenties.

One mounted her while the other stuck his penis into her mouth. She cried out and they hit her.

When the two vehicles reached the wooded hill the people called Montan de la Muerte, Jose heard Sally's cries as she was tossed outside onto the ground.

At least they would both be alive, he thought.

He called out to her.

God will show us the way to recover from these wounds and be stronger.

Sally's screams did not sound like her.

They sounded like a cat having its claws pulled out one by one.

Jose was pounded in the stomach by the flat end of a shotgun.

He doubled over. Sally fell to the sand and crawled away, clutching at the bits of clothing around her chest.

She cried out and heard Jose groaning.

She called again for him.

A sharpened spade hit Sally in the middle of the back, almost severing her shoulders from her body.

She fell face down, her mouth scooping sand like a dragline.

The next blow from the shovel cut off her head.

Jose was beaten by three men in Reebok tennis shoes, that much he could see, and jeans that were not quite long enough if you paid attention to style.

His face looked like a watermelon cut open and thrown to the ground by a moving car after the eaters were done with it.

He lay on his back, barely conscious.

One of the men, older than the rest, went to the vehicle, bringing back a knife from the fast food packaging factory in town, with five-inch curved blade and broken wooden handle.

"Beans and wieners," he laughed.

The others ripped off Jose's pants.

They tied his hands and his feet. "They know not what they do," Jose said out loud and the men kicked him for it.

Jose strained to hear Sally amid the threats and the shouting and the vehicles revving engine. One of the men must have had to sit inside to keep the motor from dying, Jose thought to himself.

The man with the knife pulled a work glove onto one hand, reached down and cut off Jose's penis in three hacking strokes, then rammed it into Jose's mouth, leaving him there bleeding, dying, as the two vehicles skidded away with a tape players blaring and Eagles song that Jose could not remember before he died.

TWENTY-FOUR

"Your life is now."
— John Mellencamp

The organ chords of the Agnus Dei drifted north, unnoticed over the sticky tar roofs of the brown brick downtown buildings.

Time for Mass. The outside home thermometers ready fifty-two degrees. The crash of the switch engine hand hitches grasping and releasing clattered over the lumpy nightcrawler backyards.

The downtown shop owners checked cash registers. A US West troubleshooter and a blonde letter carrier with tired eyes and sinewy biceps sipped scorched coffee at the Hy-Vee deli and figured gas mileage in their heads.

Dust devils whirled from a sewer drain, instigating a Snickers wrapper into chasing a Marlboro soft pack around a light pole in front of the No Place Lounge.

Inside the one-story, one-color homes on the west side, after the school bus lurched away, the husbands tidied in the rearview mirror while the whores of Aspen Run pursed lips and outlined in mauve the reflection in the refrigerator.

They made sugar toast and read from hardcover bibles while surrounded by the furniture of their dreams, wondering if something might come in the mail. To the south, the melodies braided with sweet firewood smoke and drifted skyward, signals to heaven portending the awakening terror of the adults and the giggles of the children.

The musical kites fluttered up, then quickly down, riding the cool wind like kids on God's-breath magic carpets.

In the country, red and green tractors slumped silent in old ruts like leftover Christmas ornaments.

In town, the pickups and cars for the Fourth of July parade sat knee-deep in spring mud.

Old men and old women plodded to church, dragging one black shoe after another, through the outer door, up the linoleum steps, then shoved loose-skinned forearms through the swinging wood door and fell into the big, familiar room, nodding to the altar like an old uncle in the living room.

The men swiped caps from heads, genuflecting before sliding into the rear seats. They steadied on the curled backs of the pews.

Men accompanying women tramped farther up.

The women knelt with heads up, backs straight. Each wore a scarf or a handkerchief with bobby pins.

Outside in Fords and Chevys on Washington Avenue, drivers leaned forward to listen to the hog reports, the last school lunch menu of the year and stormy season advice over the sound of heater fans stuck on full-blast.

Men in upstairs bank offices listened half-heartedly to the radio on the window ledge. Requiring the big picture, out of their windows they oversaw the stalled flood control project to the west and the abandoned feed lots to the east.

Fredrick Manfred had christened the region "Siouxland." He had written about the Indians and first white settlers.

His genius paved the way for Siouxland Doppler Radar, Siouxland Coop, Siouxland Laundry, and the Siouxland Chinese Chef.

The Friedman twins "Popo" and "Eppie," born on July 4, began giving each other advice on the swingset of their backyard in town. Sergeant Charles Floyd is buried along the banks of the Missouri nearby, the first member of the

Lewis and Clark expedition to die, contracting appendicitis in 1804.

High school drinkers by the Floyd Monument could see within 360 degrees the blinking red lights at the tippy top of ten grain elevators, marking ten towns in Woodbury County.

Inside the church, the sacristy screen door wheezed and slammed.

The wooden door brushed over the new carpet.

The young priest bowled into a boy asleep standing, a surplice over his head.

A man pulled a black comb from his billfold, straightened the trim grey locks and slipped the comb back.

He flipped the snap to the coin pocket and pulled out a stapled plastic bag holding two rose petals. He kissed the bag, pulled the rosary from the jacket pocket and knelt.

He laid his seed corn cap in the pew behind him, at about the same time as Michael and Mark, in the jail cafeteria, began shoveling in spoonfuls of hash browns and scrambled eggs mixed together.

"Hey, Zapata," Mark said, taking a breath.

"When I was in high school I was the best this, the first that. My best friend was a skinny kid who couldn't walk past a basket of kittens without getting nervous. He's still one of the best people I ever knew."

They both looked toward the kitchen as a tray of silverware dropped.

"You look around if you ever get out. You see if the best people out there ain't the misfits."

Mark waited to chew and swallow.

"The interesting ones don't know whether to sit down or go blind," he said.

Michael looked at him, trying to eat and listen.

"But they're the only individuals out there. The rest are just imitating some fool on TV or over in the living room," said Pontiac.

"Who was the other one, the other good guy?" Michael asked.

"My old man. A bricklayer with dust in his hair, on his shoes, up his nose and his ass. Most of the time, if he wasn't drunk, he wouldn't say shit if he had a mouthful. He had no idea how great he was. He wasn't loud like me. You watch out for people like me. All there is, is what you hear.

"Find one good man out there, fishin' by hisself on the bank, teaching a skinny girl how to bait a hook, or stockin' shelves with high school kids, then you got something you can work with. Then there might be a reason to do what you're doin'."

"I'll keep my eyes open," Michael said.

"Otherwise, you're wasting your time, trying to save the world, 'cause it don't deserve saving," Mark said. "They know how to swim, but they'd just as soon drown. Goin' down I-90 with their blinkers on. You'd be better off tying 'em in a gunny sack.

"Like me. Don't fuck with me. Just leave me the fuck alone."

"I'm really just trying to save me," Michael said.

Mark put his spoon down and crossed his hands over his stomach.

"Diogenes. Searching the streets with a flashlight for an honest man," Pontiac laughed through closed eyes.

Back in the block, Pontiac followed Zags into his cell, thumbing through Zags's letters.

"You got any candy?"

Zags said he didn't think so.

They each climbed to a top bunk and began to smoke.

"I'm listenin'," Michael said.

Pontiac continued a story begun on the walk from the cafeteria.

An unlit cigarette balanced on Michael's lower lip as he snored. Pontiac lit another smoke, lay back with his head against the wall, crossed his legs and kept talking.

Meanwhile, Michael Zags's brain had said time again for the recurrent dream.

He's sitting in high school history class.

"You. You want to be a good guy. You want people to like you."

Michael Zags sat in the third seat in the third row in Mr. Theobald's class.

Theobald placed an index finger on the middle bar on his glasses and pushed.

"You, Mr. Zags, don't have to fight for your rights, your food. Life for you is not a struggle."

Michael ground his teeth and peeked out the edges of both eyes to see if anyone was noticing this. Of course they were.

"You don't know what you would do if you have to fight to live, do you?"

By this time Michael wanted out of class bad enough to kill.

He glared at Theobald and thought, "Yes, I would kill. You come one step close and I will grab that skinny tie and choke you with it."

Theobald's pasty little hands and arms formed an "X" across his chest as he gripped his own shoulders.

"Theobald X," thought Michael.

As soon as the bell rang, Michael grabbed his things and booked, the first out the door. He opened his locker, threw his stuff inside and slammed the locker door.

TWENTY-FIVE

"A SINGLE DEATH IS A TRAGEDY.
A MILLION DEATHS IS A STATISTIC."
— Joseph Stalin

Mark Pontiac had volunteered for maintenance in order to get out of the cell, which he did whenever his sentence got below twenty days and time stopped.

Whenever he came to jail, even doing ten days or thirty days he worried that he might never get out. Someone could kill him or he could kill somebody and they would have him forever. Getting out to mop let him run some time off the clock.

Burton had him mopping the floor between the visiting room and the kitchen. Mark already felt a sense of freedom, being somewhere better than the last, getting away from the TV and the chatter.

At the end of the hall he heard keys.

The fat woman guard led the prisoners from A-Block to the visiting room. The guard stared at him and he froze. He wasn't supposed to see the women.

He mopped, looked up, mopped. After months inside any sighting of a female was almost more than a male prisoner could imagine. Even the fat, motley disasters herding into the glass room seemed to Mark like Georgetown debutantes entering a White House state dinner.

In the middle he caught sight of a young white woman who looked him in the eyes hard enough to make him look away. He watched her move to her chair, her small butt resting comfortably in the seat of her orange pants.

She kept watching him.

Mark saw himself in the window, a sad, old man in need of a shave, with a mop in his hands. Way past too late for graduate school.

He set the mop in the bucket and pushed it down the hall, around the corner, whistling "Dixie" as Martha entered the visiting room.

Martha smiled and extended her arms to hug Elana through the Plexiglass. They put their hands together on the window and reached for their black phones.

Two days later, Mark made sure he was mopping by the visitor's room at one o'clock.

Again Elana appeared, in the middle of the A-Block group.

Mark smiled wide and nodded.

To him, the smile was enormous and too obvious, a big fag grin, but Elana saw only a slim gap between his lips. She waved her left hand from the waist.

Mark's heart pattered. It pittered.

He watched her and saw his mother coming in to visit.

Martha waved at Elana over her head. Elana motioned back toward Mark.

Martha looked all around and spotted Mark. She waved both hands over her head. Mark nodded and moved with his mop and bucket down the hall.

That evening he wrote to his mother to ask about Elana.

Elana wrote back to Martha words she knew would find their way to D-Block.

"Your son's one person who did not do it right. I like that in a person."

Martha wrote back asking if Elana saw the Sioux City Journal in jail.

"This thing is full of the Bush visit," Martha wrote. "But none of it means anything. It's all about flag burning and the war on drugs and the glory of the Gulf War. Oh, how I wish you were able to tell the truth about this thug."

Francis Pontiac sat at his regular table in the chow hall.

His son hunched across the room, his back to his father. They both faced the mural.

All the blocks were let out at once to eat breakfast because of the low numbers that usually wanted to get up at six.

Burton leaned on one leg by the coffee urn, yawning.

He pulled his mouth shut when Mark got up from his table and carried his try to sit across from Francis.

The blocks were supposed to eat at their own tables. The two were the only ones eating that morning.

Neither Pontiac looked to Burton to ask permission for a family sit-down meal. Mark sat and scooped a spoonful of eggs, then looked across to his father.

"How's it going?" Mark said.

"Good. You?"

"I'm fine. You seen Mom lately?"

"Been awhile. You?"

"We write."

"She all right?" said Francis.

"Yeah. Luke came home. Martha asked her because of you. What's up?"

"Nothing," said Francis. "I got nothin' goin' on. You're the one in on the action. I heard about that new guy Zax. What you guys go over there? You got ..."

He looked at Burton and lowered his voice.

"You got Burt all upset. He thinks I'm in on something, too. He's funny."

"Well. Maybe you oughta know," Mark said.

He took out a smoke and slid one to his dad. Francis reached for an ashtray from the table behind.

"Five minutes," said Burton.

Mark told Francis about the plans to assassinate former president George Bush when he came to Sioux City.

"You oughta draw straws, matches," said Francis.

"Looks like it's me," Mark said. "I'm the only one getting' out in time. Same day."

Francis stared at his son, then over his shoulder at the drawing on the wall.

"So, this is how it turns out. I'll be damned."

He picked up his tray and limped to his cell, balancing with a hand on the wall. Francis asked one of the young guys for paper and pencil, another for envelope, another for a stamp. He sat at the table and turned off the television.

He began to write a letter.

Three of the young men woke up and stood at the table, implying they wanted him to move so they could play cards. One tried the set and hollered down the hall.

Francis looked at them hard. One flipped the knob on the television and they all went back to bed.

Francis dated the yellow paper at the top left.

Dear Mr. Former President George V. Bush,

Hello.

I am a prisoner in the Sioux City jail, but I will be getting out soon, in time for your visit to this city.

I don't like you.

When you come, I will kill you.

I don't want to kill you, and you don't want to be dead.

Francis pulled back to admire this sentence then leaned low to begin again.

But this is what will happen if you come to Sioux City, Iowa.

Sincerely,

Francis Ford Pontiac

Cell 5 C-Block, Bunk By The Hallway

Francis sealed the envelope and set it in the bars for Burton to pick up, then went back to bed.

The young boys shuffled out again and called down the hall for a guard to turn on the TV.

Don Burton hurried through the kitchen.

He joked with the trusties and the cook and sneaked a french fry from the deep fat fryer. He let himself out the opposite side into the hall running past A-Block. He stuffed the check from Martha Pontiac into his shirt pocket and stopped in front of Elana Usak's cell.

"Hey! Oozick!

"Here. This come for you."

Elana walked out in bare feet, rubbing her eyes.

"What?"

She took the long Radio Shack box through the bars.

It was duct-taped and had not been opened.

"What's this?"

Burton was already on his way out.

"For you," he said back over his shoulder.

The thick door boomed, leaving the secluded women's block again silent as a living tomb.

Careful not to let her sleeping fellow prisoners see that she, the only white woman, was getting more mail than they would ever receive, either here or at home, in their whole lives, she hurried the large package into her cell.

Elana laid the package across the bed and crossed her legs.

She looked at it.

She reached for her cigarettes and prepared a smoke while admiring the gift. There was no return address, and turning the heavy rectangle over and over, Elana could not find her name anywhere.

She flicked the butt and it fizzled. She began ripping the tape, pulling, biting it. She ducked and pulled in her shoulders to be more quiet.

She removed one end flap and looked down into the tube.

"Oh-my-God!"

She put her hands over her mouth and dropped the box to her bed.

She picked it up and began pulling out pieces.

She found a new microphone, antenna, coaxial cables, plug-ins, micro-transmitter.

She shot her nose up at a noise.

She began to breathe too fast.

She stuffed the equipment back into the box and bent the box to get it all back inside. She shoved the box under the bed.

She lay on her side with her rough blanket over her head and tried to think about what she could do.

Her chest pounded.

She felt it and watched her hand move up and down.

Her hands sweat.

She got up to smoke, walked into the open dayroom to look back into her cell to see if she could see the box from there.

Jesus, Martha.

I didn't ask for this.

You bitch.

You can't run my life. You don't know what it's like in here, you yuppie liberal what don't know shit.

That night, after supper, after cards, after the television was turned off.

After lockdown.

After the eleven o'clock count when the others were smoking their last cigarettes or visiting between cells or writing letters, Elana flushed her toilet, then again, and again.

In the middle of the roars she pulled the box from under her bed.

She sneaked a peak at the door, and a flurry she started yanking out and connecting.

She used the tape from the box to attach the open wires

to the pipes above the drop ceiling. At the midnight count she shoved everything under the blanket and did big wide jumping jacks as the guard walked past.

She pulled it all out again and flushed the toilet as she flipped the switch.

Someone yelled for her to light a match to get the stink out of there.

She flushed the toilet again. The sound covered the static until Elana could tune.

She took a deep breath, crossed herself and said quietly, "Good evening, friend … this is Elana.

"… Radio Free Siouxland is on the air."

No way could she know if it was working.

She let out a breath and smiled just as well, and leaned her back against the cold cell wall and crossed her ankles.

"She talkin' to herself agin," came a voice from another cell.

"Now a word from our sponsor …"

She listened in the dark for movement.

She wrapped her legs around the microphone, bowed her head and with eyes closed, opened her mouth slowly, then breathed.

"You can't kill the spi-irit."

Elana Usak sang softly from her American jail.

"She moves like a mo-ountain, old and strong, she goes on and on and onandon."

She hummed and repeated the verse for five minutes while rocking back and forth.

First one then another and another of the others still awake in the other cells joined her in singing, softly, humming, swaying back and forth, raising their hands into the air.

They sang louder, louder.

"This is KREV at 97.4 coming to you tonight from the porch of Sheriff Jeremiah Williger."

This has to be short, she told herself. They will find me.

"Short show tonight, friend, sort of a test run.

"… seek not the anonymous, joyless life, friend. We've got too many grocery baggers and bank clerks already, you know? Seek ye the fire, friend. Burn, baby, burn."

A door slammed hard somewhere.

"Wait."

Elana listened in the dark silence. One of the other women sniffled, somebody rolled over and a bed squeaked.

Elana imagined a man in an occupied country, trapped between compliance and death.

"Just one thing before this quick sign-off," she said.

She crossed her legs and leaned forward into the microphone.

"This one's for you, Daddy. … You folks need to know about George T. Bush. You need to know that he killed innocent people in Iraq, Panama, and El Salvador, for starters. You need to know that the man you will honor with your parade and your flags and banners and grilled wieners is the same one who steals from you your freedom.

"… It's true."

Elana talked for another thirty minutes about the Reagan and Bush presidencies, things never before mentioned in a Sioux City newspaper over on a Sioux City radio station, or in any Sioux City high school or college classroom.

The roving FCC tracking van was finally able to find her signal and narrow the search to three city blocks.

With her feet resting on a flowered cushion, Martha smiled in her dark living room, the breeze blowing the curtain into the room.

Her radio sat in her lap. She bent over to hear Elana's voice.

"Just one thing before sign-off …."

The signal went to fuzz.

Martha flicked off the radio, plucked her jacket from the wall hook and walked out into the children's-book night for her walk.

TWENTY-SIX

"HE'S OLD YEARS BEYOND HIS TIME, NO THANKS TO THE
WORLD AND THE WHITE PORT WINE."
— GUY CLARK

With the visit of George Bush only two weeks away, the chamber of commerce, the gladioli committee and the city council were busy. The Nature Lover's Group checked Myrtle Mourning Dove's email each day.

The assassination plans continued apace each evening in D-Block after supper.

Mourning Dove, Mendez, Pontiac and Zags played spades and planned. They smoked, kept the television up loud and posted Al Arthur and Bobby Ford on either end of the dayroom, listening for the night guard.

Matthew Pontiac talked on the phone each morning to Luke Pontiac and Ryan Mahoney, guaranteeing the former president's safety.

"Those prisoners are not going anywhere. The only other bunch we might watch would be the so-called Nature Lover's Group, but they're not really dangerous, just nuts. Plenty nuts."

Johnathan Pontiac kept in touch with his younger brother to make sure his plans for the Bush visit were passed to Ballantyne, the council and the various committees.

The national press would be there as well as state and local.

Pig's Style Beer would get exclusive television advertising rights.

He would even have ads on National Public Radio and CNN the day of the Bush flight to the Sioux City municipal airport, the National Guard facilities being too small for the expected crowds of dignitaries and onlookers. The B-2 would eventually be flown across town to be stored at the 185th.

Johnathan Pontiac considered it all as he stood on the deck with one foot on the railing, overlooking his plant, squeezing the brass, seeking an even deeper impression.

"The airport!" he said out loud.

It's too damn small for a B-1, two bomber. Fuu-uuck!

He hadn't thought of it till just now. No one had. Had anyone even bothered to check it out?

He ran down the hall to his office, his tie stretched over his shoulder.

"My wife will put the pistol in a locker upstairs."

Mourning Dove said, then bid four.

"Four? I hope you got something," said Pontiac.

"Table talk," said Mendez. "Go 'head, take it."

"A pistol?" said Pontiac. "I need a deer rifle. Ain't you got any Injun' deer guns?"

"And a getaway painted pony," said Mendez. "Gimme three."

"Diamonds," said Mourning Dove.

"It's a .38, with a white bone handle. It was at Wounded Knee, you should be honored."

"Yeah, right," said Pontiac. "Gimme four."

"Get right up on the curb," said Zags.

"Actually, a pistol is the only way to go. Step up and take him with a head shot through the back window while he's waving."

Pontiac looked around the table.

They were really talking about him killing someone, a president of the United States. Former.

He began to sweat, first his hands, then beads forming on his forehead.

"She will rent a locker," Mourning Dove said. "I'll get the number. She won't lock it. She'll wipe it and afterward you don't know where it came from."

"What's your middle name?" Mendez looked at Pontiac.

"Why?" said Pontiac.

"They always use your middle name when you kill somebody big," said Mendez.

Pontiac got up and climbed to his bunk. He lay on his back with his hands folded over his stomach.

"You out, man?" shouted Mourning Dove.

Pontiac didn't answer.

"Yeah. He's out," said Zags.

Stephen Baltimore and Martin Mumford waltzed out to stand by the table.

Mumford slipped the top card from the deck and palmed it.

He sat down in Pontiac's spot and began shuffling the cards, putting the king under his leg.

A pencil rolled off the table and crashed to the cement floor.

Mourning Dove walked into his cell.

Mendez stared at Zags.

Bobby Ford looked around from watching the television. He shook his head and turned back to look straight up at the set.

Mumford nodded to Baltimore. They walked into Pontiac's cell and stood next to his bunk. Standing they were level with Pontiac lying down on the top bed.

It was not according to code for someone to walk into another cell without being asked. Pontiac rolled to his right side to face them. The parts of his body got ready while his face gave them cover. He stared at the two black men, keeping his left hand behind his legs as if he might have a weapons.

"We want to pray with you," said Mumford.

"Shamasha shalakam and shit, like that," said Baltimore. "Martin has brought me to the Muslim faith."

Pontiac let his fists go free.

"And where's he taking you? In the Muslim faith and shit."

Pontiac sat up and grabbed his cigarettes.

"Wherever the spirit leads," said Mumford.

It was the first time Pontiac could remember seeing Martin smile.

"You need our help," said Pontiac. "You have a heavy burden that has been put upon you. C'mon."

He offered his hand to help Pontiac down.

Pontiac stared at him.

"Brothers."

Martin waved his hands to herd the other men toward him. He walked down to collect Mourning Dove and Mendez.

They squeezed into Pontiac's cell.

Pontiac sat now on the lower bunk. The others sat where they could find room. Bobby Ford stayed out under the television, staring straight up.

"Brother Ford," said Mumford. "Please join us."

Ford shook his head.

"Huh, uh." He crossed his arms tight around his chest.

"Join us when you see fit," said Mumford.

Mumford asked the men to join hands. They refused en masse.

"Fuck you," said Al Arthur.

They shook their heads and scooched, trying to gain precious space between them and the person next to them.

"Just go on," nodded Baltimore to Mumford.

"We pray today for our brother Pontiac who has been given this load to carry."

Martin went on about the rightness of the cause, then asked the men to join him in singing, "We Shall Overcome."

Zags sat in the corner with his back against the wall, his legs crossed, head bowed and hands folded in his lap.

He tried to sing as quiet as he could, managing only his customary growl. He was surprised at the voices of the others. Mourning Dove and Baltimore sang harmony. Mumford tried and then backed off gracefully.

Arthur beat a subtle reggae rhythm on the cement floor with his palms.

Mendez let it all hang out on the high notes. Ford turned the TV sound up.

Pontiac began to cry. He bowed his head and said he didn't think he'd be able to go through with it.

"I mean, man, killing someone, anyone, a real person, a human. Doesn't that make us, make me, just as bad as the guy who's doing the killing? I can't. Even someone who has killed lots of people. I still can't do it."

He looked up with tears chasing each other down his cheeks and glanced quickly around at his friends.

He put his head down again.

"I'm sorry.

"You guys are my family. I'd do anything for you. Don't make me do this."

He looked up and could not judge their glares.

"Just think about all the motherfuckers in jails like this that the gubment don't care nothin' about," said Baltimore. "We got to do something. We got to."

He grabbed Pontiac's hand.

"You be Catfish Hood. Hood-tiac. Mark Hood, Da Hood. Robin The Fish. You it."

"And Mr. and Mrs. Mendez," said Mourning Dove.

They took turns reciting the litany of the offenses of George Bush and others in power that they had repeated each night for weeks.

"Just give him some time to think," said Zags. "Let's play some cards. My back is killin' me, I got to get up."

Mumford said a final word. They got up, each stopping to shake Pontiac's hand like a mourner.

Bobby Ford watched it all.

He waited until everyone had left and with his hands clasped behind his back and his head bowed low walked over to Pontiac and asked if he could get a smoke.

Mark sat on his bed and began to undress.

He walked to the shower, turned on the water and waited silently, howling with his contorted facial expression, his face flushed red, his fists clinched tight, his knees bent his back hunched over, without making a sound, as the mist dotted the metal floor.

In the morning, before breakfast, Elana was told to get ready for court.

She said she didn't have court that day.

"'Spose to come get you. You get ready. C'mon now."

Elana dropped her clothes to sit on the toilet. When the guard looked away, Elana reached her foot to kick the box farther under the bed. She flushed the toilet and pulled up her jumpsuit and began buttoning.

"I'll be right there," she said.

"You're coming with me," said the guard. "By the time I get back here again they'll have something else for me. Just make that bed."

Elana smoothed the covers and checked out the wires, trying not to move her head. It would have to do. She'd take things down when she returned. She stood in front of her door. The guard spoke into her walkie-talkie. Elana's door opened. She walked out. The door closed behind her. She glanced quickly back over her shoulder.

Elana waited for three hours in the holding tank in the front office. She heard the morning guards come on duty and the night crew shout their goodbyes.

At nine she was let out by a guard who said he didn't know she was in there.

"We been lookin' for you."

Elana rode the elevator with three new male prisoners still wearing street clothes. Outside the courtroom she was locked into a holding tank alone for another half hour before she was shown in.

Martha perched on the aisle four rows back from the front. She waved as Elana yawned.

Don Hargrove and Jeffrey Fry stopped their car in front of the jail.

"Here?"

Fry shrugged his shoulders.

Elana was the last of four prisoners.

When her name was called she walked to stand in front of the bench still squinting at the light.

"Operating a radio station without a license?"

The Asian woman judge read the charge and looked at the deputy standing by the door. She looked down at Elana with her hair sticking out in six directions like cold mashed potatoes.

After half a minute of incredulous silence, the judge asked Elana how she pleaded.

"Do I get a lawyer?"

"You can, yes. I would have to bring you back."

She looked over at her calendar.

"I could see you in thirty days."

"Not guilty," said Elana.

The judge ordered Elana released on her own recognizance and asked the deputy to bring Elana's clothes and a hair brush up from the jail.

Elana began to object, to say she needed to go back to her cell, then put her hand down.

She changed clothes in the holding tank.

Hargrove and Fry showed their identification at the front desk and asked to be allowed to look around. Don Burton volunteered to give them a tour. He showed them the men's blocks, kitchens, volleyball court and visiting room.

"Where is the women's unit?" said Hargrove.

Burton took them around the blocks again and past the visiting room twice, through the cafeteria and the kitchen and then back to the locked cave of A-Block.

"Raaght cheer," said Burton with a wave of the hand.

"A-Block. Anything else I can show you today gentlemen? He began to close and lock the door again.

"Just a minute," said Hargrove.

The agents walked down the hall looking in at the six black women in the cell dayroom. The women stared back, combing each other's hair, scratching, yawning, sitting on the toilet.

"There!"

Fry pointed at Elana's cell.

"That cell! That cell!"

"Well," said Burton. "I'd have to get the keys. These aren't the right keys."

He moved slowly out the door and through the kitchen, stopping to talk to the cook, then to the front office as Hargrove and Fry waited, exchanging silent glares with the women, watching "Love Boat" through the bars.

Richard hunched alone in the Computer Center playing chess against the middle computer. He took a drink of warm Pepsi and walked to the work station to his right.

He called up the "Check e-Systemz" program that Verlin had invented and found Myrtle Mourning Dove had mail.

Richard was able to open Myrtle's message from her sister in Rapid City without Myrtle having any idea. Richard clicked on "open" and went to the middle table for more cold fries.

When he returned he found out that Myrtle's sister would be "sending the package UPS" today.

Richard called Verlin on the red phone at work.

The line was busy. He put a message at Brigita's and dashed out the door.

TWENTY-SEVEN

"I was once like you are now, and I know that it's not easy,
to be calm when you've found something going on. But
take your time, think a lot, why think of everything you've
got. For you will still be here tomorrow,
but your dreams may not."
— CAT STEVENS, "FATHER & SON"

Just get it done," Johnathan Pontiac talked to Matthew Pontiac on the phone.

"Ballantyne will do it. Besides, it won't make any difference. Those width and length requirements are always excessive. There won't be any problems."

"Mahoney's sniffing around," said Matthew.

"Remind him of the Contra cash," said Johnathan. "Remind him that Bush will need help if he's getting back into things. Remind him that it's hard to find good help these days.

"And make sure you've got everything covered before he brings it up."

"And he will," volunteered Matthew.

Ryan Mahoney sat at his desk in Washington, D.C. Out his window he saw the White House dome.

He wondered which office would be his.

He thumbed through the mail and came to a pre-opened letter in a manila envelope marked "Immediate Attention Required."

Mahoney read Francis Pontiac's letter and pushed the

button to phone Matthew Pontiac at the statehouse in Des
Moines.

Luke and Martha Pontiac sat in the visitor's room.

Luke pulled a chair over for his mom. They watched the
others coming in, including a woman who looked Indian.
The rest were white, nobody they recognized.

Luke picked his mother's hand out of her lap.

"It'll be okay, ma."

He tapped the Plexiglass.

"He can't get through that."

"Yes, I know. I know he can't get through that."

She looked all around her. Two of the most important
people in her life had spent most of their days in this place.
It hit her.

You got yourself in, get yourself out had been her motto.

You like those people so much, I guess that's your family.

And that's how it had been.

The seal cracked on the prison side. A guard opened the
door and stood with a clipboard marking names. Francis
Pontiac was the first in line. He surveyed the visitor's side
and made like he didn't see Martha and Luke. Then he
looked right at them and smiled. He swooped down and
picked up his phone.

Luke picked up their phone and said hello.

He handed it to Martha.

"H'lo, Marth. You're looking good."

She stared at him, not speaking.

"You don't look good, Francis. You better get out of
there."

That made Francis and Luke laugh.

"I will tell the officer my wife says I should go," Francis
said.

"Why don't you come on home after you get out," said
Martha. "I can still cook, ya know. It's lonely. Not like you
here with all your friends."

"Yeah, they're a neighborly bunch," Francis laughed again.

Martha and Luke stared at him. Martha saw the shadows in the lines in her husband's face. She saw his deep, thick stubble and thought his mustache might look good if he grew it back.

Luke saw birthdays in the house just him and Martha, a pickup just pulling into the drive after being gone for days.

Francis thought how beautiful she had become, always was.

The grey in her long hair belonged there and her fit body from the walking made a fine background for the light in those brown eyes.

She had pledged the sorority of women who grow calm and pretty with added years as they meld misfortune with courage and will it into glittery blue steel sculpture.

Her hands, folded on the damaged desk of a county jail visiting room, with strong veins and thick, white nails, lent grace to the shithole.

They talked about school and about driving truck.

Martha asked about Mark.

Francis said he had spoken with Mark just the other morning.

"Yeah, I see him all the time. He looks out for me in my old infirmity."

The door behind Francis opened.

He did not look, but could see in Luke and Martha's faces.

Francis turned and saw the jail guard tugging him away from his family once again, with just his pointer finger.

In the hall behind the guard stood two men in the shadows, in suits and ties, serious, tanned faces.

"I gotta go," said Francis.

"Love you. I'll be there."

He put his hands up to the window and Luke and Mark matched his with theirs.

Then he was gone and they had nowhere to go but home.

TWENTY-EIGHT

"I HAVE SPENT A LOT OF TIME WORRYING ABOUT THINGS
IN MY LIFE, MOST OF WHICH NEVER HAPPENED."
— WINSTON CHURCHILL

The Nature Lover's Group gathered in the Command Center with the doors closed.

Richard stood in the middle of the room, frantically relating Myrtle Mourning Dove's email message while Mickey called it up on the screen.

"It's going down."

Richard spread his hands flat toward the floor.

"I thought you didn't believe in this shit," said Rodger Tipple.

"This is different," said Richard. "It's real."

"It's always been real," said Verlin. "I really thought all of you people knew that."

"Whatever," said Richard.

He waved his hands in front of his eyes to erase all irrelevant data.

"If this is going to happen, we have to be there and help capture the ones responsible. I think Verlin was right before. Whoever is planning this probably also blew up the shuttle."

"The shuttle?" said Brigita. "Earth to Richard. His whole family is weird." She pointed a hitchhiker's thumb at Richard.

"If there's any more room up there, try sticking this up your crotch."

Richard gave her the finger.

She hacked a loogie and lobbed it at him like a missile.

The Tipples, in their new black caps and black T-shirts, stepped between the two like rock concert security.

"Geezuz! Would you just shut up?"

Verlin pushed Richard toward the door, away from Brigita.

"We need to make some serious decisions, fast.

"Mickey, start making a list.

"One. We'll need a mobile command unit."

"A what?" said Brigita.

"A car," said Rodger.

"And a video camera."

Verlin stalked up and down the room.

"Two cameras. One in the mobile and one on foot.

"You getting this, Mick?"

TWENTY-NINE

"AND THE VETERANS DREAM OF THE FIGHT,
FAST ASLEEP AT THE TRAFFIC LIGHT."
— Jackson Browne

Pontiac sat at the table with Michael Zags.
The others were also up early that morning, moving around, smoking.

Pontiac would be getting out, supposed to get out before lunch, but it all would only go according to how Burton wanted to play it.

Pontiac dealt himself solitaire.

He vowed to himself to be stoic. He wouldn't walk up and down the bars like some damn Bobby Ford begging to be let go.

Burton walked up unnoticed to stand by Pontiac.

"You miss anything lately?" he asked.

"Nothing I can think of," said Pontiac.

"Red nine on the ten." Burton pointed.

Pontiac moved the card.

"Don't do nothin' stupid out there to come back," said Burton conspiratorially.

"Never do," said Pontiac. "I just like it here."

"Yeah, right," said Burton. "Your old man, he …"

Pontiac swiveled his head.

"He got moved yesterday. Feds came and took … coulda been Springfield … Missouri … psych hospital."

"What for!" said Pontiac.

"Shhh," Burton hissed. "I ain't s'posed to be telling you that. S'all I know."

"He was in on a misdemeanor. He wasn't federal."

Pontiac stood to talk.

"Guess he got another charge while he was in here," Burton said. "I'll come back for you in a bit. You might want to get your shit packed up."

Zags sneaked a cigarette inside Pontiac's perfect pyramid.

"Which one is it?" Zags said.

Pontiac took a deep breath and let it out slow.

"Can't really tell. Guess you are one of us. Congratulations."

"Whatchoo gonna do?" Zags asked.

"About what?" said Pontiac. "I don't know. What do you suggest? I thought I might put in an application at Sears."

"Don't do it for anybody else," said Zags. "Don't do it for any people with brown or black or white or red skins that you don't know. That little bit of good feeling will leave you when you're faced with a hundred years in the penitentiary. If it's not for you, deep down, you can't do it, you just can't. It's not your fault, you just can't."

"How do you know that?" said Pontiac. "How is it you are now so deep you can't touch bottom?"

Zags twisted on the bench to rest half of his bony bottom.

"You think I didn't understand what I was doing?" he said with big wide eyes. "I suppose I look stupid to you?"

"Yeah, kind of," said Pontiac.

"Listen," Zags moved closer. Pontiac held his ground.

"I can sit here for however long they want to feed me," said Zags.

"Because, I didn't want to kill anybody. I just wanted people to think about killing George Bush.

"I didn't want to talk about fishing, about women, or beer, or cars.

"I sat through months of hours of coffee breaks like that,

smiling, waiting for somebody to talk about something that meant anything to me.

"Now they are.

"Talking about it.

"That's what I wanted." Pontiac opened his mouth as if trying to swallow a giant Cheerios "O."

"You need professional help," he said.

"No."

Zags put up a hand.

"You need to be getting out of this what you want. If you can't come back here and sit and be contented, head towards where you can. And run."

Pontiac picked Zags' cigarette from his stack and the pyramid collapsed, sending rollies both ways across the yellow table.

"You're weird," Pontiac said. "Do you know who I am, son?"

"Cap that motha," Al Arthur walked over to shake Pontiac's hand, thumb around thumb. Each of the men took their turn in saying goodbye to Pontiac and bucking him up.

Pontiac looked over to Zags as Mendez walked away.

"I've spent all my life in jail and never been in a real prison," Mark said. "Might be kinda cool. You get yard, go to the commissary, a real library, have a job, a little freedom. Some decent convict clothes, blue shirts buttoned at the neck you know what I'm talking about? Instead of these orange janitor's uniforms. It'd be a definite career advancement, is how I'm lookin' at it, ya know?"

Zags grabbed the opposite side of the table and pulled himself in, leaving him within breath-smelling distance.

"Ya know the parable of the sowing of the seed?" Zags said. "Uh-huh. Some fell on rocks, others didn't give a shit, and some grew like freaking beanstalks, ya know?"

Pontiac nodded slightly.

"They bury you guys underground here and forget about

you, pile shit on top of you in layers. But shit is fertilizer to those it don't choke out, you understand what I'm talking about, huh?"

Pontiac nodded.

"Some seeds push through the shit and blossom. Some beanstalks bust right through the goddamn barn roof."

"My mother ..." Mark said.

Keys jingled.

Bobby Ford shuffled to the north corner to wait for Burton.

"Hey, Burt, hey ... I get any money on my books?"

"I don't know," said Burton without looking at Ford. "I'll check, Mark-you-ready?"

Burton whispered to his walkie-talkie and the inside jail door opened.

Pontiac walked around the cell again, shaking hands. He slid a pack of cigarettes into Ford's front pocket.

He grabbed his pillow case of dirty laundry and his carton of letters and papers and stepped into the sally port.

Burton told the front desk and the door closed behind Pontiac.

The outside door opened and he stepped through. Burton told the second door to close and it did.

Pontiac walked past the cell block slowly.

The gaps in the bars flashed the faces of the men like the frames of a silent movie.

In the dark cave of Mourning Dove's cell he saw a clenched, tattooed fist raised.

Mendez read a magazine on the toilet.

Bobby Ford waited in the corner, clutching the bars, his head wedged into the last space.

George Bush was scheduled to take off from Andrews Air Force Base that morning and arrive at Sioux City municipal at noon.

In the meantime the parade would run through town the first time with the high school bands and city officials. This would serve as a run-through for the official Bush parade later in the afternoon.

Bush would turn the bomber over to the Sioux City National Guard in a runway ceremony with Sioux City state legislator Matthew Pontiac.

Bush would speak at the evening Rotary meeting.

Following, Bush would tour the Pig's Style Beer brewery and then attend a cocktail party at the home of Johnathan Pontiac.

George and Barbara Bush would be the guests of the Pontiacs in their home that night for an invitation dinner and pool party. The Bush's would stay over with the Pontiacs and take Pontiac's Cessna to Texas the next morning.

Johnathan Pontiac hurried around town making final adjustments and arrangements, in constant contact with everyone everywhere on his cell phone. His wife stood in the driveway, swinging the catering vans into position like a flight deck traffic cop.

In Washington, Ryan Mahoney worked his phone, trying to reach the Pontiacs or Charles Ballantyne. He found out through the U.S. Marshall's service that Francis Pontiac was being flown to the federal penitentiary in Springfield for a psychiatric examination. A U.S. attorney would meet him there with a summons to appear in court for threatening the president, former.

Mahoney finally found Matthew Pontiac at his mother's home, having cake and coffee.

"That runway of yours is too damn small," Mahoney said.

"Too small for what?" said Matthew.

"For a B-2 bomber flown by the former president of the United States. Have you ever had a DC-10 on that ginger bread highway? What is the rating of that concrete? I need to know. Now! Call me back in three minutes, senator. Two."

Matthew found Johnathan in his redwood Jeep Cherokee

driving the motorcade route, advising the police to come and tow parked cars.

"He says he'll cancel the whole damn thing," said Matthew. "I think he'll do it."

"Well, he can't," said Johnathan.

"It's all planned. Call Ballantyne. Get him to have the airport manager get out there with a damn tape measure and make sure he knows how wide it's supposed to be. Tell 'em what they want to hear, little brother.

"They just want to be assured. They don't want the actual necessarily, just enough so their own asses don't get burned. That's what he's asking for. Trust me, Matt."

Richard, Brigita and Mickey pulled into the Ford dealership where Verlin and the Tipples were renting a used van for the day. They waited until twelve-thirty to save half a day's rent. They asked for no side windows. Like on Hawaii Five-O, Rodger said.

None available.

The kids followed Verlin and the twins downtown.

They stopped in the McDonald's parking lot.

Brigita and Mickey stood outside Verlin's driver's-side window. Verlin again told them how to run their camera, rented from Radio Shack until noon tomorrow.

Rod filmed Verlin talking to the three.

"Shut that thing off."

Verlin slapped at the camera.

"Got it," Rod smiled.

"They will seek triangulation," Verlin said. "Remember your notes. Just after the left-hand turn onto Douglas from Seventh Street. Right around City Park, probably just before the motorcade gets to the Oasis, after that they get to the four-lane and pick up too much speed. No good for a shooter after that.

"Look for someone high, one low, look for crossfire. Look for people who don't belong there, who look out of place."

"Like us," said Brigita. "Look for anyone who looks like us."

"That's it," said Verlin. "Any questions?"

Rodger tuned the scanner on the dash.

"We better git," he said. "It's busy. We don't want to miss nothing."

"Meet back at the CC after the parade," Verlin said. "Do not turn your film over to anyone no matter what credentials they show you. Got it? And make sure you get any such requests on tape."

"Let's go Verl," said Rod.

The van pulled from the lot.

Richard and the girls jumped into the Bel Air.

"This is way cool, you gotta admit," said Richard from the back seat.

"Just think of being in Dallas that day, just as it was going down. This is awesome. I'll bet we get on the History Channel, you think?"

Brigita began to smoke.

Mickey checked traffic and pulled away.

Verlin parked the van on the west side of Seventh Street near the turn onto Douglas.

Rod placed the hand-lettered "Press" white poster board signs on the front side of the van. Rodger listened to the scanner and the police account of the citywide preparations.

Verlin leaned on the window and kept his eyes monitoring, memorizing the various movements. Across the street he saw Mickey pull into the park. The three doors yawned open. Three heads appeared and the doors squeaked shut.

Richard held his recorder at his hip, then aimed it across the street at Verlin and swished his arm high over his head. Verlin violently waved Richard off. The three began moving aimlessly about, trying not to look as though they needed to be apprehended. Richard snuck up to a squirrel eating walnuts, gradually sank to his knees and began filming.

Pontiac stopped by Ford, with his head stuck in the last set of bars of the day room. Burton waited.

"Those stories I tell," said Ford. "It's just something to do. I'm not nuts, I'm not. They're just stories, ya know? That's all."

Pontiac moved. Ford grabbed his arm.

"And I didn't take your list like some think I did."

Pontiac, his hands full, looked directly into Ford's eyes and waited for them to turn up.

"I know," he said.

Burton waited behind Pontiac.

"You watch out for thin ice," said Ford. "You be careful where you walk."

"We're all on thin ice, all the time," said Pontiac.

"Hey!"

Ford looked at Burton.

"Check my books when you get up there this time, okay?"

"We get store today?" Arthur yelled out.

"Can we get this TV turned on?" said Mendez.

Pontiac moved down the hall, Burton in tow.

As they passed his father's empty cell in C-Block, Burton asked Mark to stop.

"Get me that book there! Please?"

Burton addressed one of the young prisoners, pointing to a paperback sitting in the bars of Francis Pontiac's cell. Burton passed it to Mark.

"He's been after me to get you that," said Burton.

"Stick it in your property."

"Red Badge of Courage."

Mark read the coverless title page.

"Shit. He knows I already read this. We musta went through it ten times when I was a kid."

Mark opened the book where the page was dog-eared.

He read the line underlined in pencil.

How could they kill him who was the chosen of gods and doomed to greatness?

258

Mark opened his mouth to ask Burton what he thought of the passage, then stopped.

Burton asked his walkie-talkie to open the door.

The two disappeared through the grey mausoleum slab into the lobby.

Mark walked past the desk and stood in front of the window, the shades pulled back. Jennie said, "Quite a big deal out there, huh? The parade." Mark talked to the outdoor window glass.

"Uh, I wouldn't know. It's been ninety days. There's a tree."

Mark stood at the front desk signing a sheet to receive his property.

Jennie poured the contents of a manila envelope onto the counter and checked it against the receipt.

"Wallet. Three dollars. Comb."

She lined the items on the counter.

"Sign here and be eligible for our grand prize," she said. "You're not coming back anymore, right?"

She scolded Mark with a bob of her head and a raise in her eyebrows.

"No, I won't," he said. "I have been rehabilitated. You people do good work."

Burton took the laundry in the pillowcase and walked around the corner. Mark followed to the locker room to get his street clothes.

Mark slipped into his jeans and pulled out the waist to show how much weight he had lost.

"We feed you," said Burton.

"You be careful out there. It can be a nasty ol' world, remember?"

"Since when," Pontiac smiled.

"Since forever," said Burton, flinging the laundry bag onto a pile. Burton let Pontiac out the front door and let it close and lock.

Mark looked and couldn't see through the darkened, bullet-proof glass.

He boarded the elevator alone.

He backed to the wall and considered an amazing list of life options. In the next moment he longed for a safe afternoon nap under his grey cover.

Mark inched into the lobby with its meatloaf cafeteria smell and carpeting and blur of voices and faces. The television in the corner showed Dan Rather standing in the middle of an intersection in Sioux City. Rather wore a Navy ball cap and Desert Storm camouflaged jacket and smiled into a microphone.

Mark walked past the set into a dark hallway lined on one side with two rows of rental lockers, each a foot tall and a yard deep. Mark walked down the line, searching for a key left in one, hopefully No. 39.

He spotted it, marked it and walked past, down to a set of windows.

He stood and saw Rather in the middle of the street, someone combing his hair for him, then someone running up to him, someone with a ponytail and headphones.

Mark looked down the deserted hall.

Everyone must have been on the street. Everyone but that one heroic FBI agent, thought Mark. The one who would tackle him as soon as he turned the key. He walked toward the locker, his feet crunching the stiff AstroTurf carpet.

He looked both ways and took a deep breath.

He twisted the key, opened the door and took out the padded manila envelope and its irregular contents. In the rest room, in the handicapped stall, Mark ripped off the duct tape, took out the bone-handled pistol and box of shells. He figured out how to open the roller.

He flushed the stool, locked the stall and fed six bullets into the chambers.

He lifted the gun and aimed it at the door, testing the weight and grip.

Someone came in and used the urinal. Mark flushed again and waited for the person to leave. He pulled the trigger back just barely and pointed at the door.

Mark reached the envelope into the bottom of the trash can. He put the pistol in the inside game bag of his green camouflaged jacket. He unlocked the door, washed his hands, and held them under the power dryer, looking around the room behind him.

He pushed, then yanked on the door and entered the now empty lobby.

Mark headed to the outer doors and went through the civilian sally port.

When the air hit his face he stopped and choked in a deep breath. He looked down and saw the glass-block, blurred windows of the jail.

Not a sound or smell or sight filtered through.

He sidled closer to the building, putting one foot in the muddy lawn.

He leaned down, pretending to tie his shoe and smiled at the intro music to Bobby Ford's "All My Children."

THIRTY

"I don't care if it rains or freezes, long as I got my plastic
Jesus, ridin' on the dashboard of my car. Comes in colors
pink and pleasant, glows in the cark, 'cause it's iridescent.
Take it with you when you travel far."
— "Cool Hand Luke"

Ryan Mahoney picked up the phone, cutting the
first ring short.
"Yes."
"I talked to Ballantyne," said Matthew Pontiac. "It's okay.
He's been out to the airport half a dozen times talking to
the manager. No problemo."

"How wide?" said Mahoney. "How wide is the fucking
runway. How long? If he's been there he knows."

"Gotcha," said Matthew. "Got it right here. He gave it to
me."

Matthew grabbed a pad and pencil and drew a rectangle.

"Uh. Wide. One hundred yards wide. Hundred and fifty
let's say. Uh. Long. One thousand yards long. Probably
more."

"One thousand?" said Mahoney. "Won't make it."

"That's just the first half," said Pontiac.

"There's a shed and some grass, then there's more. Each
half is a thousand. Didn't I say that? Total, two thousand
yards long, plenty, way enough. Right?"

Mahoney picked up a phone on his left and punched a
worn button.

KGB

Paul sat in his car a block from City Park, under the Marlboro billboard behind some tall weeds. He watched the downtown city scene. He checked his watch.

Three hours to wait to see George Bush. He turned the key to listen to the radio.

After thirty minutes he moved to the park and spotted Verlin's van.

Rod slumped in the front seat, filming, with his cap turned backwards, trying to use up the roll that they would have to pay for anyway.

Paul leaned forward to see better.

Somehow. They're doing it, he thought. It's happening right now. When Bush comes past that van in three hours they will shoot him unless I do something. Right now.

Paul grabbed his Reds cap from under the floor, slapped it on the seat, straightened the bill and pulled it down to his eyebrows.

He got out of the car, not taking his eyes off the assassin team.

With his teeth Paul Novotny ripped two blue balloons from a parking meter and tied the strings to his wrists.

"Let's go," he said, letting the balloons carry his arms head-high, with a little help.

He walked across the intersection.

Paul walked up to Rod Tipple's window, took a deep breath and flung the door open, sending Rod out of the van and onto the curb. His head and shoulders bounced off the cement. The video camera clattered on the curb.

Blood ran down a crack in the sidewalk toward the gutter.

Rodger Tipple flattened his nose against the back window to see out. His eyes went wide and his mouth flattened against the fogged window, calling to his brother on the walk.

"Oh, my," said Paul.

Mark Pontiac looked up from tying his shoes and saw

Elana Usak standing over him, wearing new white cowboy boots, tight jeans, her thumbs in her belt loops.

He stood, passing a layer of perfume on the way up.

Mark hunched his back and put his weight on his right leg.

"Hey," he said.

Elana had washed her hair. It hung just a little in her eyes. She wore a new emerald button down shirt with the front tied at the belly button, and tiny transistor radio earrings.

Mark touched one.

"Pretty cool," he said.

"Yeah. Your mom took me to the mall. Well, congratulations!"

"For what?'

"You're out!" she said. "Out of that place, ugh!"

She shook her whole body like a dog drying off.

"What now?" she said. "Wanna get a room?"

She punched him in the shoulder.

"Just kidding."

"Nah," he said like a junior high kid being asked to dance. "I got something I got to do."

"You don't need a ride somewhere?" she said.

"C'mon, let's go have a drink, a big meal. Your mom gave me money and her car. Let's go."

She tugged at his arm, pointing to the Chevy.

"I know what you're trying to do," said Mark. "And Mom."

"I'm planting flowers," said Elana. "Daisies. Call me. Or knock on the wall. I'll be in the room next to yours. I stay up late. Be good."

Mark nodded and waved goodbye as Elana backed up to the Chevy parked the wrong way next to the curb.

He flinched when a squad car yanked out of traffic, flashed on its lights and crashed into the front end of the Chevy. Elana's hands shot to her face. With blinking light on the dashboard, Hargrove and Fry skidded in behind the Chevy with a squeal.

Elana ran from them and into the arms of two policemen who put her face down into the sidewalk.

They handcuffed her behind her back.

Elana screamed in Czech.

She cried and kicked and wrenched her arms.

Mark stepped up to her and tried to kneel down.

He was pushed out of the way by Fry.

Two more police cars arrived and the officers began shutting off the area around Elana, still on her stomach on the walk, still shouting in English and Czech.

Mark stood, able to see above the cordon of officers as they put Elana in the back of a squad car.

She turned and hollered again, asking the people around her to do something.

Mark watched them swerve into traffic and surge away.

After they took Elana, he continued down the street, backwards, trying to see where they had gone.

He would call her, call Mom, after things quieted down.

Nothing he could do right now.

He breathed deep and sang.

"Get yourself a sweet Madonna, dressed in rhinestones sittin' on a pedestal of abalone shell."

Mark walked down the street, noticing every damn thing, he realized, like a first grader out for his first walk. He watched the young flowers in the planters outside We Care travel agency.

The streets were lined with lawn chairs and people, coolers and kites.

His heart began to pound hard and his lips tightened.

He focused on the path ahead, through the oncoming one's, two's, three's, everyone carrying United States flags on sticks.

Yellow ribbons adorned each parking meter.

The loudspeakers on the reviewing stand blared, "I'm proud to be an American ..."

KGB

Mark leaned against the brick front of the Oasis Bar. He pressed his back against the sharp bricks to gain some space from the crowd. He heard every voice as if he were an invisible observer.

There was nobody there that would understand, he thought. About where he had just been, understand living underground in a locked cave for three whole months, not seeing the sun or the sky or cars. Not drinking a Pepsi whenever you wanted or switching off the TV 'cause you were sick of the noise.

Not one person in this crowd could appreciate how he had spent thirty years learning to shit in full view of other people and sleep with a rolled washrag over his eyes.

And I'm proud to praise the men who died to give this life to me.

He could roll cigarettes with one hand and cut a card deck with the other.

But he couldn't live out here, not with these people.

Not with them and their motorcades and their squat little tubs of Ben & Jerry's and their matching lawn chairs. He petted the gun through his heavy jacket.

Mark felt the sweat on his forehead and remembered the three dollar bills in his wallet. He stepped to the front door of the Oasis and jerked it open.

The air turned black as soon as he entered. He let the door close behind him and stepped just one more step and stood there, pinned between the crowd and the wall of dark.

The only light came from the television above the far corner of the bar.

Then the jukebox came into view and the Hulk Hogan vs. Jesse The Body pinball machine appeared next to it.

His eyes continued to adjust and Mark saw two could-be construction workers at one table.

At the bar sat an older guy with a fishing cap pushed down to his eyebrows.

He and the bartender were watching the tube, enjoying viewing the national report on the scene just outside the door.

It was cooler to watch it on the television than to bother to go outside the door and see it for themselves. Mark could understand that.

Mark walked past the one man at the bar, down to the end and seated himself under the television. The bartender brought a Pig's Style Beer.

"On the house," he said. "There's free beer everywhere in town. Cheers."

"No," said Mark. "I don't drink. "Pepsi, no glass. Thanks."

That bartender picked up the beer and turned to the man at the bar.

"How soon?"

"How soon, the motorcade? How soon it supposed to come downtown?"

"Soon," the other guy said. "Right past here." He pointed toward the door.

The bartender pointed at the television, then at the front door, looking at Mark, showing him they were the same damn thing.

He cackled loud and walked back to the old man and picked up his cigarette in the bean bag ashtray on his stool behind the bar.

Mark saw that the two were friends.

Where are my friends, he thought.

He reached into the left side of his coat with his right hand and felt the book. He reached with his left hand for the gun.

He picked up the pop bottle and knocked it back.

Mark knocked it softly on the bar and pointed to it when the bartender looked.

He brought out the book and began thumbing through.

The bartender pulled on his cigarette, got up, put the cigarette back into the ashtray and moved toward Mark while keeping his eyes on the TV screen. He grabbed another pop from the glass case on the way and shoved it under the bar to an invisible opener. Whoosh! went the top. He picked up Mark's empty and wiped the bar with a towel he pulled from nowhere just as Mark grabbed for empty air.

He set it down without smiling and walked back.

"Ahhh, I don't freaking believe it!"

The older man was pointing at the screen with the cigarette in his left hand.

Mark looked up and saw Dan Rather in front of the khaki van with what had to be a Danish film crew standing around it in the background.

The logo Special Report ran across Rather's beltline.

"This is Dan Rather, reporting live from Sioux … City … Iowa."

"What was scheduled to be a test run for a possible re-entry into national politics has turned into a scratch.

"Only minutes ago, as former President George T. Bush was seated in a two billion dollar black B-1 Stealth bomber on the runway of Andrews Air Force Base, scheduled to fly the plane here to Sioux City for delivery and then a celebratory parade through this blue-collar American city, followed by a speech many have said would announce his future plans, the trip was canceled."

Rather read from notes blowing in his hands.

"Ryan Mahoney, chief aid for Bush, said the trip was stopped because the Sioux City runway is not equipped to handle a B-2."

A photo of Michael Zags appeared in the upper right corner of the television screen.

Pontiac pointed and looked at the bartender and his friend and began to tell the all about the county jail and D-Block and Burton, and then put his hand down.

"You will recall," Rather continued, "that Michael Zags, Sioux City resident, was jailed weeks ago for threatening the president, former president's life, and we have it from an unidentified source, in of all places, a Sioux City dental office, that another jail inmate was taken into federal custody just yesterday for another threat on the life of George C. Bush.

"How or if … these were connected … we … perhaps … will never … know.

"But it does seem that Iowa is too dangerous for George D. Bush today.

"What this whole fiasco … will do … to … Bush's … plans … to enter the Republican primaries … we can only guess … at … this … time.

"But … many … are … saying … that … George Bush is dead.

"From Sioux City … Iowa. I'mmm Dan … Rather."

Rather dropped the microphone to the pavement, walked directly to the Cherry Red Jeep he and his producer were using and floored it, headed down Douglas. He spotted the cocktail glass neon sign of the Oasis. He skidded the Jeep to a stop and charged the front door.

He lunged through, stumbling over a table and reaching in the dark for the bar.

"Whatdya got?" he asked the bartender, standing tall with a white bar rag inside a glass.

"Pig's Style?" he smiled. He wiped the table with one swoop and set the bottle own.

Mark pinned two dollar bills under the empty Pepsi bottle.

He walked past the old man in the fishing cap.

"What a screw-up," the old man muttered. "Somebody should be shot."

Mark moved past the growing crowd that had followed Rather inside. He reached the front door, then looked back over his shoulder. He walked back to the bar, leaned on it with one arm and asked the bartender, "How much for one of these?"

The bartender looked at the bill in Mark's hand.

"One dollar," he said.

"Perfect," Mark said.

Mark pulled one of the flags on a stick from the glass vase on the bar and turned and went out the door.

The crowd was beginning to thin out, the word running along the street.

A steady sweaty stream began to trickle into the Oasis.

Mark stepped aside then began pushing his way through oncoming foot traffic, carrying lawn chairs and coolers and crying kids.

He spotted an open space on the curb where he could stand for a moment.

He pulled out his flag and waived it.

A white-haired lady limped past behind him humping a folded lawn chair.

She stopped and clutched Mark's elbow.

"He's not coming," she said with a frown.

"Yeah, I know," Mark said.

He waved his flag in her face and bent low.

"I know, I know. I know."

He turned and waved the flag over his head and yelled.

"Hey! Hey! God Bless America! Hey-Hey!"

As the Heelan High School marching band came down Douglas, split in two for spare traffic, then joined again, like it had practiced it every day.

George and Barbara Bush huddled in the officer's lounge in the mid-section of the black Stealth bomber at the tail-wind end of Andrews No. 3 runway.

They accepted scotch and water in clear plastic glasses from the waiter and settled into deep black straight-backed chairs. A triangular black mahogany table on rollers sat between them. Barbara tore pieces from her black napkin and rolled the pieces into balls, setting them in a pile, like cannon shot.

The former president put his chin in his hand and stared wistfully out the small window. He saw Mahoney's white and gold Camry racing up. "Maybe I won't do this after all," he whispered to the window. Barbara clutched her crotch with one hand and jogged to the ladies room.

George watched Mahoney scramble out of his vehicle carrying a briefcase. He sprinted up the steps in leaps and bounds and entered the lounge after wiping his feet on the black mat in the foyer.

George Bush was still looking out the window wistfully as Mahoney approached the table.

"Bab's pissing, George said without looking at Mahoney. He pointed both thumbs backward over his shoulders at the women's restroom.

"I wonder if ..."

He looked up and asked Mahoney to have a sit down.

Barbara Bush returned, running her hands down her skirt.

She reached across the table and drew her cannon balls over without upsetting the stack.

Mahoney ordered a drink and buffalo wings and asked Bush if he was upset.

"No. No, you did what you had to do. Can't go running one of these puppies off the edge into a soybean shed."

He looked back out the window.

"Maybe it's for the best. It's a lot of trouble."

Mark waved the flag over his head.

He saw a red Jeep Cherokee pull a squealing U-turn.

It screeched up to him.

The driver leaned over and scowled at him with stretched eyebrows.

"You fucking ... loser."

"Hello, Johnathan," Mark said.

He leaned and put a hand in the open window.

Johnathan slid over.

"You had to do it, didn't you. You had to ruin this whole thing. You two aren't even safe in a jail cell."

"Not too bad," said Mark.

"How 'bout yourself, little brother."

He squatted on his thighs, still holding his flag aloft.

"You don't know what you're talking about and neither do I."

He stood and waved the flag inside the window.

"Nice day, huh? I just go out.

"Why don't you buy me a soda? Wouldn't that be the Rotary way?"

"You! Sonofabitch!"

Johnathan slapped at the flag, pushed open the door and knocked Mark back onto the sidewalk.

Mark hit his head against a parking meter.

The pistol clattered out.

"My God!" said Johnathan.

"You were really going to do it. They were right!"

He picked Mark up by his jacket and yelled in his face.

"Do you have any idea how much this meant to me! Of … course not. You know nothing!"

He pushed Mark away.

A tepid crowd began to form around them.

Johnathan's body quivered.

His white shirt and red tie looked out of place in a street fight, the old lady thought, still stationed behind Mark.

Mark studied his brother.

His hands smoothly formed fists.

He eyed the gun.

Johnathan looked down and lunged for the pistol.

"You going to kill somebody?"

Johnathan's face was blood red. He screamed and pointed the barrel at Mark, holding the gun with both hands, still trembling.

"You going to kill the president?

"Why don't you try killing me first!"

Mark put one foot up on the curb and held out his arms sideways.

"You get your freedom and what do you do with it!" Johnathan screamed.

"You are all alike, you get things given to you and you have no idea what they cost."

"You can't give me my freedom, John. I took it."

Mark took one step forward and Johnathan fired.

Mark put his hands up, spread wide.

No, no, no.

I got things to do.

I can't die today. Elana. Mom.

They're expecting me, making pie.

He stepped back and began losing his center of gravity, falling away. He saw the wide look in Johnathan's eyes as he began to understand what he had done.

Somebody stop this, do something, doesn't anyone see me here?

This is me.

I'm somebody's son and I count for something.

He put out his hands, trying to stop the bullets.

The shots went through the palms of each of his hands.

The first shot lodged in the grass behind the sidewalk.

The next spinning shot bore a neat hold through the lower half of Mark's heart and then struck the elderly lady in the middle of her forehead, tossing her body into a rain gutter along the west wall of the Oasis like used clothes, her blue flowered dress thrown up.

The pavement tore skin from Mark's left shoulder through his coat.

He did not move. The book lay beside him.

Johnathan aimed the gun at the crowd.

"Get back! Back! Out of here! Go! There is no parade!"

"Go fucking home!"

He fired over their heads until he ran out of bullets.

He threw himself into his vehicle and shot away.

Brigita, Mickey and Richard pulled away from the park just as Paul assaulted the van crew.

They drove west down Seventh Street.

An ambulance and police car passed them going the other way with lights flashing.

"I know what I want to do," Richard said.

"Turn here, right here."

"Everyone's downtown," Richard whispered.

They tried the east loading dock door and it opened.

"Forget this," Mickey said.

"C'mon," said Brigita. "Smell that."

She smiled.

"Good ol' 'merican hops and barley. Salt of the earth. We are Amuricans. We're just looking around."

They passed the box room and crawled under rows and rows of loading racks. They reached a gigantic hall that workers called The Planet of the Pigs. The ceiling stood fifty feet above the floor.

The room contained randomly spaced shiny copper vats that could have been a captured alien landing force. The floors were shiny cement.

The block walls were sea gull white, repainted every May along with the four-color mural on the north wall.

American flags sprouted from the wall every ten yards in a ring twenty feet high.

Next to the maintenance room door hung an eight-by-ten colored photo of Johnathan Pontiac shaking George C. Bush's hand at the White House.

Along the walls the work jackets, broom and mops rested on hooks in neat rows. Above the floor a walkway encircled the room. What could have been a jogging track was the private observation deck of Johnathan Pontiac.

On the north breathed the company mural.

A hundred yards long.

Pigs at the Oasis bar.

Richard pointed to the mural.

"Over there."

He nodded at the winding steps leading to the walkway. "I'll be right back."

The girls stealthily made their way to the edge of the steps.

Richard arrived with a five-gallon bucket of white paint and three brushes still in the plastic packs.

Richard led. They wound up and upward.

On the balcony they could appreciate the enormity of the room.

Large enough to store and service three black, Stealth B-2 bombers, Mickey guessed.

Richard disappeared down the stairs again and came back huffing and hauling two step ladders.

He opened the paint with a screwdriver, assigned tasks and went to work.

Martha and Luke Pontiac sat in their favorite chairs in the living room.

Martha rested her hand on the clicker on her knee, watching the various accounts of the debacle in Sioux City.

"Pie?" she asked Luke.

"Maybe later," he said, his eyes on the screen.

"Francis had something to do with this."

Martha spoke to the television.

"Prob'ly Mark, too," said Luke. "He was supposed to get out today I thought."

He got up and headed for the phone.

"I'll give a call down to the jail and see what's the hold up. He should have called for a ride."

Brigita climbed down from her ladder by stutter-steps.

The three leaned on the railing to view their work.

Richard thought they should go below.

They scrambled down the steps and ran to the middle of the brew gallery.

"Cool," said Mickey.

"Mighty fine," Brigita repeated twice.

Richard goose-stepped twenty yards to his right, then to the left to get the full effect.

"Works for me," he said.

"Definitely."

They stood in the middle of the golden vats, arms around each others waists, beaming at the mural, the pigs now whited out, leaving only the bar and the floating caps.

"You free the pigs, you free the people," Richard said.

"We'll work on that," said Mickey.

"Whatever. I think it's just weird," said Brigita.

"Let's just get the-fuck out of here."

She tugged on Richard's sleeve.

"To the Command Center, Batman," she said.

They ran laughing across the hall, hair and shirt tails flying.

Michael Zags occupied the table with Bill Mourning Dove and Miguel Mendez.

Bobby Ford stood under the set, staring up with his arms crossed.

Stephan Baltimore and Martin Mumford lounged in front of their cell on the floor, backs against the bars. Al Arthur's outline was visible under the cover in his bed. Skinny, long, clenched.

The men watched Dan Rather, his tie loosened, his hair messed, standing in front of the Oasis Bar, with ambulance workers and policemen scurrying in the background.

"It has been an incredible day in Sioux City," Rather concluded. "We return you to your local weather."

Don Burton's keys announced him. He talked into his hand machine. The man next to him held his jail kit in his arms. He worked to memorize the men in D-Block.

His eye sockets deepened and his face grew even more pale as he stared into the dayroom, at the ugly, chipped, thick steel table bolted in the middle of the floor. Michael Zags smiled at the familiar likeness waiting in the sally port.

That didn't take long, he began to say. The sentence formed in his mind. He opened his mouth then the sound sucked away as in a vacuum.

Bobby Ford stared at Johnathan Pontiac as he walked by.

He stepped in front of him and stood in the doorway of his cell, both hands on the bars, denying access.

Johnathan Pontiac stood by the table. Each cell door was blocked.

Arthur stood in the entrance to Mark Pontiac's former home.

"No room at the inn, Burt," said Mourning Dove. "Try C-Block, they got extra."

"Felony," said Burt. "Got to go here. You'll find room."

He walked off, keys jangling, his machine speaking to him as he held it to his right ear, his head bowed, watching the concrete range.

Pontiac watched Burton disappear, then sat down at the table.

He set his stuff on top and picked up the bent, faded deck of cards.

He began shuffling.

Ford walked to stand under the television.

Mumford went to bed.

Baltimore stalked by in a towel, headed for the shower, staring hard at the new man.

Mourning Dove moved into Mendez's cell.

Pontiac detected taunts directed at him in their conversation.

Al Arthur dropped his pants and sat on the toilet, staring at the newcomer, his penis in his hand.

Michael Zags took a piss, then grabbed his cigarettes and walked into the dayroom.

He sat down across from Pontiac.

"You Mark's brother?"

He dropped a cigarette on the table.

"Yeah," said Johnathan, continuing dealing solitaire.

"Seems like there's always a Pontiac in this jail," Zags tried to smile.

Johnathan shot his head up, angry.

He saw that Zags was not impressed by the look.

"Yeah, I guess that's about right."

He returned to examining his cards.

"What time you eat around here?"

"Four, four-thirty."

Bobby Ford watched the television, his hands across his chest.

He balanced on his tiptoes, trying to see under the weather woman's dress.

[POSTSCRIPT]
"We are not deceived by their pretenses to piety. We have seen their kind before. They are the heirs of all the murderous ideologies of the 20th century. By sacrificing human life to serve their radical visions, by abandoning every value except the will to power, they follow in the path of fascism and Nazism and totalitarianism. And they will follow that path all the way, to where it ends, in history's unmarked grave of discarded lies."
— George W. Bush, Sept. 20, 2001,
  speech to Congress, declaring war on terror

KGB

KGB

KGB

Printed in Great Britain
by Amazon

73537541R00168